PENGUIN BOOKS

THE LIGHT OF STARS

Leslie W is the pen name of Kayce Teo, who is the Regional Team Lead at TheSmartLocal.com, one of Singapore's top lifestyle portals. Her debut fantasy novel, *The Night of Legends*, was written under the mentorship of award-winning writer, Dave Chua. When she is not busy working and parenting, she is dreaming up new and exciting stories to tell. Follow her writing journey on Instagram @lesliewwrites.

OTHER BOOKS IN THIS SERIES

The Night of Legends, Penguin Random House SEA, 2019

ADVANCE PRAISE FOR *THE LIGHT OF STARS*

'I loved *The Night of Legends,* book one of The Night of Legends young adult coming-of-age fantasy trilogy. *The Light of Stars,* the second book, beats it hands down. In the first book, our team of six heroes discovered everything they'd been taught was a lie. Now, in *The Light of Stars,* they have to find their own truths. And what a journey they must make to do so.

This is a gripping read, with many unexpected plot twists as kick-ass girls Keix and Vin fight unexpected enemies in a city that changes its configuration every dusk and dawn. Be prepared for self-discovery, loss, love and a dramatic changing of loyalties as the two young women and their six companions journey on towards their destinies. A must-read. Can't wait for #3.'

— Audrey Chin, award-winning author of *The Ash House*

'Lots of riveting action and astounding set pieces, with fascinating world-building that blends fantasy and science fiction seamlessly.'

— Dave Chua, award-winning author of *Gone Case*

'With a razor-sharp plot and strong emotional arc, the sequel to Leslie W's *The Night of Legends* raises the stakes and makes for a dangerously compelling read that is impossible to put down and hard to forget.'

— Joyce Chua, author of *Land of Sand and Song*

'A page-turner at every chapter. Riveting, action-packed, and full of exciting plot twists, I couldn't put it down. The world-building is stupendous, peopled by relatable characters that I rooted for. Leslie W's storytelling prowess and prose left me wanting more.'

— Eva Wong Nava, author of *The House of Little Sisters*

'Leslie W weaves magic into her words to make each action scene as vivid as if you were watching a movie. The world she's built is foreign yet familiar in its themes, with compelling characters that will stay with you long after you've turned the last page.'

— Catherine Dellosa, author of *Of Myths and Men*

'*The Light of Stars* is an electrifying YA fantasy rich in suspense, action and tender moments. Leslie W's evocative prose, exceptional world-building and compelling characters drew me in from the get-go. A praiseworthy sequel to *The Night of Legends*!'
                    —Vivian Teo, author of *My BFF Is An Alien* series

'Keix, an awakened soldier trying to find her own way, is the perfect foil to guide us through the 1984esque Star Wars setting—paper thin trapezoidal buildings, mystical creatures like haagis and shihs, and shady organizations trying to control magic for the 'public good'. I highly recommend!'
                    —Nabeel Ismeer, author of *The Hunter's Walk*

The Light of Stars

Leslie W

PENGUIN BOOKS
An imprint of Penguin Random House

PENGUIN BOOKS

USA | Canada | UK | Ireland | Australia
New Zealand | India | South Africa | China | Southeast Asia

Penguin Books is part of the Penguin Random House group of companies
whose addresses can be found at global.penguinrandomhouse.com

Published by Penguin Random House SEA Pte Ltd
9, Changi South Street 3, Level 08-01,
Singapore 486361

First published in Penguin Books by Penguin Random House SEA 2022

ISBN 9789815058192

Typeset in Adobe Caslon Pro by MAP Systems, Bangalore, India

www.penguin.sg

To Kong Kong,
the original Leslie Albert Walter,
who instilled in me the love for reading and storytelling.

Contents

Prelude   xiii

1. Keix | Ambushed   1
2. Maii | An Opening   14
3. Keix | The Kulcan   29
4. Dace | Connections   38
5. Vin | Forgiveness   52
6. Pod | The Light of Stars   63
7. Keix | Moving Pieces   78
8. Zej | Reluctant Allies   89
9. Keix | Marked   100
10. Keix | Confusion   109
11. Vin | Illusion of Choice   120
12. Keix | Preparations   131
13. Keix | Precision and Strength 141
14. Vin | Fractals   154
15. Pod | Precipice   164
16. Keix | Replay   174
17. Maii | Crumbling Fissures 186
18. Keix | No Return   194

19. Pod | Ghost   203

20. Keix | The Ifarl's Tale   205

21. Zej | Predestined   212

22. Keix | Full Circle   216

Acknowledgements   219

Prelude

'The Night of Legends' and 'Act of Repentance' are rhymes that have been passed on, first by word of mouth, then written text, as far back as we, Ifarls, remember.

The works allow for limitless interpretations. However, our ancestors who documented our lore believe they are two halves of a riddle. Both poems begin by alluding to the nine dimmest stars before taking off in opposite directions.

'The Night of Legends' suggests a child is born when this set of stars glow the brightest they can get and form a line that divides the sky into half. This child will inherit the limitless power of the stars, but their mother will die during childbirth.

It is said that the child, although powerful, will do something unpredictable and create a problem for the Ifarls to resolve. It is not known what exactly the child can or will do, so it is only natural that people fear them. But this fear must be overcome, and the child must be taught with utmost care to tread the right path. Otherwise, disaster will strike.

So far, no one has been able to prevent the predictions of 'The Night of Legends' from becoming fact. That is where 'Act of Repentance' comes in. This second half of the riddle hints at a solution to the 'problem' this child has posed.

It is believed that the Ifarls will get a chance—only one—to right the wrongs of the child when the nine stars line up once again—but this time, when they are at their dimmest. The repentance needs to be sincere. If any single element of this act is done inaccurately, the world will be plunged into darkness once again.

The Night of Legends

Nine of Stars,
Cut sky's bars.
Traces line,
Make ties bind.
Bae born,
Mae worn.
Bae be bound, powers—unbound.

Evil dwells,
Where fear swells.
Evil thrills,
Where joy fills.
Teach right,
Tread light.
Bae be born, of Nine Stars bond.

Act of Repentance

Stars of nine,
Forgo shine,
Line the skies,
Break the ties.
Condemn,
Repent,
Bae we renounce in assent.

Failure stains,
Power wanes.
Deadly dance,
Single chance.
Chant right,
Tread light.
Plunge anew into the night.

—Excerpt from Chapter 9: A Riddle of Light and Darkness,
The Basics of Ifarl History

1

Keix | Ambushed

Darkness engulfed Keix. She took a cautious step forward and that footstep echoed around like mocking laughter. She paused. Anyone who wasn't hard of hearing would have caught her faint footfall in the eerie quietness in which she was suspended. To her heightened half-Kulcan senses, even her measured breaths sounded like a roaring gale.

A long beat passed. The air remained still.

Where am I? What was I doing before this?

Keix's mind drew a blank—as if being in this strange realm of nothingness had eliminated all her recent memories.

The silence was a threat, whispered in her ear. It sounded foreign, yet felt strangely familiar. In the complete absence of light, every single cell in Keix's body tensed for a confrontation.

Seconds stretched into minutes. Nothing stirred. For the life of her, Keix couldn't figure a way out of this maze of invisibility.

The air was devoid of odour. It had a stillness so complete, she could neither feel the slightest vibration nor a tinge of heat or coolness against her skin. That she was the cause of every ripple in this void gave her pause—her echoing footsteps and harsh breaths were amplified, only to be swallowed by the abyss.

She thought it would be prudent to remain on the spot and wait things out. There was no way to assess her environment properly, what with the overwhelming blankness. But something from deep within her gut made her take another step forward.

Two, she counted as her heart pounded in tandem.

More silence.

Keix couldn't decide if that was a good sign. She pressed on.

Three. Four. Five.

Still, no one came for her.

The emptiness threatened her to stay where she was, while her intuition urged her to go forward. These imaginary voices warred in her head and reached a crescendo.

Keix pressed her fingers against her furrowed brows and allowed herself to suck in a long, deep, noisy breath. On the exhale, she decided to throw caution to the wind. Striding towards a non-existent destination, she continued numbering her steps to ground her thoughts.

Ten. Eleven.

Before her ears could catch the reverberation of that last footstep, she saw a flash of yellow eyes an indeterminate distance away. In a split second, ghostly orbs appeared—red, orange and blue—and rushed her. But what made her knees buckle was the spectre leading the troop. As solid as a ghost could ever be, it wore the face of her late mother.

A flood of memories surged through her, the shocking sight lifting the shroud that had concealed them.

'Hell, no,' muttered Keix as it became clear what she was up against.

This is a dream. And it isn't my first time here.

The moment the thought crossed her mind, everything around her slowed down. The caricature of the only family member she had ever known moved towards her in slow motion.

Keix was frozen to the spot. She squeezed her eyes shut, willing herself to wake up. There had been countless times in her life, whenever night fell, when she had desperately wished she could catch a glimpse of her mother's ghost. Keix knew the immense pain that she would feel if she were to be touched by a spirit, having experienced it during her Atros training. The incident had left her pale and shaking, but she held on to this naive dream of hers—to bid a final farewell to her mum. The fact that Keix never managed to do so because her mum had died while at work, a few days after she turned eleven, was a weight that she would carry for the rest of her life.

However, this apparition wasn't her mum's real ghost. Keix was certain that this was a recurring dream and all she had to do to get out of it was to touch the imposter.

But what if . . . this was truly her mother's soul? Keix shuddered at the thought of being assaulted by the grievances and the ugliest thoughts, magnified to the extreme, of a person who had been her only family. What was her mum's greatest regret in life? Would she hate the Kulcan who'd left them when Keix was born, shirking his responsibilities of a father and husband? Or would she rue the fact that she brought Keix into this world more?

Keix took an unsteady breath and braced herself to face the translucent spectre head on. It was just a hair's breadth away now, reaching a finger towards her. At the contact, a wave of relief washed over her. Just as she had suspected, this wasn't real, so not one resentful ghostly memory assaulted her.

The respite was brief, however, because she was immediately struck by a pain so pure and so thorough that everything else ceased to exist. Time, and even the emptiness of the space that was hosting this dream, fell away as she relived the ritual that had burned every last trace of paranormality out of her.

* * *

Keix sat up with a start. She had fallen asleep, seated with her back braced against one of the sturdiest-looking trees in this part of the forest she had ventured into.

Through wisps of moonlight peeking past the dense canopy, she could just about make out the outlines of a cluster of trees a few steps from where she was. Their thin tree trunks reached high into the sky and looked like they were interlaced from where she sat. Cool air rushed in to fill the gap that the nightmare had carved out from her, helping to soothe her frayed nerves a fraction.

Keix shook her head to clear her thoughts. She felt like she had lived a decade in the past two-plus years. Yet, she'd only been awake for less than a handful of months in that entire duration. At sixteen, when she graduated from the Atros Training Institute—or ATI, as everyone in Atros called it—she was all set to protect her city from whatever and whoever threatened its safety and peace.

But the Sector at which she had been stationed was swarmed by ghosts, and she had had to make one of the most difficult decisions of her life. She sacrificed her best friend and fellow troopers to prevent the paranormal beings from advancing into Atros and causing the deaths of more people. However, because her account didn't fit the agenda being peddled by the organization to which she had pledged her loyalty (they had wanted to play up the threat of the rebel groups to justify their twisted experiments), they made her disappear. Then, she had been used as an experimental subject, tortured, and subsequently put into a medically induced coma and imprisoned underwater.

Two years later, her friends Zej and Pod rescued her from the underwater prison in PEER, the Paranormal Electromagnetic Energy Research Centre, one of Atros's top research institutions. Keix thought the rescue marked the end of the betrayals against her. But no, the treachery kept coming, pelting her from every direction. Zej and Pod stood aside and did absolutely nothing as she was turned into a host for a parasitic soul and put up as sacrifice in a ritual to close the portal between the living and the dead. In the grand scheme of things, which was to make sure that spirits could never haunt their world again, Keix was nothing more than collateral damage.

Yet, fate had other plans for her. The rite was a success. But she had miraculously survived it when she should have died. However, despite having been given a new lease of life, she found herself depleted of energy. A level of detachment that she had never felt in her life inundated her senses. Her anger and disappointment dissipated. And with that came the realization that she had, and would have, done the same when and if she were put in her friends' shoes. Atros had taught her well. They had brainwashed her so completely she didn't even know who she was aside from being an Atros trooper and citizen.

That was why she had to get away from the city and escape from the organization's sphere of influence. That was why, just a little over a week after the ritual was concluded, she had left her friends and the lake house at which they were staying without telling anyone. She was chasing the words of a memory she couldn't even determine was real, embarking on a journey to look for her Kulcan father.

And now she was lost . . .

'Damn it,' Keix swore through gritted teeth as she drew up her knees to her chest and pressed her eyelids to the bony joints. She released a long exhale. Her heart was still beating frantically. It seemed reluctant to let its guard down after the nightmare she had just had. The pain that had assaulted every last inch of her body in the dream felt fresh, but the image of the fake ghost of her mother seared into her mind was what rattled her the most.

The first time that Keix had had the nightmare was after the ritual. Back then, she'd assumed it was a one-off incident, a remnant of the trauma she had undergone. However, the horrific dream started invading her sleep more and more frequently. Now, it had turned into a nightly ordeal.

Her wall of resistance against the emotional battering was crumbling, as was her body's patience—although for an entirely different set of reasons. An unwelcome trio of lightheadedness, headache and hunger pangs had been assaulting her at different intervals for the past week since she ran out of food and water. At present, she was having all three at an intensity that was impairing her senses.

And that was saying something, considering her father was a Kulcan, a race of warriors who were known to be one of the best fighters in the universe. Keix's genes not only gifted her with innate and immaculate control over her physical abilities, but she was also able to tune her senses to a level of sensitivity unmatched by beings from other races.

However, even with her hearing ramped up to maximum awareness now, she had to strain to hear the low hum of the forest. The cacophony of sounds here was unlike the melodious songs of the electric green qiues that resided in the woods right outside the Atros Sector borders. There was also a somnolence to the air, as if it had fallen into the deepest sleep.

Having been in this part of the woods for several days, Keix knew that very soon, a soft muffled gurgling would rumble through the forest. She hadn't been able to figure out which creatures made those sounds, but she was sure that there would be enough light for her to continue on her journey in due time, even though a fog had gathered in the night. Before the wake-up call came, however, a sharp chirp pierced the air.

Apprehension crept through Keix. She had never heard the likes of it in this patch of the forest before. In fact, she hadn't managed to catch a glimpse of any living thing in the past week. As if affirming her wariness, the lightening sky faintly illuminated a frozen haagi a few steps away from where she sat crouched. Had it made the warning sound that she just heard? Keix knew these palm-sized creatures were impossibly fast, had an impeccable sense of direction, but would be rendered immobile whenever they sensed danger. But she didn't know if they made any calls—and if they did, what they sounded like. This one right in front of her was grey in colour and could have passed off as a rock.

Regardless, I must get going, thought Keix, standing up in one swift movement. But the second she straightened her legs, her body rebelled.

Dizziness and hunger overwhelmed her. Doubling over, she retched while her stomach roiled and she got all upset with herself. What were the bad decisions she had made that landed her in her current predicament? Everything she had done since she left Atros.

'Check. And checkmate,' she mumbled sarcastically, after disgorging nothing but bile.

The ominous chirping filled the air once more. This time, its urgency was clear.

Keix ignored the foul taste in her mouth and looked at the haagi. It hadn't moved at all. Was the call made by some other creature? She swept her gaze around. That was when she saw something that made her stomach churn even more.

A group of four, dressed in unitards, was flitting through the thicket in her direction. The figures were covered from head to toe: gloves, hoods and goggles. Their shimmery black attires, under the eerie shroud of the fog, blended perfectly into their surroundings.

Keix's heart raced erratically at the sense of déjà vu. It was as if she had been teleported back in time to when she came across Odats in Atros's PEER after Zej and Pod rescued her from the underwater prison.

But these were clearly not Odats, who were thickset and clumsy, not to mention, repulsive. While Keix couldn't ascertain the attractiveness of these beings, it was as apparent as day that there was absolute grace, agility and dexterity in the way they moved. Even the weapons slung on their hips (Keix could make out a couple of guns and a baton) moved silently in tandem with them. These shadowy figures' swiftness surpassed even the gentlest of breezes as they made zero disturbance while chasing her.

Keix couldn't decide if she should confront them head on or flee.

For a fist fight, she would have to wait until they were almost close enough to touch. The trees in this area were too close together for her to manoeuvre advantageously. Add to that the thickening mist and the fact that she had never fought these figures before, the odds didn't seem to be in her favour.

Her other option was to flee. But for that, she would have to move faster than her pursuers and hope that she could lose them in the fog. Getting to a clearing might also add to her chances of winning a fight against these figures.

Keix would be confident of facing these strangers and taking them down effortlessly had she not been in such a weakened state. Now, she couldn't even be sure that she could last five minutes whether she chose to fight or flee. She knew she only had herself to blame for her current dilemma.

After she had left Atros, she came across a small hut which reminded her of the safe house to which Pod and Zej had taken her. It was there, at that safe house, that she saw first-hand the ugly side of Atros, when a hybrid (a human whose soul had been fused with a ghost) called Seyfer killed Rold, a friend she had just made.

Keix couldn't bear to face the painful flashbacks, so she had taken off in the opposite direction. Since then, she had been avoiding any signs of life, preferring to starve than ask for help.

Fuelled by pure adrenaline at the prospect of getting captured, Keix channelled her leftover strength into her limbs and prepared to run. But the immobile haagi, a mound of grey on the brown-black ground huddled directly in the path of the approaching black-clad figures, caught her attention. She was suddenly reminded of the chilling fear that had petrified her in her nightmare.

Before Keix realized what she was doing, she had scooped up the furry creature. Its heart was beating so rapidly it was positively buzzing in her grasp. Then, she ran in the direction where she thought the undergrowth looked sparser, dodging and ducking under tree trunks that were leaning over at odd angles.

Just as Keix threw a glance over her shoulder for the fifth time, a sudden pattering of feet exploded. She rammed into a warm, solid body and let out an involuntary oof. A familiar voice echoed her. Turning around, Keix had to blink twice before registering the identity of the person into whom she had collided. When her brain finally got with the programme, she couldn't keep the shock out of her voice.

'Vin? What are you doing here?' she demanded.

'Following you, of course,' replied Vin. She looked in the direction from which Keix had been fleeing and cursed. 'Who the hell are they? Why are they chasing you? And why in Atros's name are you holding a haagi?'

* * *

The surprise of seeing her best friend had an invigorating effect on Keix, chasing away the pain and nausea she was battling.

Her pursuers had already covered about half the initial distance between them and were closing in. Still, Keix remained rooted to the spot,

unable to tear her eyes away from Vin. Keix just needed to soak in the sight
of her friend, whom she had known for more than a third of her life.

Vin's hair had always been shocking pink, shaved on one side to reveal
a tattoo-like intricate maze of pink lines on her scalp—both of which were
distinctive features and traits of the enigmatic race of Ifarls, who were her
ancestors. But she was now sporting brown hair, in a shoulder-length,
layered cut that made her look . . . serious. It was a symbolic change to
distance herself from her heritage after the Ifarls had offered her up as a
sacrifice in that same ritual to close the gateway between the living and dead.

Like Keix, Vin had been tortured by Atros and turned into a hybrid
like Seyfer. She became a vicious and ruthless soldier imbued with
inhuman strength. The hybrids did the organization's bidding because
their sole enjoyment in life was to see the world burn. They were worse
than mercenaries. Atros had allowed them a long leash because the
organization's end goal was to create a ghost army; hybrids had the ability
to control these spirits. Together with Seyfer, under Atros's orders, Vin
even set out to capture Keix again.

Eventually, all of them—the hybrids and Keix—fell into the
Ifarls' clutches.

Zenchi, the Ifarl elder, said that anyone who had been at the brink
of death or had crossed the threshold but came back to life one too many
times 'straddled both worlds'—the living and the dead—even if they hadn't
yet become a hybrid. Keix was one of these people because the torture that
Atros had put her through primed her for that transformation.

Maii, the Ifarl whom Zenchi had deployed to investigate and thwart
Atros's shady activities, as well as gain Pod and Zej's trust, completed
Keix's conversion into a hybrid. It was a pre-emptive measure to make sure
that nothing would go wrong during the ritual, reasoned Zenchi.

All of these hybrids had to die. Zenchi was afraid that keeping anyone
around who had a link to the afterworld, no matter how tenuous, would
render the rite a failure, and she wouldn't be able to close the portal
completely.

Zenchi also believed that Vin, a descendant of Iv't, the Ifarl who
opened the gateway between the living and dead (basically, the origin
of all their problems), had to be sacrificed to right the wrongs of her
forefather.

Keix understood her friend's need to become a different person. She
herself had chopped off her hair into a bob after her mother's death. Before

that, she had kept it long for as far back as she could remember. Wearing her hair short accentuated her huge, round eyes. Each and every time that she caught a glimpse of her reflection was a stark reminder that she was on her own now.

Vin probably felt the same way; her brown hair serving as a constant self-reminder that she wanted nothing more to do with the Ifarls.

What an ironic way to escape from one's past . . .

'Sure, you can stand there and admire me all day. It's not like we've got a set of weirdos chasing us down, right?' demanded Vin in exasperation, picking up her feet and taking off away from their pursuers.

Keix took a beat to throw her friend a cheeky smile before following her cue. The coordination between them, honed by instinctive rapport and years of training at Atros, was seamless. In fact, with her ally in the picture, Keix's confidence of taking the group down had now quadrupled. The task should be a breeze, given their Atros training.

But as the minutes passed, the 'set of weirdos' pursuing them showed no signs of fatigue. They were still moving without a sound and at the same speed, neither escalating nor de-escalating their pursuit, despite having one more warm body to chase down now.

A thought struck Keix. 'Do you think they are droids?' she whispered to Vin. Droids, as far as she knew, were ancient machines that had served a host of purposes—from cleaning the streets to assembling weapons. Atros used to rely heavily on them, and they could be found everywhere in the past. However, when the portal between the living and the dead was opened decades ago, these droids were put out of commission because they malfunctioned in the presence of paranormal activity and energy. No one knew why, but when there were ghosts around, inanimate machines such as communication devices and other electronics would sputter and die. But droids, perhaps due to their extensive range of motion and mobility, would turn destructive, posing a danger to anyone nearby.

At least that was what Keix remembered, having spent a grand total of fifteen minutes listening to Sabul, a wizened old man who taught Atrossian history at ATI, talk about these things that she had neither seen nor had any interest in.

What did droids look like anyway? The stray question wandered into Keix's mind.

Vin gave her a wary look. Keix's deduction was not impossible. The portal had been closed recently, which meant that Atros could bring these droids out of 'retirement', programme them to do their bidding and let them loose to roam around without risking harm to their citizens.

'Only one way to find out,' said Keix, all of a sudden convinced that confronting the figures instead of running from them would give her some answers. But just as she turned around, she saw another set of pursuers heading towards them from the left of her peripheral vision. Keix did another count. The odds had reset to one to four, and the fog was getting thicker by the second.

Keix and Vin exchanged glances. They swerved away from the newcomers and, minutes later, found themselves in an area with a much sparser undergrowth. Surely they would be hitting some kind of clearing soon?

'Wait a minute . . . they are corralling us!' said Vin.

'They are *what*?'

Vin didn't have to answer Keix because at that moment, they almost tipped into a crater. It was a clearing, all right; but not the kind that either of them had hoped to see. Keix would bet her life that the semi-circular dent in the ground—more than five times Keix's height deep, and double that in diameter—was created by Atros's black-hole bullet. What alarmed Keix even more was that in the dead centre of the crater, a pillar had been driven into the ground. This served as an ignition point for the shot, because once the bullet left the barrel, the first thing it hit would be the core of its spherical 'kill zone' or suction range.

Black-hole bullets were Keix's curse. Eight years ago, her mother's workplace was attacked by ghosts and Atros troopers used the rounds—newly developed then—to get rid of the vengeful spirits. Keix's mum had been caught in the kill zone and classified as dead because Atros said everything that was sucked into the vacuum had disappeared forever.

Then, years later, as a loyal Atros soldier, Keix had fired one of the shots at an army of ghosts that attacked the city Sector's security outposts where she was stationed. Vin had been in the bullet's effective range. Even though Keix knew that her best friend and fellow troopers would die, she had squeezed the trigger; Atros soldiers put the safety of the city and its civilians above all other things, their own lives included.

It was only much later, after Zej and Pod rescued her, that the former told her that black-hole bullets didn't kill or make people and things disappear forever; they only teleported them to a secret Atros facility (which turned out to be PEER) for the organization's twisted experiments.

Learning about this lie gave Keix pause. It crossed her mind that there was a chance that her mother could still be alive; but rationally speaking, she knew that this possibility was next to zero. Her mum, although resilient, wouldn't have been able to last through Atros's systematic tortures. Not for eight years straight.

When Keix broke into the secret facility to save Vin and the rest of the Atrossians imprisoned there, there was no sign of her mum.

If their pursuers had access to the black-hole bullet technology exclusive to Atros, they were definitely working for the organization. There was no chance in hell that Keix would allow herself to be captured by them again.

In the heat of the moment, Keix turned to Vin and said, 'Weirdos want fight. Weirdos get fight.' Once the words left her lips, she ground to a halt and waited. When the first figure came within reach, she spun around and raced towards it. She dropped her shoulders to land a high kick at its head. This trick had never failed to knock out an opponent, but this time, she was shocked to see the black-clad figure dodge her booted foot easily.

Keix bent her knees, bracing herself for a hard landing because of her unsuccessful manoeuvre. She almost extended her hands to break her fall, but realized that she was still clutching the haagi in her left hand. To protect the creature, she landed on her right shoulder and grunted as she hit the ground. Sharp pain rammed through her body.

Beside her, Vin was trying to land a punch on one of the two figures circling her.

The two girls' opening moves hadn't managed to tip the scales in their favour. The attackers were clearly skilled, and Keix was suddenly doubtful about prevailing in this fight if it dragged on.

The edges of her vision were getting blurry; she couldn't tell if it was because of her recent starvation, or if it was getting foggier. But there was no time to dwell on these morale-dampening thoughts as four more figures joined the fray. The group had split up and were trying to separate Vin and herself, simultaneously herding them closer to the lip of the crater.

The smoothness of the concave pit would make it difficult for anyone who had fallen into it to climb out.

'We have to push them back,' Keix said to Vin. 'They are trying to drive us into the crater!'

'Over. My. Dead. Body.' Vin's reply was punctuated by grunts.

Keix feinted left and landed a right hook on the temple of one of the figures attacking her. The impact, which vibrated from her knuckles all the way up her arm to her shoulder, caused the figure to fall to the ground and stay there, prone. Shaking the pain from her arm, she shot a satisfied smirk at the haagi in her hand.

'One down for me!' Keix shouted to Vin, looking around, trying to locate her friend in the hazy surroundings.

'Vin!' Keix couldn't keep the panic out of her voice.

'Still four. Don't gloat!' Her friend's reply came from somewhere to her right, not too far away.

Relieved, Keix almost laughed as she bent into another crouch and threw her leg out, aiming for one of her attacker's ankles. She managed to knock it off its feet, but it scrambled up in no time.

Continuing to mix up her moves, Keix tried to find a spot of weakness in these hooded figures. But every time she gained a bit of ground, they would redeem their advantage and then some a couple of moves later. It was as if they were learning in real time to predict her moves. Cradling the haagi didn't help matters, and Keix wished she had never picked it up. But because she had, she didn't think it was fair to leave it to fend for itself.

A scream from Vin distracted Keix and one of the figures circling her moved in. She took a step back only to realize that she had been cornered and was right at the edge of the crater. She felt a swooping sensation in her stomach and let out a startled cry as she hit the ground and rolled down to the lowest point of the hole. The air was knocked out of her when her back slammed against the pillar.

'Keix!' Vin shouted.

Keix scrambled to her feet, but she couldn't spot Vin. Instead, through the murky mist, she caught sight of a shadowy figure looming at the edge of the crater with a gun drawn. She tried to run up the trap, but as she had foreseen, she slipped on the smooth surface and slid back to the bottom of the pit.

The hair at the back of her neck stood on end. Certain that the figure was going to fire the black-hole round any second now, exhaustion struck Keix. She was going to be captured again; Vin along with her. The only comforting thing she could tell herself was that she had fought a good fight. But once again, it just wasn't enough. Who knew what would happen to them at Atros? Would they be used as lab rats again? Would Atros attempt to turn them back into hybrids? Was that even possible now that the portal was closed?

Keix scoffed and wondered whether getting turned back into a bloodthirsty hybrid might be a welcome respite, for then she would no longer feel guilty or ashamed. There would only be a cold rage coursing through her and the need to make the people who crossed her pay.

She looked at the haagi, still humming, still motionless in her grip. If she had left the unfortunate creature on the ground, would it have survived? The hooded figures might have just ignored it and it could have hopped away after they left. Keix felt an irrational bubble of mirth in her throat as hot tears scalded her eyes. *When will I ever learn that I'm just not cut out to save people—not even a tiny creature?* she chided herself.

A sudden gust of wind made her look up, befuddled. Everything seemed to slow down as a blurry figure approached her. Instead of readying her fists as the figure neared, she found herself holding the haagi closer to her heart protectively.

A gunshot sounded.

The figure finally came into focus and it took Keix a split second to see that this person had his back to her. There was something familiar about the silhouette . . .

A sharp image of the Kulcan with whom she had once crossed paths—the one who had cut the lock of the cage in which she was trapped during the portal-closing ritual—snapped into her head. Before she could fully register her new discovery, she saw the Kulcan jump high into the air, unsheath the broadsword strapped to his back and—to her even greater shock—in one smooth move, slice the bullet hurtling towards the pillar. In. Half.

2

Maii | An Opening

Maii was willing to bet her Ifarl powers that if someone had told her a year ago that she would be living in Atros, she would have scoffed in their face. And she would have lost the wager. Sorely.

Not only was she doing just that, she was now preparing to stride into the city's most prestigious club with Dace, an Atrossian, to 'mingle' with Atros's elites. It was rare to encounter instances where the two races interacted freely, so what they were doing would definitely attract eyeballs.

'Ready?' asked Pod over the intercom. He was back at the safe house with his screens and keyboard, trying to make sure that everyone in their group stayed off the radar of Atros troopers. All of them—Dace and Maii, who were approaching the club, as well as Zej, who was waiting in Dace's hovercar at the building's basement parking area to help them make a quick getaway later—were wanted by the organization.

Maii murmured an assent and stepped out of the elevator that she and Dace had ridden to the top floor of the building where the club was situated. Her boots clicked on the polished stone floor of the lobby as the mermaid tail of her slinky halterneck dress rippled around them. The flowy movement reminded Maii of the way the tall grasses of the field beside her home would sway whenever a breeze caressed them. She used to train her less-than-stellar fighting skills on that patch of land every day, before sunrise. Memories of the solitude she had felt and the tang of the crisp morning air caused an ache to form in her throat. She missed her carefree days in the Ifarl village, where only the pursuit of knowledge mattered.

Since her departure from her hometown, Maii had had to build relationships and betray friendships, as well as deal with emotions like anxiety and discomfort. She didn't know where she stood among this group of people she had tentatively come to call her friends: Pod, who wore his emotions on his sleeve; Zej, brooding, carrying the weight of the world on his shoulders; and Dace . . . ?

Maii tilted her head to look at her partner-in-crime for today's mission. The air of unpredictability that hung around him had quietened down the moment they stepped out of the elevator. His eyes were narrowed, and one corner of his lips lifted mockingly as he surveyed the entrance to the club—one of the tallest and widest set of lacquered doors Maii had ever seen.

A rich, soothing voice resounded through the lobby. 'Dear valued patrons, welcome to *A*. We strive to provide the best experience, so please do not hesitate to approach our staff if you require anything.'

Maii stifled a snort at the clichéd and pompous announcement. How exactly did she end up here, miles from where she predicted her life would go? Perhaps the unravelling started when Zenchi, the leader of the Ifarls, sent her here a little over a year ago on the pretext of helping a rebel faction called Oka.

The resistance group wanted to stop Atros from building a ghost army; they felt that it was unethical of the organization to surreptitiously capture their own citizens and turn them into ghost-human hybrids just to strengthen their defences. Zenchi offered them a permanent solution—the Ifarls would close the portal between the living and the dead. No ghosts equals no hybrids equals no justification for twisted procedures. In return, Zenchi asked for crucial information and resources that they needed to perform the ritual.

In the course of this partnership, Maii helped Pod and Zej, Atros soldiers who had secretly defected to Oka, break their half-Kulcan friend called Keix out of a high-security water prison. But Maii didn't tell them that she would eventually need to make Keix's transformation into a hybrid complete. She also held back the information that Keix would have to die during the portal-closing rites to allow the two worlds to have a clean break from each other.

Pod and Dace were shocked, to say the least, when Maii used her Ifarl compulsion to get them to hold Keix down to merge a ghost into her body.

Having been friends with Keix for years, Pod and Zej were understandably upset when they discovered that Maii had kept them in the dark about the Ifarls' true plan. Nevertheless, readily accepting the need to think about the bigger picture, they stood back as the ritual went ahead as scheduled and the portal was closed according to plan . . . somewhat. Ghosts would never wreak havoc on the human world again. But for some mystifying reason, Keix and the rest of the hybrids didn't die. And the Ifarls, Maii included, lost their powers.

Zenchi suspected that the last two outcomes might have had something to do with a half-Ifarl called Vin. While the Ifarl elder sought to figure out how to get their powers back, she requested Maii to continue to keep an eye on Vin. So, Maii had returned to Atros along with Pod, Zej, Vin and Keix—these four were a tight bunch who went to the ATI together—as well as Dace and his girlfriend, Lana.

It was a simple task, really. And even though Maii was grappling with the loss of her powers, she hadn't expected herself to fail so spectacularly. More than three weeks ago, Vin had disappeared in the middle of the night from the lake house that they had been living in since their return to Atros after the Ifarl ritual. So had Keix. And Lana.

Maii wanted to sigh, but with an exemplary show of self-discipline, locked away the jumble of thoughts in her mind and schooled her features into her usual detached expression. This was not the time to get sidetracked. She needed today's mission to be a success in order to find Vin. Pushing her shoulders back, Maii adjusted her arm that was looped through Dace's.

At her movement, Dace cocked his head and flashed her his lopsided smile, his signature irreverence on full display. 'Oh, what I wouldn't give to get a peek inside your head.'

Maii didn't reply, but she returned a tight smile of her own. On any other day, she would have turned the full blast of her icy glare at anyone who dared intrude into her personal space. Coupled with the scar that ran from her right temple across her cheek, that withering look which she had perfected served as a great deterrent to keep others at bay. Physically and emotionally. But she had to at least pretend to be on good terms with Dace today for the sake of their current mission.

There was actually another reason for her cordiality. On the night when the three girls disappeared, Maii had seen Lana sneaking out of their safe house by the lake. Although there had been no signs of a struggle,

Dace, Pod and Zej jumped to the conclusion that Atros had kidnapped them and started drawing up plans to locate and rescue their friends.

Maii had to find Vin—Keix and Lana weren't her priority—and she didn't know where to start looking, so she went along with the boys' assumption. She tried to rationalize that she had kept mum about Lana because, even though she could have left of her own accord, there was a chance, albeit small, that Atros *did* abduct her. After all, among the seven of them, only Vin, Keix and Lana had been imprisoned by the organization previously. Furthermore, Maii didn't want the group to be distracted and go off on tangents searching for the three girls separately. Four heads were better than three, right? But the longer she kept her silence, the deeper the truth gnawed at her.

Now, under Dace's scrutiny, the thought of them finding out that she had withheld information again felt like an insect crawling across her nape. No, she wouldn't—couldn't—allow the guilt to eat her up. She pretended to shake the fringe out of her eyes to clear her thoughts.

Even if Dace wasn't trying to bore holes into her skull with his eyes, Maii had always felt a little unsettled in his presence. The Atrossian was forever a hair's breadth too sure of himself, too glib. The sinister gleam in his eyes whenever he said something fatalistic felt at odds with Zej's self-righteousness and Pod's optimism. Tonight, she realized why.

His curly ginger fringe that usually grazed his eyes had been combed back, making him look exceptionally suave. Under the warm lighting, his teal-coloured eyes shone like polished amber, twinkling, exuding an easy warmth.

His grey bespoke suit. The self-assuredness of his bearing. Even his towering frame. Every aspect of him looked at home here, in a space frequented only by the richest, most influential people in Atros who held sway over the Atrossian government. There was no way a person could blend in so seamlessly into a foreign environment.

He must be one of them, thought Maii.

But this wasn't the time to consider the implications of her deduction, especially since she had no way of proving it. So what if Dace was an elite Atrossian? He was hanging out with wanted criminals, which made him complicit as an accomplice. Still, Maii resolved to be extra cautious from now on. She drew herself to her tallest height. Her pride refused to allow her to pale in comparison to Dace. She was an Ifarl. And in her sixteen years of life, she had never failed to excel in whatever she set out to do.

Until you lost Vin. Maii dismissed that stray mocking voice with a blink of her eyes, restoring her cool façade.

'And we're in.' Pod's pronouncement came through crisply over the intercom tucked in Maii's ear. 'Well, technically, not "we". I'm not in. You two are. In. Physically. And'—he let out a low whistle—'I'll never get tired of seeing those gleaming, double-panelled doors folding so sleekly into their wooden frame. The interiors are even more impressive than I'd imagined. I mean, whatever I can see of it through these two measly security cameras they've installed at the entrance. But what a name for a club! *A*. Pfft.'

Maii allowed herself a half smile, welcoming the distraction provided by Pod's incessant jabbering. Reticent by nature, Ifarls preferred to be economical with words.

When Maii had first met Pod, a master of long-winded and convoluted conversations, she was irritated by his rambling. Over time, however, she grew to find his chattiness endearing, although it still irked her when he lapsed into his stream-of-consciousness monologues. These usually happened whenever he was not in the thick of the action—in other words, now.

Taking in the view in front of her, Maii tapped on all the knowledge that she had gained from living with Atrossians in the past months and tried to understand Pod's fascination with *A*. The unimaginative name aside, the club looked to be the epitome of Atrossians' obsession with materialism. Situated on the top floor of the highest building in the heart of Atros's city centre, *A*'s real estate was as prime as it could get.

Sure, the attention to detail could be considered impressive. The music was just loud enough to camouflage whispered conversations, and its bass and beat, coupled with the pulsating lights, were made to coax even the stiffest person in the room to groove. Cushioned seats were arranged in cosy configurations around the dance floor, and Maii could almost feel the velvety softness of the luxurious upholstery just by laying her eyes on them.

However, the fact that every surface not obscured by a partygoer was either gleaming or glittering made her eyes hurt. Simplicity ought to be key to everything material. Opulence was gaudy. If one had to possess something, it should be knowledge, not material goods. And what would be one's life purpose if not to uncover the secrets of, well, life? And the secrets of life one would not find in a place where appearances are everything. Maii couldn't stop herself from judging.

'Okay. I'm losing my eyes on you because those doors are closing behind you and there are no security cameras inside this dratted place.'

Pod's wistful tone shifted to one of annoyance in a split second. 'I mean, which moron refuses to install cameras in this day and age?'

Dace made a show of bending down and putting his face next to Maii. She resisted the urge to swat him away as he whispered right beside her ear—or intercom, rather—'A moron with something to hide, of course.'

'That was a rhetorical question! Of course, I know that there's something fishy going on here, duh,' retorted Pod.

Dace straightened up with an insolent expression. He looked ready to banter with Pod, but the instant another voice came over the intercom, the smirk slid off his face and his eyes narrowed.

Zej's voice was sharp. 'Can we focus on the task at hand? Please.'

'All right. Task at hand. Let's get a drink,' said Dace in a false cheery tone, steering an exasperated Maii towards the very-prominent circular open bar island in the middle of the club as if he were showing off some trophy to his fellow patrons.

Maii stopped herself from shaking her head. It was an understatement to say that Zej and Dace had history. As to what kind of history, Maii wasn't sure. She wasn't interested either. She only knew that they harboured an obvious and mutual dislike for each other. Observing them interact was like watching someone mix two unknown chemicals together to find out what reaction it would yield. So far, it had been fizzles and sizzles. There hadn't been any major 'explosions'. Yet.

'You'll need to keep your wits about you.' Zej's disapproval was apparent.

'Just one,' insisted Dace.

Maii was amazed at how she could literally *hear* Dace rolling his eyes when he said that, although she doubted that he would keep his word. Still, babysitting him was the last thing on her to-do list.

They came here today to steal someone's fingerprints. By hook or by crook, they would leave with the prints. And when they did, Maii hoped that not only would they be able to find Vin, she might also learn Atros's deepest and darkest secrets.

* * *

Within five minutes of perching herself on a barstool beside Dace, Maii had suppressed the urge to walk out of *A* at least a dozen times. The bartender had appeared with two sickly red drinks in thin-stemmed glasses and delivered a self-important greeting, 'Welcome drinks, on the house. Enjoy,' then vanished. But everyone else in *A* had snuck at least three glances in her direction. There were even a handful of people who were openly gaping at her and Dace.

Pod's voice sounded over the intercom again. 'Relax, Maii,' he said. 'You're an Ifarl. That's why everyone's looking at you.' Even without his 'eyes', he had read the room correctly. But he was wrong about the cause of Maii's nerves. The stares, she could handle.

Atrossians viewed Ifarls as an enigmatic race so it was only natural that their curiosity would be piqued, seeing Maii with the race's trademark neon pink hair undisguised, mingling among them. It was the niggling feeling, manifesting as a knot at the back of her throat, that their careful planning might go horribly awry, that was hard to ignore.

'You're worried.' Dace's keen observation took Maii by surprise.

'Wha—why? Who's worried? Maii? Our plan is simple and easy to carry out. We know Raye has a weird obsession with Ifarls, so it won't be hard for Maii to get him to touch something and swipe it afterwards. You guys will be out before you know it.' Pod was, as usual, the irrepressible optimist.

Zej was the one who had first floated the possibility of stealing the prints of an Atros trooper called Raye, the only son of Atros's most decorated general. This was because Pod had been running into dead ends trying to find proof that Atros kidnapped Lana, Keix and Vin. Even with Pod's exceptional skills, it was hard to get into the system remotely unless he had an authentication key, like a set of fingerprints.

It wasn't as if Pod and Zej could waltz into any of Atros's offices after their last expedition to PEER—even if Pod vowed that he had erased all traces of their records off the organization's system. Keix had wanted to return to the research centre to rescue Vin after Pod, Zej and Maii got her out of the underwater prison there. Then, triggered and encouraged by the half-truths that Zenchi had fed them about how Keix and those selected by Atros to turn into hybrids were key to stopping the organization, they devised a plan to try to infiltrate PEER again.

But Pod and Zej's covers were blown when they ran into a hybrid called Seyfer, who captured all of them and locked them up. When Oka helped them break out of their holding cells, they released a bunch of other prisoners and fought their way out. They didn't just cause a commotion. It was a full out revolt against Atros in one of their most important and highly secured buildings right in the city centre.

So, they didn't just have one good reason to never set foot into another Atros building; they had millions of them.

Nonetheless, that didn't stop Pod from gasping in excitement as soon as Zej made the suggestion. Pod's fingers flew over his keyboards, and he started digging up every kind of private and professional information on the target using his uncanny ability to find the most vulnerable points of anything or any person behind a screen.

'He frequents *A*.' Pod sounded both awed and disappointed after a minute of furious typing.

'A what?' A confused Maii asked.

'*A*? The invite-only club in the city centre!' Pod's exasperation was clear. 'Only VVVIPs can get in.'

Maii rummaged through her memory and recalled that she'd come across the name of the place when she was doing research to infiltrate the rebel group, Oka, that Pod and Zej had been a part of.

Zenchi had used the word hedonistic to describe it.

'Isn't there another place where we can catch him?' she asked, sensing from Pod the impossibility of getting an invite into the prestigious club.

Pod turned back to his screen. 'We stand the highest chance of getting him alone at *A*. Everywhere else he goes, there's always someone tagging along.'

'I can get us an invite to *A*.' Dace's announcement earned him looks of disbelief from the group.

All he had ever done since Lana's disappearance was skulk around, throw thinly veiled insults and make snarky comments mostly aimed at Zej. But once the group realized that Dace was serious, they had been drawn into a whirlpool of mapping out the details of how to carry out this plan—a plan cobbled together in just five days.

Caught up in her thoughts, Maii let the silence stretch. However, the lack of conversation seemed too much for Dace because he suddenly asked, 'Why are you really here, Maii? Are you on a secret mission? Are you here to spy on us? Because I wonder all the time why I'm here. Unlike you, I have no family or tribe to turn to.' His eyes took on a faraway look.

Maii stared at him. She was more than aware that Dace had his reservations about her since the day they were introduced to one another. Even though that undercurrent of distrust hadn't intensified after that compulsion incident with Keix and the portal-closing ritual, she had noticed that he was always openly observing her. Now, under the influence of the 'welcome drink' that he'd downed in one gulp, he seemed to be going off on a tangent to see if he could catch her off guard and make her inadvertently let slip a truth or two.

Pod, who was oblivious to the fact that the air around Dace had turned heavy, chimed in. 'Hey. Get off Maii's case. Maii's done with secret missions—right, Maii?'

If only you knew, Pod, thought Maii with another pang of guilt. She wondered what he would do should he discover that she was here only because Zenchi had instructed her to keep an eye on Vin. Pod was the one who had advocated for her after the ritual. He reasoned with Zej that she had merely been carrying out orders, and that every one of them had to bear responsibility for what had happened with Keix. *Each one of us has betrayed Keix and Vin in our own way,* he had said.

Before Maii could reply, Pod turned the tables on Dace. 'And speaking of family and tribe, who did you approach to snag an invite to this place at such short notice? Every time I ask you something remotely personal, all I get from you is a shrug.'

Right on cue, Dace raised his shoulders and gave Maii a crooked smile that didn't quite reach his eyes. 'I'm sure you can find out easily, if you really wanted to know,' he said in reply to Pod.

Pod sniffed, offended. 'Well, it's common courtesy not to dig into your teammate's background, however great the temptation.'

Maii might have applauded Pod's dogmatism if she hadn't been fighting the urge to glance around to check if anyone was eavesdropping on them. Anyone with more than one brain cell could have sensed the oddness of the conversation.

Fortunately, Maii was spared the need to remind them of the mission at hand because, within seconds, Pod's voice came through the intercom again. This time, the urgency in his tone was apparent. 'Target's approaching. His hovercar is pulling into the building.'

'I have eyes on his hovercar,' confirmed Zej.

Tense seconds passed.

'Wait,' said Zej in a grim voice. 'He's not alone.'

The foreboding in the air thickened. Maii and Dace tried to look nonchalant and unaffected by this new development because people in the club were still observing them closely. Over the intercom, the clicking of keys on Pod's end intensified.

'This can't be,' started Pod. 'He's never come with a plus-one bef—'

Pod gasped at the same time as Zej said, 'He's with an Ifarl.'

Every coherent line of thought that Maii had flew into a mass of confusion. Why would an Ifarl come here of their own accord?

But then again, she was here, wasn't she? *Under Zenchi's orders*, she tried to reason. She knew in her heart that she was reaching, but she was adamant that Ifarls wouldn't be here for recreational purposes.

This other Ifarl might be on a mission too. Yes, that would be the most logical explanation. Or they could be just a half-Ifarl or quarter-Ifarl with no loyalty or link to her tribe. Maii nodded to herself. Those of mixed heritage who were not brought up in accordance with their customs tended to be rogue operators.

Or . . . it could very well be an imposter! An Atrossian could easily try to pass off as an Ifarl by colouring their hair pink or getting a maze tattoo on their scalp—both distinctive features of Ifarls.

'We should abort the mission.' Zej's reluctant but firm voice interrupted Maii's internal monologue.

'Yes, we should. You guys can avoid running into them if you leave now,' said Pod, the words rushing out of him. 'This Ifarl is a wild card that we didn't plan for.'

'No,' whispered Maii. 'I need to find Vin. *We* need to find her and Keix. And Lana,' she added belatedly, avoiding Dace's eyes in case she gave herself away. 'Besides, it's too late to abort. We've already created too much of a commotion here. To leave so abruptly—and right before another Ifarl walks in—would be too suspicious. She could be a fake, for all we know.'

'She? It's a guy, Maii,' clarified Pod. 'And judging from the colour and lustre of his hair, I would say that he definitely looks like a full Ifarl.'

Maii levelled her gaze at the entrance to *A* as warring thoughts filled her mind. This mission was a mistake from the start. She knew the risks when they had started detailing the plan. But she'd felt desperate enough to attempt it.

The alternative was for Maii to go back to Zenchi and admit that Vin had gone missing. Somehow, Maii had a feeling that her elder already knew what had happened, and didn't contact her because she trusted that Maii would figure things out as she had always done.

Maii wanted to blame the smooth-sailing lead-up to their entry into *A* for lulling her into complacency. But they were now eyeballs deep in the muck they'd waded into. Getting out without a scratch was a non-option.

Maii also hated to admit it, but the appearance of the unknown Ifarl had ignited in her a ravaging need to find answers. Her curiosity overriding logical reasoning, she found herself saying through gritted teeth to her team, 'I'm seeing this through.'

Locating Vin—and by extension, Keix and Lana—notwithstanding, Maii had to figure out why this Ifarl was hanging around an Atrossian, and one who was part of the governing organization at that. To do so, she couldn't have Pod and Zej screaming in her ear to abort the mission.

Decision made, she removed her intercom by pretending to adjust her hair. She leaned on Dace's shoulders and slipped the tiny earpiece into the inner pocket of his suit. The move earned her a look of disbelief, then a wide smile from Dace, who was ever the nonconformist.

After what seemed like an eerily silent forever, the double-panelled doors opened up and Maii had to stop herself from staring at the pair of newcomers like the rest of the Atrossians around her.

When Maii had been on the receiving end of the stares, she assumed that everyone was just gaping because of the novelty of seeing an Ifarl-Atrossian pairing.

The height difference between Dace and her was also striking; he was one of the tallest Atrossians she had met, while she was the size of an average Ifarl, whose builds tended to be more petite compared to other races. And the scar that ran from her right temple to the corner of her mouth would have tipped the gawk-able factor over the edge.

But Raye and his Ifarl plus-one were a whole different level of eye-catching. Both of them, who were about the same height, had ivory-cream skin that looked untouched by the sun. Their paleness was set off by the indigo shades of their sleek suits. Both sets of garments were cut to perfection, and while the Atrossian's suit was made of velvet, the Ifarl's had a more subdued matte finish.

The Ifarl's hairstyle was quite something too—in a shade of pink so bright it was almost glowing (usually a sign of high abilities). His longish hair was gelled into an old-fashioned spiky style, with the right side of it shaved to show off the reddish maze of lines that marked every Ifarl's scalp.

Raye, their original target, on the other hand, had midnight black hair, unshaved, but similarly styled.

The moment the newcomers stepped into *A*, they moved towards Maii and Dace in a synchronized and purposeful manner.

'Fancy seeing another Ifarl here, in Atros's most exclusive club,' the Ifarl addressed Maii as if Dace were invisible. His voice was melodious—another distinctive trait of their race—and had a deep, rich timbre to it. 'I wonder . . . what brings you here?'

Maii imitated one of Dace's shrugs, the kind that was so vague, one couldn't tell if it was indifferent or sardonic. 'Wouldn't you give the nine stars to find out,' she replied with a downward inflection, alluding to the nine dimmest stars in the skies, a symbol of mystery in Ifarl lore.

Dace laughed at her gibe, and the Ifarl looked at him as if he were a speck of dust on his perfectly polished shoes—a feat since Dace was so much taller.

'I am Shin. I don't believe we have met . . .' The Ifarl raised a gloved hand to his heart and inclined his head towards Maii in a gesture widely accepted by their race as a polite salutation.

'Maii. This is Dace,' said Maii, without returning Shin's gesture. 'No, we have not met.'

Shin smiled, as if Maii had not just slighted him. 'This is Raye.'

Raye waved in typical Atrossian fashion and muttered a greeting. His voice was a little high-pitched and squeaky, which made him seem juvenile. He brought his hands together a little too gleefully and said, 'Fate must have brought us together. Since we're all here, why don't we head to my private booth in that cosy little corner? It's quieter, and we can get to know each other better away from prying eyes, and ears.'

Before Maii could reply, however, she was blinded by a burst of light. She saw Raye outlined in chartreuse, Shin, in a subtle shade of maroon, and Dace, in azure. The auras evaporated as quickly as they had appeared.

It can't be . . . Maii found herself blinking rapidly.

Ifarls had the ability to see and sense the energies emanating from people because their innate sensitivity to spiritual elements was so strong. Some called this talent 'aura reading'. But it was a little more complex than that. The skill required acute observation of the subject's energies and facial expressions to deduce what they were thinking because everyone was different.

Pod, for example, had this orange glow when he got excited. But Zej radiated that very same colour when he was upset. Dace's expressions and gestures were a mystery to Maii because she hadn't known him for very long before she lost her powers.

I haven't been able to 'see' since the ritual, Maii thought in a mixture of hope and dejection. The memory of that fateful night when she had

lost her powers was seared into her mind. The Ifarls, hand in hand, with
Zenchi leading them, had recited the spell to close the portal that one of
their own accidentally opened years ago. This was what they had been
working to achieve for generations—to restore balance to the world by
banishing the ghosts that didn't belong here.

The words uttered in the Ifarl's ancient language formed a haunting
song. Even to this day, it remained a phantom chant in her ears.

> *First star,*
> *Witness us line the bar.*
> *Second,*
> *Deity of all unknown,*
> *we beckon.*
> *Tri-star,*
> *The all-seeing eye, never marred.*
> *Quartet,*
> *Hear our call to repay debt*
> *owed—we would never forget.*
> *Pentagon,*
> *We submit.*
> *Six of Sins,*
> *We repent.*
> *Sevenfold,*
> *We repent.*
> *Octet,*
> *We repent.*
> *Nine of stars,*
> *Shine!*
> *Line the skies!*
> *Break the ties!*

As they recited the words, the wind built up in speed and strength, heating
up within the circle formed by the chain of Ifarls who were holding on to
each other's hands. This tornado that they summoned had stayed within its
drawn boundaries. Until it didn't. At that flashpoint, everyone knew that
the balance had tipped. Something had gone wrong. In a split second, all
of them were knocked unconscious.

Maii remembered waking up to a scene that looked like the aftermath of an explosion. Some of her fellow Ifarls were lying on the ground, still passed out. Others who were awake looked as disorientated as she felt. The locks on the cages that imprisoned the hybrids had been cut. Several of the captives, including the one called Seyfer, who was designated as the head of Atros's hybrid army, had disappeared.

When Maii realized that she had lost her ability to see the auras of others, she had pulled Zenchi aside. 'What went wrong? Did we succeed? If so, why can't I *see*?'

Her mentor's eyes, ever bright with wisdom, looked uncertain. Zenchi knew that Maii wasn't talking about her actual vision. Gesturing in the direction where Pod and Zej were huddled over the unconscious Keix and Vin, Zenchi sighed. 'They didn't die, as we expected them to. But yes, I think we succeeded in closing the portal. I felt something click into place, even as we were flung backwards.'

'Then why can't I see?' repeated Maii. The desolation she felt threatened to swallow her whole.

Zenchi reached out to hold her hands, but Maii found no reassurance in the elder's soft, lined palms.

'You need to stay with your friends,' said Zenchi, sidestepping Maii's question once again.

But I just betrayed them, Maii wanted to whine as relief and guilt warred within her. *How can I claim to be their friend when all I did was manipulate and lie to them?*

While Maii was glad that Keix and Vin had survived, she had never considered a scenario where she would have to face the very people whose trust she had just broken. Yet, here was her mentor asking her to do exactly that.

'Apologize to them. Even if you don't mean it. I know how proud you are. But this loss of our powers after closing the portal might well be another test for us. We need a plan. But one of us needs to be with Iv't's descendant in the meantime, just in case this abnormality is due to the fact that the hybrids didn't die.'

Maii jerked her hands out of Zenchi's clasp. While she understood her mentor's need to figure out a way for all of them to get back their powers— it was something she wanted too—she couldn't help but feel her stomach heave at the plea.

But an Ifarl never disobeyed their leader's direct instructions, much less one framed like a favour. Maii tried to retain her composure. 'You will send word when there is a plan?'

Zenchi nodded. 'You will be the first to know.'

Maii found herself having misgivings about her elder's words for the first time in her life, even as she dutifully followed Pod and the gang back to Atros.

In the weeks that followed, she had held out hope that Zenchi would get in touch with her and let her know exactly what else she was supposed to do other than keeping an eye on Vin. But no news came.

Maii felt like a forgotten melody, adrift in the familiar yet strange Atros, trying to find her way back into a score that she was supposed to be part of.

And now, all of a sudden, she was assaulted by a storm of emotions, reminded of how vibrant and magical it had been, to be able to see people outlined in ever-changing colours. Yet, her powers disappeared as quickly as they had returned.

Without their vivid halos surrounding them, everyone had gone back to looking dull, lifeless.

Maii thought she saw Shin's smile faltering at her disappointment and she hoped that the rest hadn't detected the rapid change in her mood. They were still looking at her expectantly, waiting for her answer to Raye's invitation.

But Maii had only one thought in her head—*could it be possible that I'm getting my powers back?*

3

Keix | The Kulcan

Keix couldn't believe her eyes. How was it possible that someone could hit a tiny speeding object like a bullet and split it in half? She watched wide-eyed as the Kulcan who had come to her rescue ran up the half-sphere of doom effortlessly, digging the tip of his sword into the hard ground and using it like a lever.

He moved with an uncanny swiftness—even faster than the figures in black—and charged at the attacker who had fired the bullet, felling the hooded assailant with a single slash of his sword. Then, he disappeared into the fog.

'Vin!' called Keix. She tried clambering up the crater but kept slipping back down. Just as she was preparing to yell her friend's name again, the Kulcan appeared next to her and put a long, slender finger on her lips to shush her.

Keix froze at the cool touch. It took her half a second to react and push the man's hand away. Even though she wanted to express her displeasure, she bit her tongue because she could sense the tension rolling off the Kulcan and deduced that the danger was not over yet.

The fog was dissipating, and a starburst of gold was creeping up the horizon now, turning the sky a powdery purple. With the soft illumination, Keix was able to get a proper look at the person who had come to her aid.

Dressed in an inky-black, full-length robe that had nary a stitch of decorative detail, he cut a sombre figure. The heavy material of his attire, coupled with the equally nondescript sash tied at the waist, accentuated his broad, squarish shoulders.

The hilt of his sword, which was back in its sheath and strapped to his back, jutted out at an angle from behind his head. At this proximity, Keix was struck by his height. He towered a good head over her. His dark hair of indeterminate length was pulled into a messy knot at the back of his head, with flyaway wisps framing angular cheekbones and intense eyes that looked half brown, half black under the muted lighting. The light stubble that swept across his jawline added an air of rawness to his deadly demeanour.

When he spoke a couple of seconds later, his voice was low and crisp, with a lilt that she couldn't quite place.

'Your friend is unconscious. Here, I'll get you out,' he said, holding out his hand.

Keix's stomach roiled. She needed to check on Vin, stat. But just as she was about to reach out, a bout of dizziness overcame her. The adrenaline from the earlier fight was fading, and she could feel the last of her energy reserves depleting.

Mistaking her delayed reaction for hesitation, the Kulcan clasped her clammy hand and added in an urgent whisper, 'Come. Their backup will catch up soon. We need to get you and your friend out of here.' He unsheathed his sword and the sharp hiss it made reverberated in Keix's ear as he towed her out of the crater.

As soon as they were out, he led Keix to Vin, who was lying on the ground by some trees. Suddenly realizing that she was still holding the haagi, Keix thrust the tiny animal into the Kulcan's hands. She knelt beside Vin and ran her hands along her friend's body, feeling for signs of injury. Although she couldn't detect any, she turned to the Kulcan with an accusatory look. When she saw him stroking the animal between its ears absent-mindedly, she felt a surge of anger. How could he look so unconcerned?

'I didn't see what happened.' The Kulcan's tone was matter of fact, but he was still whispering. 'I wasn't the one who knocked your friend unconscious,' he added disgruntledly.

He's right, thought Keix. Why would he do such a thing when he had just saved them from their attackers? Keix looked down sheepishly and wondered whether she should be a little more polite to her rescuer—even if she had reservations about the impeccable timing of his appearance. It just seemed too coincidental. Had he been stalking her? If so, why? Or was he sent by Atros to gain her trust? He had, after all, taken out the hooded figures so easily.

To cover up the awkwardness of the moment and to allow herself some time to think, Keix continued inspecting Vin. Her blood turned to ice when she saw a needle with an attached syringe sticking out from her friend's neck. The object was similar to the receptacle used to hold a kind of sedative shot that could be fatal to Ifarls. Fighting down her panic, Keix checked Vin's wrist for a pulse and heaved a sigh of relief when she found one.

A sudden burst of rage rose from the core of Keix's being. Why wouldn't Atros leave her alone? What did she have that was so important to them? She had left Atros because she wanted to regain some semblance of control over her life. But the organization that had stripped her of her identity seemed intent on driving her to the edge.

She stalked towards one of the attackers that the Kulcan had taken down, intending to strip off the figure's mask. She needed to put a face to her enemy—any face. All too long, Atros had pervaded every aspect of her life. From now on, she swore to herself that she would memorize the appearance of each and every one who attacked her, and treat it as if she were chipping away a small piece of her previous life to reveal her true self beneath. But before she could take another step, the Kulcan put a hand on her arm and stilled her.

'There is no time,' he said, the urgency in his voice obvious. 'We need to leave. Now.'

Keix opened her mouth to protest, but the Kulcan continued with a touch of acerbity, 'Your senses are dull right now, so you can't hear a new group of them drawing near. Whoever these people are, they're still on our tail. We'll need to shake them off. Try to be as quiet as you can, so I can hear if anyone's approaching.' He held the haagi to his face and whispered something to it.

To Keix's astonishment, the haagi shook its short furry ears and came back to life. 'You speak haagi?'

The Kulcan's displeasure vanished in an instant and he seemed to suppress a smile at Keix's disbelieving tone, amusement apparent in his twinkling eyes.

'Come,' he whispered, putting the haagi gently down on the ground. He then lifted Vin's limp body and slung her over his shoulder with the same level of care.

The next thing Keix knew, the haagi had hopped off confidently with the Kulcan right on its heels.

'This area is made to trap anyone who ventures in. Without it'—the Kulcan jerked his chin in the haagi's direction—'leading the way, we might be running around in circles the entire day.'

Keix rubbed the tender spot on her shoulder that she had landed on in order to protect the haagi. *At least I hadn't borne the pain for nothing,* she thought.

'How is it that you're saying we're in danger and yet the haagi is up and about? It froze up when I was getting chased, you know?' she grumbled, her breathing laboured as she struggled to keep up with her rescuer's longer strides.

'Well, its senses aren't as keen as mine.'

Keix wanted to snort at the Kulcan's boast, but she decided to err on the side of caution by suppressing it in case he was telling the truth. Her senses were also tuned up, yet she couldn't hear a thing except for her blood making its merry way past her ears. That said, she knew that her body was crashing. She had used up all her adrenaline during the chase.

Her feet confirmed her disheartening diagnosis as one tripped over the other, and she pitched forward. The Kulcan threw out his free arm and caught her before she fell. Then, he looped his arm under hers as support.

'We need to move faster. And quieter. You have to trust me.' His tone was even lower now.

The sincerity in the Kulcan's plea made Keix draw a deep breath as noiselessly as she could to ground herself.

After the recent series of betrayals she had encountered, it was only natural that she was reluctant to put her faith in anyone—except perhaps Vin. *Yet, why do I still feel an inexplicable urge to trust this Kulcan?* wondered Keix. There was a strange familiarity to him. Was it because he bore a resemblance to the one who had cut the lock on the cages after the ritual? Or was it the frank, attentive way with which he handled both the haagi and Vin?

'I have no choice, do I?' she conceded. She was starved and could barely stand upright. Vin was unconscious. And a bloodthirsty band of who-knows-what was chasing them down, armed with black-hole bullets.

The Kulcan tightened his grip on her arm ever so slightly in reply to her question, and the two of them spoke no more as they tried to keep up with the haagi which looked set to go missing in the undergrowth.

* * *

Keix could tell that they had escaped from the trap when the formation of the trees in their surroundings looked more random than replicated. The fog had also cleared. With it, the tension in her chest, which had caused her breathing to be more laboured than usual, also disappeared.

The haagi, as if sensing that its mission had been accomplished, turned around to look at the Kulcan with bright eyes and twitched its ears. The action caught Keix's eye, and she noticed a white triangular spot at the tip of the furry creature's right ear. In response to the haagi's gesture, the Kulcan nodded in appreciation.

A mixture of relief and regret flooded Keix and she had the silliest urge to call out and ask the animal to take care of itself as it sped off into the bushes for the last time.

By the time the Kulcan lugged both Keix and Vin to an abandoned hut, it was twilight. The remnants of the retiring sun's rays cast a purplish tint on the tiny derelict structure in front of them, turning it a nebulous shade of brown and emphasizing how ancient it looked. Age had settled into the grooves of its walls, made with horizontally stacked logs.

Not that it mattered to Keix. After hours of leaning on the Kulcan for support, all she needed was a place to rest. She let herself crumple to the soft ground by the door of the cabin. Her leg muscles felt like they were on fire. It was by sheer determination that she'd managed to stay conscious throughout the whole journey. She had to, because Vin was still out cold.

The person carrying Vin, on the other hand stood tall. His breathing was slow and rhythmic, and he showed no signs of exertion. With his recently freed hand, he pushed open the door. The entrance to the cabin was wide but low, so he had to duck his head to go through it.

A fusty odour that had been trapped within the hut wafted out. Keix forced the offending air out of her nostrils in short rapid bursts and turned off her sense of smell completely.

'I've laid your friend on the couch inside,' said the Kulcan as he emerged from the door.

An image of Vin lying on a pile of dusty cushions flashed across Keix's mind. Vin would not be happy when she woke up.

'You should take a rest as well. It will be completely dark soon, but you should be safe if you stay inside the hut and don't make too much noise.' The Kulcan turned to leave unhurriedly.

Even though Keix hadn't expect him to stay long, she couldn't fight the bubble of panic rising in her throat. What if the people chasing her and

Vin caught up with them before she regained her strength? Would they be able to fight them off? Before she could get her emotions under control, a volley of questions tumbled out of her.

'Wait . . . where are you going? Who are you? The weirdos who attacked us—are they droids? They must have been sent by Atros. Who sent you? And why did you help us?'

The Kulcan paused in his tracks. He pondered for a while before breaking into a small smile. 'Which of these questions should I answer first?'

Keix told herself to ignore his teasing tone and the fact that his smile lent a boyish, disarming charm to his otherwise serious appearance. She was also trying to wrap her head around the vast contrast in his behaviour—the deadliness he had displayed when there was danger, compared to his insouciance now.

Start with the basics and don't get sidetracked, she thought to herself. She was glad when her question came across firmly. 'Who are you?'

'My name is Jūn Gantulga.'

Keix waited, expecting him to elaborate or answer the other questions that she had previously posed to him. Instead, all the Kulcan said after an extended pause was, 'You can call me Jūn.'

Keix stared at him. He sounded like he was doing her a favour. All right, next question. 'Why did you help us?'

'I helped you and your friend because you were in trouble.'

'How did you know we were in trouble? How did you know we were there? Were you stalking Vin? Or me?'

Jūn raised his eyebrows at her last question. 'I heard scuffling.'

'And you just happened to be in the area?'

'It would be within reason to say that I was in the area. Otherwise, I would not have heard the scuffling.' He crossed his arms.

'Why did you help us? Why are you helping us? What is your agenda? What do you stand to gain?'

'Shouldn't you be thanking me instead of interrogating me?'

Keix could tell that he was getting a little exasperated now. His lips were pressed into a thin line, but there remained a hint of amusement in his eyes. When he realized that Keix wasn't going to answer his question, he sighed.

'I helped you because you were in trouble. It is that simple.'

This conversation was going in circles. Keix resisted the urge to kick him in the shins—although she couldn't very well do so when she was seated on the ground. The back of her neck was aching from having to look up at the Kulcan, but she couldn't summon the energy to stand up. 'The weirdos who attacked us—are they droids?'

Jūn tilted his head. 'Droids?'

'Ancient machines that look like humans?' Keix didn't know if Jūn was pretending to be obtuse, but he looked like he was considering the question seriously.

'Hm. They did look like humans.'

At Keix's glare, he admitted, 'I've never seen them before. But didn't you hear them coming?'

Keix was affronted even though Jūn looked genuinely concerned. She sidestepped the question. 'You've seen—heard them. They move without a sound.'

Jūn cocked his head at her denial but didn't press further. 'Didn't you hear my warning?' He puckered his lips and emitted the loud chirping sound that Keix had heard just before she saw the attackers.

'That was you? Wait a minute . . . Are you admitting that you've been stalking me?' Keix's temper was flaring again.

'I was in the vicinity.' Jūn shrugged.

Keix huffed and looked away. Her head was spinning now and she closed her eyes to try to alleviate her intensifying queasiness. She wasn't going to, and couldn't afford to, expend any more energy on a conversation that was going nowhere.

'There's a town nearby,' came Jūn's voice. 'I'll need to go there to get some food for you, but it's quite a walk so I need to leave now. I will only be back at dawn.'

'You're coming back?' blurted Keix. Noticing that she hadn't managed to keep the relief out of her voice, her cheeks reddened. It wasn't like her to show this level of reliance on anyone, much less a stranger.

Jūn nodded. 'You look like you're on the verge of fainting. You should rest first, then eat something to regain your energy.'

Grudgingly touched by his thoughtfulness, Keix scrambled to her feet and planted herself right in front of him, trying hard to not wobble. She spat out the question that had been bugging her since she met him. 'Are you the one who came to me on the night of the ritual?'

When Jūn had first rushed to her side in the crater, she didn't have any doubt that he was the very same Kulcan who had slashed the locks of the cage that she was in after the Ifarls separated the realms of the living and the dead. But now, she wasn't so sure. Her memory was hazy and the only prominent characteristics that Jūn and the Kulcan from weeks ago had in common were that they were both, well, Kulcans, and extremely tall.

'You don't remember.' Jūn's shoulders drooped a fraction, his disappointment clear.

'If you are one and the same, prove it,' pressed Keix.

'How?'

'What did you say to me then?' Keix looked at him expectantly. She might be physically weak right now, but the Kulcan's words still rang clear in her head.

'I was riding on my shih, and I said to you, "If you want to look for your father, head north out of Atros. I'll meet you at the woods that's a two-day ride outside Sector L." And I was there, as promised. But you lost your way,' said Jūn without inflection.

The pink spots on Keix's cheeks darkened. She felt mortified thinking about how rude she had been to the very person she was looking for, the same person with whom she'd have to amicably coexist, at least until he brought her to her dad.

But she was also indignant at his insinuation that she couldn't find her way around. Putting aside the fact that she had grown up in Atros and was only familiar with the city, how would she know how far exactly a 'two-day ride' was? A two-day ride on what? A hovercar? *His* shih?

These historic animals were extinct, as far as Keix was aware. She had only read about them in books, which always depicted them as majestic creatures with intelligent eyes, thick manes and muscular bodies and tails. It never crossed her mind that she would one day be able to see a living, breathing shih with her own eyes.

'You could have told me this right at the start of this conversation,' accused Keix.

'I was waiting to see when—*if*—you'd remember.' Jūn looked up at the sky. 'Time is running short. I'd best get going,' he said, stepping to the side to get past Keix.

Once again, Keix found a jumble of thoughts scrambling for attention in her head. The first question that made it out of her mouth was, 'Will you bring me to him?' Her voice was barely a whisper, but she knew that Jūn had heard her. There was also no need for her to specify that the 'he' to whom she was referring was her father.

Jūn turned to face her and nodded.

'Why do you want to find him?' There was no judgement in Jūn's voice, but Keix could see compassion and concern in his eyes.

Keix paused. There was, at the same time, none yet so many answers to his question. 'Leave your sword here,' she commanded in a steely tone.

Jūn raised his eyebrows. 'Why?'

'I need to know that you will return.'

'You have my word.'

Keix held his gaze. She wasn't ready to accept someone's word as currency at the moment. 'I need a weapon to protect myself.'

Jūn let out a short laugh. 'I'll be back before you know it. But if it makes you feel better . . . that pendant you are wearing . . .'

Keix's hand shot to the semi-polished stone charm that hung around her neck on a dainty chain. The trinket was a family heirloom from her Kulcan father, gifted to Keix by her mother on her eleventh birthday. A few days after that, her mum died in a ghost attack in one of Atros's Sectors.

'It is important.' Jūn reached under his collar and pulled out a long chain—black, of course—that was looped around his neck. At the end of the chain hung a semi-polished stone similar to Keix's charm. The only difference was that Jūn's stone was black and twice as large as her purple one.

With the same swiftness that he had used to take down her previous attackers, he slipped his chain over his head, drew Keix's left hand to him and deposited his necklace into her palm. He frowned for a moment, holding her hand.

Keix wasn't sure if she should extricate her hand from Jūn's grasp. His hesitation, and the warmth from his leftover body heat on the accessory and where his skin made contact with hers, conveyed the gravity of the gesture.

When he released her hand, he said, 'I will leave this with you instead of my sword. It is far more valuable, so you can be sure that I will come back for it. And I need this'—he tapped the sword strapped to his back and gave her a small lopsided smile—'more. For now.'

Keix closed her fingers over Jūn's charm as she kept her eyes on his retreating back, contemplating the meaning of his words. When he disappeared from view, he left nothing but a buzz in the air and her heart racing, for reasons she couldn't fathom.

4

Dace | Connections

Dace liked to push others' buttons. There was just something satisfying about seeing someone's unguarded reaction whenever he made an outrageous or cutting remark. These moments were golden opportunities to judge a person's true character. And they helped take his mind off things he would rather not think about—Lana, the girl he liked; his parents; and Atros.

However, he couldn't help but feel concerned when he saw a look of pure shock cross Maii's face at Raye's invitation to head to a private booth to 'get to know each other better'.

'Maii?' Dace prompted the Ifarl.

Today's original plan to saunter into *A* and sneak out a set of Raye's fingerprints without getting caught had been upended when their target appeared with Shin. Now, playing it by ear, accepting this invite seemed to be the best course of action. So why was Maii hesitating when she was the one who didn't want to abort the mission in the first place?

Although Dace didn't dislike Maii, he didn't harbour overly positive feelings towards her either. He suspected that she'd followed them back to Atros on Zenchi's orders. After all, she didn't divulge the fact that the Ifarls had always intended to sacrifice the hybrids during the ritual until she completed Keix's transformation. But since Pod and Zej had accepted her back into the group, Dace decided that he could be civil to her as long as she didn't use her compulsion on him again.

Still, Maii was a tough nut to crack. To peg her attitude as cool was euphemistic. The Ifarl's frostiness was at an absolute zero. Granted, she would sometimes ease a few degrees warmer when Pod was yammering, allowing the corners of her mouth to quirk up, but that was about it.

Yet twice today, Dace had witnessed her eyes widening. The first time was when she heard that Raye was with an Ifarl, and then again when Raye and Shin had approached them. Now, he watched as she fought to steady her nerves, taking in a deep breath and giving a small nod in assent.

'Lead the way,' she said to Raye.

'Maii? What's wrong with Maii? Maii, are you okay?' Pod seemed to have sensed that something was amiss. His customary babble sounded a touch hysterical. As usual, Dace couldn't decide whether he was naive or plain annoying. Pod's unbridled enthusiasm for tapping away at the keyboard sometimes grated on his nerves. How could anyone be so . . . cheerful? That was why Dace never missed an opportunity to tease Pod or get him flustered. But the last thing Dace wanted right now was for Pod to throw a fit, so he didn't tell him that Maii had taken out her intercom.

Steering Maii in the direction that Raye and Shin were heading, Dace appraised his surroundings.

A's interiors hadn't changed much since the last time he was here. He used to frequent the club back when he was fifteen, when it became apparent how much it irritated his father to have to arrange for someone to pick up his wastrel of a son in the wee hours of the morning—a son who was too drunk to do anything except pass out on whichever available surface there was.

There came a point when his father stopped caring, and Dace would wake up in one of the emergency stairwells of the club, locked out of *A*, his clothes crumpled, stinking of the alcohol that he had downed the night before. That was when he decided to join the rebel group Oka, disappearing from his father's life altogether.

Being back in the club felt surreal. Dace never thought he would ever again set foot in this place. If he were to nitpick, he would say that the ostentatious decor had only gotten gaudier. The entryway leading into the spacious corridor, which was the backbone of the private section of *A*, had been brushed with gold paint on his last visit. Now, the tall arch was gilded with a pattern of silvered geometric shapes.

Dace recognized the shimmery veils that hung like sheets of mist, dancing beguilingly and cloaking the spacious circular booths behind them. These semi-translucent curtains provided *A*'s patrons with an illusion of privacy.

He almost scoffed. Everything that happened in Atros was monitored in one way or another. It was merely a question of whether one's security clearance was high enough to access the data. For instance, he was willing to bet his most treasured hovercar that it would be recorded in some system that at this second, he and Maii were scooting into a curved seating booth reserved under Raye's name in *A*. Dace could only hope that no one was paying attention to this blip in the massive amount of data running through Atros's systems at any given point of time.

'Drinks?' asked Raye, the obnoxious, self-appointed host of this impromptu tête-à-tête.

A skittish waitress in a black, knee-length sheath dress materialized from behind the glimmering partition.

Slipping into the booth seat that enclosed a circular table, Dace said without preamble, 'Two *A*'s special blend. Neat.' This was the only thing he missed about this place—the smoky and sharp drink with a hint of sweetness that he used to overindulge.

Maii sat down beside Dace, close to the edge of the circular bench, as if she was ready to bolt at the drop of a hat. In tandem, Shin and Raye made themselves comfortable on the plush, cushioned seats and adjusted themselves to face Maii and Dace. Neither pair scooted to the middle of the circular bench, preferring to keep the width of the table between them—an arrangement which was more than fine with Dace.

'I see your tastes haven't changed.' Raye smirked at Dace before adding to the waitress, 'We'll have the same.'

The waitress nodded and slunk away.

'Wait, do you know him?' Pod's disbelief was evident.

Even Maii turned to Dace with a questioning look.

'Have we met?' Dace was pretty sure they hadn't. Raye looked no older than Dace had been when he first started frequenting *A*.

'We haven't had that pleasure until now. Although I've heard lots about you from your father, Dace.'

Dace tried to not wince when Pod let loose an ear-splitting 'What!' over the intercom. Dace knew that there was a chance that Raye knew— or, at least, knew of—his father. After all, his dad was a highly ranked

Atrossian officer too. Forcing his fists to unclench, Dace remained silent, ignoring Pod's string of questions and Maii's scrutiny.

The tension was palpable when the waitress returned with their drinks, and she had the good sense to disappear as quickly as she appeared.

'Come—' began Raye, looking extremely pleased with the fact that he seemed to have rattled Dace.

But before he could utter another word, Shin turned to him and said with that unmistakable singsong inflection that marked the Ifarl compulsion charm, 'You'll stay still, not make a sound, and be unaware of the conversation that is happening from this moment onwards.'

Okay, that was unexpected, thought Dace. Shin's agenda was definitely different from Raye's.

As Raye's eyes glazed over at the compulsion, his body relaxed and settled down until he was as still as a statue.

Dace saw Maii's bewildered expression from his peripheral vision.

'You have your powers . . .' Maii's voice was a bare whisper.

'And you don't.' Shin looked neither gleeful nor disappointed.

Pod was shrieking by now. 'You don't have your powers, Maii? Why didn't you tell us? How did you lose it?'

Dace suddenly wished that he had taken out his intercom too. At least that way, he wouldn't have to bear with Pod's outburst right now.

Zej, being his silent and brooding self, wasn't of much help.

Shin's revelation about Maii having lost her powers let Dace put two and two together. He had sensed that she'd been different since the night of the ritual—she seemed less assured of herself, and her attitude, a little more brittle.

Maii's panic and distress were written all over her face now, and Dace found himself feeling a little sorry for her. What must it feel like to lose something that you've had forever?

'What's it to you?' He decided that regardless of what he thought about Maii, they should at least present a united front to Shin. Dace threw the offensive Ifarl a steely stare and heard Maii let out a breath.

Shin's lips twitched. 'Nothing,' he said. 'Whether or not she has her powers is of no consequence to me. But it might make a difference to you. And your friends.'

'Quit beating about the bush.' Dace tried to sound bored.

'I'm here to make you a proposal,' said Shin.

'What makes you think we're going to listen to your crap?'

Shin looked irked by Dace's cheek. 'Well, for one, you're here, aren't you?'

Dace grabbed Maii's wrist and stood to leave.

'Sit down.' The compulsion in Shin's voice was sharp.

Like a silky thread creeping under Dace's scalp, Shin's command overrode his intended action. Dace sat back down and threw Shin a glare so sharp it could have cut through glass.

'Did Zenchi send you?' asked Maii when she finally found her voice.

Dace heard a mixture of hope and helplessness in her words. He wondered if she knew Shin from before.

Shin ignored Maii's question. Instead, he said, 'It was foolish of you to come here. It's one thing to fail at the task given to you, but another level of recklessness to waltz into one of Atros's most high-profile establishments and think that they'll let you walk out of here.'

Maii looked chastised, but the moment Dace opened his mouth, Shin said to him, 'And you. The arrogance must have gone to your head after you and your friends escaped unscathed following that fiasco at ATI. I bet you didn't know that it was because your father had intervened. The other Atros council members were unimpressed, so they tossed him into one of their cells.'

Dace's throat tightened. His nails cut into his palms as Pod yelled, 'Your father is a council member on Atros's—'

Pod paused for a split second and gasped. 'Zej? What are you doing here? Aren't you supposed to be waiting at the extraction point for Dace and Maii?'

Zej's firm voice came over the intercom. 'I'll explain later. But we need to leave. Now,' he said. 'Dace, you need to get out of *A*. We'll meet up at the place that we discussed before.'

'W—what's this discussion? Why wasn't I in it?' Pod's anger was clear. 'I thought we were supposed to be a team!'

'I'll explain on the way. Atros troopers could be here any second now. Do you trust me, Pod?'

Pod didn't answer, but the next moment, Dace heard a flurry of movement and he knew that Zej had somehow convinced Pod. Dace wanted to sneer. He hated Zej's guts and the way everyone looked up to him. If not for Zej, Lana might never have become a hybrid or left him . . . Yet it was precisely because Zej was a righteous ass, whose moral compass could withstand a battering by the entire army of Atros troopers, that Dace couldn't help but feel a grudging respect for him.

Dace unclenched his fists. He tried to keep his voice neutral as he asked, 'And you are telling us this because?'

'I'm here to make you a proposal,' repeated Shin. 'We need your help.'

Dace stared at the Ifarl. Shin could be lying for all he knew. Why would his father step in to stop Atros from dishing out punishment to his rebellious son? His dad had all but disowned him when he fell off the radar after he joined Oka. There had been no missing person notice nor any attempt to track him, at least as far as Dace knew.

The only thing that his father did was to vacate the lake house in which they used to live and never returned—something Dace found out using Oka's resources. He supposed it was his father's way of saying that he was done with his unfilial son.

That was why when their ragtag group had run into trouble and needed a place to regroup, Dace felt confident enough to shelter them at the lake house. Now, Shin was telling him that his father had been keeping tabs on him all along?

Right. I'll buy that story when I'm dead. Dace snorted and rotated his ankles. They seemed to be doing his bidding. Shin had told Dace to sit down, but he didn't say that Dace couldn't leave.

Dace flashed Shin his most insincere smile. 'Well, I'm afraid we're not much in the business of *helping* dodgy people we've just met. It's been a plea—'

'Atros has Lana,' interrupted Shin.

Dace froze. He didn't want Shin to know that he was concerned about both his father and Lana. He tried to sound as nonchalant as possible when he asked, 'Is this the best leverage you have over me? A man who hasn't been in my life for years and a girl I've broken up with?'

Over the intercom at Pod's end, Dace vaguely heard him muttering something about daddy and relationship issues, and Zej shushing him.

But Dace couldn't care less. His heart was pounding, his mind flooded with images of Lana. She had come to his room the night she left the lake house and told him that she needed some time alone to process what happened to her.

Dace remembered looking into her eyes, those that were once bright with optimism and life, now hollowed out, replaced with a permanently haunted look. He thought of Keix, who likely went through the same 'experiments' as Lana when they were held captive by Atros—tortures to prepare them for their transformation into hybrids. He recalled the sense of kindredness he'd felt towards the half-Kulcan when he first met her, the fact that Keix remained genuine and undaunted, even in the face of the countless betrayals—and the spark that she managed to hold on to that Lana did not.

We'll work through this together. I'll be there every step of the way. If you want me to remain invisible, I will be invisible. Ignore me. Talk to me. Don't talk to me. Just let me stay by your side, he wanted to tell Lana, gather her into his arms and rub his chin on the top of her head like he used to. Yet all he managed to croak out was, 'Are you sure?'

Even when Lana had nodded, Dace couldn't bring himself to reach for her. There wasn't merely an abyss between them. It was as if the ghost that had been bonded to her ripped out a part of her along with itself when the portal between the living and the dead was shut.

Dace didn't know how long he stared at the door after Lana closed it behind her, but when he finally accepted that she was gone, he'd found himself outside Keix's room.

Zej had just left and the first thing Dace did after knocking and entering the room was tease her about the late-night visit. Then, Keix asked him about Lana, and all he could do was skate over the depth of his true feelings.

When Keix smiled at him, he reached for her hand on impulse and clasped it between his own palms as if it were a lifeline. He felt the wild beast within himself calm down. A glimmer of hope crept in. Hope that Lana might, in her own time, come to terms with what had happened to her, just like Keix had.

But maybe he was wrong; the hybridization process had damaged their spirits irrevocably. Because the next morning, Keix was gone from the lake house as well. So was Vin.

On the surface, it seemed as if the three girls had vanished into thin air together, so it was only natural for Pod and Zej to assume that Atros kidnapped them. But Dace knew that Lana had left of her own accord. He just didn't want to share this information with the rest. It also felt too coincidental that the three of them would decide to leave on the same night, so Dace didn't want to rule out the possibility that Atros had indeed abducted Keix and Vin. That was why he'd gone along with this mission: to uncover the truth.

And now Shin was telling him that Atros had Lana? She must have been captured after she left the house! Dace tried to calm himself down. His fists itched to land on something. Right now, the long, hooked nose on Shin's face looked to be a great target.

'You should know by now that lying to me doesn't work,' said Shin.

Dace felt Maii's hand grip his under the table as if she were trying to reassure him. He shook it away and bit out his next words.

'What about Keix and Vin? What does Atros want in exchange for them? What do you want? What can we do that Atros can't?' he asked, letting loose a bitter laugh.

'Atros doesn't have Keix and Vin. They left Atros. In the direction of Tilsor.'

'Tilsor?' asked Maii. 'That's on the way to Yurkordu.'

Shin nodded.

Atros's cameras must have caught them leaving the city, thought Dace. Shin must have access to those footages since he was hanging out with Raye, whose security clearance was pretty high. Dace's gaze flitted over to Raye. The Atrossian was still seated like a lifeless puppet.

'Tilsor? Your—what?' Pod resurfaced in the intercom.

Dace shared Pod's confusion, but he thought that voicing out the questions would increase Shin and Atros's leverage against them, so he settled for exhaling a breath of relief instead. At least Keix and Vin were free. Two fewer people to break out of Atros's clutches.

He also made up his mind that if Maii was unwilling to leave *A* with him, he would knock her unconscious and haul her out. They needed someone to explain what and where Tilsor and Yurkordu were.

'Atros has been detecting an abnormal level of erratic magnetic waves outside the city,' elaborated Shin when neither Maii nor Dace spoke.

'But it can't be paranormal activity. The portal's been closed, right, Maii?' demanded Pod, still oblivious that Maii was offline.

She furrowed her brows. 'Do you think . . .'

It was Shin's turn to frown. 'Unlikely.'

'What is unlikely?' Dace butted in.

'It's unlikely that the portal was not closed successfully, if that's what you're thinking,' explained Shin.

Maii bit her lip, as if trying to stop herself from saying something.

'And you're telling us this—why?' Dace had an inkling that every second this conversation dragged on made it a fraction harder for them to get out of *A*. Shin could be stalling for time while Atros soldiers prepared to swarm this place any moment now.

'Because the Kulcans are our best chance at defeating whatever's coming. And your friend, Keix, is our only connection to them.'

'And what's the "whatever's coming"? Would you care to elaborate?'

'Groups of attackers have been hitting up some of the warehouses where Atros keeps their weapons,' explained Shin. 'They only take a few weapons each time, and they have been so stealthy that Atros hadn't discovered the thefts until recently.

'It could be an inside job or the rebel groups, for all we know. But Zenchi and I think it could be a group of Atrossians we call ExA, who'd been sent into exile by this current organization decades ago. ExA used to govern Atros back in the day, but because the citizens were unhappy with them, the people banded together and threw them out. After the revolution, the current Atros government was formed.

'We believe that ExA are stealing and accumulating arms and ammunition to seek revenge or to take back Atros,' concluded Shin.

A revolution? The tale sounded so similar to what Oka was trying to do that Dace had to snort. 'You Ifarls have already closed your dratted portal, haven't you? So why do you care about Atros now? I have a hard time believing you are a bunch of do-gooders.'

'You're right. The Ifarls care because if the attackers are who we think they are, and Atros falls to them, the Ifarls might be next. I'd give you the details, but we're running out of—'

A shrill alarm cut through the placid instrumental music that had been droning in the background.

'Is that the alarm? I didn't trip that.' Pod's exclamation over the intercom was almost drowned by the piercing bell.

'Dace, you've got to get out. NOW,' shouted Zej.

Dace had to hand it to Shin on his quick reaction. As if the Ifarl had been anticipating this moment, he slid a gun over the table to Dace.

'Take this and go,' said Shin.

Dace felt the thread of compulsion that had tied him to his seat loosening, and he caught the weapon with one hand. As he and Maii stood up from the booth seat, he saw, through the veil, the blurry silhouette of the skittish waitress walking over to them. He stepped out from behind the translucent curtain right on Maii's heels and saw that the waitress had dropped all pretence of docility. She now exuded a ruthless energy as she stalked her targets. The moment she moved her hands, Dace trained the gun to her side and fired a warning shot.

The bullet hit one of the columns at the side of a booth and the surface of the plaster disintegrated. Even through the screaming siren, the shot rang clear. It sent half the customers at *A*, who had gotten to their feet at the sound of the alarm, scrambling.

The other half, who had been peeking out from behind the veils to find out what interrupted their conversations, now looked panicked as they made up their minds to forgo all decorum and dash out of their private booths.

In the ensuing stampede, some of them tripped and trampled on the waitress who had dropped to the ground and rolled behind one of the chunkier pillars for cover.

Dace turned back to the space that he and Maii had just vacated to see Shin pushing the curtain aside. The Ifarl had in tow Raye, who was still glassy-eyed and placid, as if he hadn't heard the uproar.

'You've got to go. *Now.* Maii will explain everything. I need to remain in Atros to continue gathering information.' Shin fished out an envelope from his suit and pressed it into Maii's hand. She gave a nod, as if responding to an unspoken conversation.

Dace fired another shot at the waitress, stepped back towards the now-exposed table at which they had been seated, reached for Raye's glass (Dace had finished his own drink ages ago) and in one swift move, downed the beverage.

Both Maii and Shin threw Dace looks of disbelief and he responded, 'What? Never let a good drink go to waste.' He slipped the crystalware into the inner pocket of his jacket. The bulge it created looked ridiculous. 'Keepsake.' He winked at Raye, who was still wearing a vacant look. This really wasn't the time for chit chat.

A ripple of movement from the entrance of the corridor caught his eye. The customers dressed in a riot of colours parted as a group of Atros troopers came through like an arrow let loose, its black tip heading purposefully in the direction of its target.

There's an exit, three booths down, to the left. You'll find a stairwell that will lead to the basement, Shin spoke directly into Dace's head. Dace knew the hidden exit that the Ifarl was talking about, courtesy of his history with *A*.

He wondered if Shin might be directing them into an ambush. But judging by the large group of troopers still spilling into the corridor, Dace thought he might as well take his chances at the stairwell. He had discussed this alternative exit plan in secret with Zej previously because he didn't fully trust Maii. He'd also made Zej promise to not share it with Pod in case the latter blabbed about it to the Ifarl.

Maii tugged at Dace's hand, heeding Shin's instructions. She tried to look for the exit that Shin had indicated.

Dace watched as Shin and Raye disappeared into the crowd. He fired another two bullets in the waitress's direction to buy himself and Maii a couple of seconds more. The waitress ducked out of the way as the bullets whizzed past her head, forcing her to drop and take cover yet again.

Breaking into a run, Dace's long strides overtook Maii in no time. When they burst through the hidden exit door of the stairwell, he was almost dragging the petite Ifarl along.

'Wait! Aren't we heading to the basement? Isn't Zej waiting for us there? We can't leave him there to fight the rest of the troopers on his own!' protested Maii as Dace pulled her up the steps.

'Glad to see that you actually care about Zej. But there's been a change of plans.'

A was located on the topmost floor of the tower and they were now climbing up the stairs leading to the roof of the building.

To Dace's surprise, Maii was right on his heels instead of delaying them with objections and questions.

After the flight of steps, Dace scaled up the rungs attached to one side of the wall and pushed open a trapdoor-like contraption. The hinge was silent as the door flew open and they emerged into an open space.

It was way past midnight now. The lights from the other high-rises in Atros's city centre glittered brighter than the stars in the sky. This part of Atros was home to some of the wealthiest people in the governmental organization. It seemed counter intuitive, but security here was the laxest compared to the other Sectors.

Dace's father had moved to one of the spacious apartments here after they'd fallen out. Whenever Dace felt down or angry, he would come to this rooftop to gaze at a particular window of one of the surrounding skyscrapers—the window to his dad's room. Dace had always found it ironic that when he was here wreaking havoc in *A*, his dad had been nearby; yet, he'd refused to fork out time to collect his son on his own.

Resisting the urge to scan the skyline now, Dace took in a deep breath of the cool, clean night air that smelled as sterile as PEER. He shut the trapdoor and secured it with a heavy-looking lock. Then, he led Maii to the cable that Zej had slipped up to secure after he dropped them off at the basement. One end of the thin steel wire had been looped and fastened around a thickset stump that seemed to serve no purpose at all. The wire connected to the adjacent building.

Dace picked up two harnesses from the ground, passed one to Maii and started fastening the buckles of his equipment.

'The new plan requires us to zip across to that building?' Although Maii's tone was measured, her scepticism still managed to seep through.

The drop that the two of them would have to take would be steep because A was located in the tallest building in Atros. Dace reckoned that the difference was about ten storeys in height, approximately spread over the width of six lanes of road.

When Dace didn't answer, Maii pressed, 'Are we doing it individually or together?'

'If we have time, we'll do it separately.'

The trap door that Dace had locked previously jiggled. It sounded like Atros solders were trying to break the lock.

'Guess we're going to have to do it together.' He gave Maii one of his trademark smirks.

'Will it hold?' Maii's hesitation was clear.

'Come on, Maii. If I didn't know any better, I would say that the encounter with Shin has rattled you.'

Securing the gripping devices, Dace tugged at them to check the tautness of the cable.

Maii was almost done putting on her harness too, a determined look on her face.

Once she was ready, Dace clipped her in, looped her into a hug before she could object and kicked off the side of the building.

He felt his stomach swoop as the cable sagged under their weight and they zoomed towards their destination—the rooftop of the other building.

As the red-bricked façade drew nearer, Dace did a mental countdown.

Eight metres. Seven.

Their feet would land on the other rooftop in no time.

Four. Three.

BAM! A shattering explosion sounded behind them. In reflex, Dace thumbed the lock of the devices that he'd been holding on to as the wire snapped, and he and Maii were hurtled forward.

They rammed into the side of the building. Dace instinctively angled himself so that he would take the brunt of the impact as they collided with the wall.

Bone-shattering pain overwhelmed Dace. He felt something pierce through his chest—the beverage glass that he had pocketed shattered when he slammed against the building. Searing heat assaulted his back and it felt like his suit was burning against his skin.

'What just happened?' Pod called from his end.

Dace's breathing was laboured. He forced out a reply. 'Can't talk now, Pod. Maii and I are hanging from a wire from the side of the building that we were supposed to reach.'

He grunted and looked upward, then down. They were dangling midway between the rooftop and the window of an apartment on the topmost floor of this building.

'Maii, we need to try to climb up. Chances the window's unlocked is twenty to eighty.' Dace panted. He tried to steady his breaths. His palms were getting sweaty—he couldn't tell if it was because of their precarious situation or the heat from the explosion behind them. He passed one of the gripping devices to Maii and let her climb up before him. Together, they inched up towards their original destination.

When Maii finally hauled herself over the parapet, she reached out a hand to help Dace over. After catching their breaths, Dace straightened up. He didn't know what to think of the sight that confronted him.

Dense smoke was billowing out from the top of the building from which they'd just escaped. At least three of its topmost floors had crumbled, and it was apparent that the explosion was premeditated.

Whoever had been chasing them up the rooftop must have been caught in the blast. Shin and Raye couldn't have survived this either.

Maii took out the envelope that Shin had passed to her and extracted a piece of paper from within. Dace wanted to be a gentleman and resist peeping, since it felt intrusive, but curiosity won out.

Still, all he saw was a script written in an unknown language and Maii's eyes gleaming as she scanned the words. To see the gamut of emotions on

Miss Expressionless's face today—surprise to insecurity to sadness—left Dace stumped, and he found himself wondering what Pod would do or say to comfort Maii if he were here.

'Speak to me! Are you guys safe? Maii?' Pod's panicked voice sounded in Dace's ear.

'Yeah, we're safe,' uttered Dace with a wry smile. 'We're heading to the meeting point. And Pod and Zej, you might want to turn on the news now. *A* just got blown up.'

5

Vin | Forgiveness

The first thing that Vin noticed when she came to was the offensiveness of the stale and stuffy air that she was inhaling. She sat up and wrinkled her nose as her eyes adjusted to her surroundings.

Where am I? she thought.

She supposed the space in which she'd woken up, enclosed with stacks of log and a thatched roof, could be classified as a room. Carved into one of the walls was a window. It was left slightly ajar, and through the gap penetrated a shard of light that fell on a small table and stool. Both items were lined up alongside the wall opposite the bed on which she was seated.

That explains the smell—the lack of ventilation. Vin stood up and dusted herself off in disgust, trying to recall how she had ended up here. Images of black-clad figures chasing her and Keix flashed through her mind.

'Keix!' exclaimed Vin. She looked around and saw a door hiding in the shadows. It took her a second to register the slumped figure seated by the exit.

Vin shouted her friend's name again. She rushed forward and grabbed Keix by her shoulders and shook her, fear rendering her almost hysterical. It was only when Keix's eyelids fluttered open that Vin let out a sigh of relief.

'You're awake,' mumbled Keix, her voice thick with fatigue.

Vin nodded.

'You're okay,' added Keix. She looked out of the window and her brow furrowed. 'It's almost noon . . . You've been unconscious for more than a day.'

'Thanks for dragging me here.' Vin smiled in gratitude. 'How did you get out of the crater, though? And fight off the attackers? I remember you fell into the pit . . . and a figure in black followed you into it . . . then I lost consciousness.' She touched her neck. The spot where she'd felt a pinprick before she fainted was still sore.

'The troopers shot you with a sedative,' explained Keix.

'So how did you manage to take them out all by yourself? I thought we were dead meat.' Vin tried to keep the dread out of her voice but wasn't quite successful.

'It wasn't—' started Keix. Before she could finish her sentence, the door swung open and hit her in the back.

She let out a yelp of pain and scrambled to stand up as a figure appeared on the other side of the half-opened door.

The intruder muttered an apology just as Vin pounced on him.

Despite having just woken up from a sedative-induced sleep, Vin's reflexes were quick. Regardless, she was no match for the tall figure.

With barely any effort, he twisted his body out of her grip and pushed her away. Though the blow wasn't heavy, Vin still staggered backwards.

Her eyes widened in recognition when the light hit the man as he stepped forward. 'You!' She pointed at him. 'Who the hell are you? You were with the group who attacked us!'

The figure answered with an appraising look and turned to Keix. 'A proper introduction is in order, don't you think?' he said.

Vin gasped. 'You know him?'

Keix took a deep breath as if she were preparing to deliver some very bad news to Vin. 'Vin, this is Jūn. He was the one who helped us fight off the black-suited weirdos who attacked us.'

Vin gaped at her friend. 'We don't know that. He could have been the one who attacked me!' How could Keix trust someone else so easily after everything that had happened to them in the past two years?

'If I had attacked you, I would have left you unconscious in the trap instead of carrying you all the way here,' reasoned the man called Jūn.

'You did what?' Vin blinked at him, then at Keix.

Keix looked sheepish. 'I wasn't . . . strong enough.'

Jūn looked almost smug.

Vin crossed her arm, imitating his stance. 'Well, carrying me here doesn't prove that you weren't in cahoots with the weirdos who attacked us.'

'I helped you and Keix fight them off too.' Jūn sounded like he was speaking to a child.

Vin scowled at him. 'Like I said, there's no proof that you aren't part of their team. Who knows? You could be a spy sent to gain our trust so that we'd follow you into a trap. We're not that stupid.'

'You're right, and you're wrong,' said Jūn mildly.

Vin wanted to smack the look of amusement from his face. 'Stop talking in circles,' she warned and looked to Keix to back her up. But her friend's face was green and she looked like she was about to keel over.

Stepping protectively in front of Keix, Vin prepared to launch herself at Jūn again, this time with the aim of inflicting serious bodily harm.

But Keix put herself between them and raised her hands. She looked like she was about to say something, but the moment she opened her mouth, she retched.

Vin looped her outstretched arm over her shoulders. 'Are you all right?'

'She needs to eat,' replied Jūn, holding out a bag in their direction.

'How do we know you're not trying to poison us?'

'You know, I should think that a word of thanks should suffice, considering that I carried you for almost an entire day to safety, and that I brought food for your friend here, who's almost fainting from starvation,' said Jūn, before muttering something unintelligible under his breath.

Vin thought it sounded like an insult. 'Excuse me?' she snapped.

Jūn waved a hand. 'All right. You're excused.'

What was wrong with this man? Vin stepped towards him, but Keix reached out a hand to still her and raised her other hand to Jūn.

'Excuse *us*,' said Keix, snatching the bag from Jūn. She dragged Vin out of the hut before she could protest and made for the clearing beside the building.

'Where are we going?' asked Vin, supporting Keix with one hand as they walked. She noticed that her friend kept glancing back. When she followed her line of sight, she saw Jūn emerging from the tiny, dilapidated structure.

He planted himself at the entrance and leaned against the door frame with a casualness that made Vin want to throttle him. His eyes followed them intently, and when he caught Keix looking at him, he gestured to the ground as if to reassure her that he wasn't going anywhere.

Vin made a sound of disgust and pulled Keix away. She needed to talk to her friend alone. However, when she stopped and opened her mouth to speak, Keix shushed her and started steering her towards a small hill in the horizon. Every now and then, Keix would pause and prick up her ears like she was listening out for something.

Finally, Keix stopped just a little over the peak of a soft rolling hill, when Jūn's silhouette had shrunk to half the size of Vin's palm. He was still outside the hut; at this distance, Vin couldn't even tell if his eyes were open.

'How did you get to know him? Why do you trust him? And why do we have to come so far to talk?' demanded Vin, the pitch of her voice rising with each question.

Instead of replying, Keix sat down on the ground and untied the bag that she had taken from Jūn.

'Are you *serious*?' Vin stared at Keix and watched her friend take out a long loaf of bread and a bottle of amber-coloured liquid from the bulging sack. Vin's eyes softened when she saw just how ravenous Keix was, so she held her tongue for the next couple of minutes while the half-Kulcan devoured the bread and guzzled the drink between bites.

Keix finally took a huge swallow and said, 'First of all—'

'All right, now she's ready to talk.' Vin pretended to grumble and made a show of sitting down beside her friend. She'd remained standing throughout Keix's 'feasting' to convey her annoyance, but truth be told, even if Keix wasn't starving, Vin wouldn't have been able to stay irritated at her for long.

The two of them had been fast friends since they first met at the orphanage. Vin had sensed Keix's grief the second she saw her. Even though no one expected children who entered the institution to be happy, the way Keix held her emotions in check made an impression on Vin.

Blessed—or cursed, depending on how one looked at it—with the Ifarl ability to see people's auras, Vin had always found it hard to socialize. It was like being able to read someone's mind, which most people found disconcerting and creepy.

But Keix was different. Her aura was blurry, and the eleven-year-old Vin latched on to this new person, who embodied calm and serenity in the sea of bright, colourful, attention-seeking Atrossians. This alone was reason enough for Vin to decide that she *had* to be friends with Keix.

It was only a couple of years later that Vin discovered that Keix's aura was different and harder to read because of her Kulcan heritage. By that time, the two of them were inseparable, and when Keix said she would join ATI as soon as she turned fourteen (because that was the earliest that the institution admitted trainees), Vin concluded that her mission in life was to protect Atros too. And protect Atros they did. During the ghost attack on Sector L, Vin, for the first time in her life, used her compulsion deliberately on Keix and forced her to fire the black-hole bullet.

Vin had been ready to die—to vanish after getting sucked into the vacuum created by the shot. Yet, she had found herself reappearing in a laboratory and turned into an experimental subject by the very organization that she was willing to sacrifice her life for. What she went through felt worse than dying. In the two years that she was held captive by Atros and tortured, she'd kept herself sane by considering possibilities of how she would live her life if she escaped from captivity.

She would try to find the Ifarls, learn more about her parents and ancestors. She would run off and explore the world—something that she had never considered in her growing-up years in Atros. She would seek out more meaningful experiences because she had come to the realization that her life, though entertaining, felt rather empty when her sole priority was to have fun.

When she saw Keix leaving the lake house after they survived the ritual, Vin panicked and followed. She wasn't ready to lose the only stable presence in her life—not when she had so much to figure out after going through the life-changing hybridization, then having her proper consciousness restored and losing her Ifarl powers in the process.

She knew that Keix was going through her own struggles, so she had given her friend space and stalked her from a distance, unsure of when she should make her presence known—until the attackers came.

'If I'd known that you were starving, I would have made my presence known much earlier.' Vin sighed.

'Okay, first things first. I do not know-*know* Jūn,' confessed Keix. 'I don't trust-*trust* him either, but it seems like I—we, if you're coming with me—have no choice but to do so.'

Before Vin could ask why, Keix rushed to clarify. 'And he's a Kulcan. That's why I had to drag you out here to talk. So that he wouldn't overhear us.'

'A Kulcan?' Vin's whisper conveyed her shock. 'How do you know that?'

Vin glanced at the Kulcan. Jūn was a conundrum and then some. She wanted to know how and why he had appeared at such an impeccable time—when she and Keix had been under attack. And how had he managed to dispatch their assailants so effortlessly?

Kulcans were outstanding fighters, Vin knew that. But she could have sworn that she'd seen at least one of the attackers draw a pistol that discharged black-hole rounds before she was knocked unconscious. How did the three of them manage to escape unscathed if that attacker had fired one of those bullets? Perhaps the hooded figures' marksmanship was *that* bad?

'How do I know he's a Kulcan? Have you seen anyone fight like that?' asked Keix.

'I was knocked unconscious almost as soon as I saw him, remember?' Vin rolled her eyes. 'I mean, was there anything that gave his identity as a Kulcan away, like . . . bright pink hair or something?'

'I just . . . know,' replied Keix.

Vin wanted to ask her friend what she meant by that. Was it a gut feeling? Could she see a halo or some sign invisible to others on Jūn, not unlike her Ifarl's powers?

Vin touched her recently coloured hair and considered for a moment. Ifarls had telltale pink hair and a maze of lines on their scalps—if they chose not to disguise them. Vin had embraced these traits because it kept the other kids at bay. Rumours about Ifarls' mysterious abilities were rampant in Atros, and laying claim to that heritage meant that everyone always thought twice about crossing her.

It was only after the ritual that Vin decided she wanted nothing more to do with the enigmatic race, so she changed her hairstyle.

And Kulcans weren't like Odats, who looked distinctly non-human. In fact, the renowned fighters didn't differ that greatly in terms of appearance compared to Atrossians, even if they did seem to be much taller on average.

Keix had always been a good half a head taller than Vin, who inherited the Ifarls' petite genes.

In the end, Vin decided not to press Keix for answers as to why or how she knew that Jūn was a Kulcan. There were other more important things that she needed to find out.

'All right,' she said. 'We can revisit this Kulcan thing another time. But I need to know this—what do you mean you have no choice but to trust him? And where are we going?'

'I first saw him after the ritual,' began Keix. She didn't have to elaborate on which event she was referring to. After that night, Keix conveyed to

Vin what Zenchi, the mastermind behind the ritual, had said to her. The most shocking and mind-boggling revelation for Vin was that she was a descendant of the powerful Ifarl who had opened the gateway between the living and dead because he had returned home one day to find his wife murdered and his daughter missing.

'Jūn came to me right after the ritual,' continued Keix. 'He said that if I wanted to look for my father, he would be waiting in the woods outside Atros to bring me to him.'

Vin thought it sounded too convenient. 'Your father? How—'

'How did Jūn arrive at the place where the ritual was conducted? How did he know I was there in the first place? How do *I* know if he's lying?' interrupted Keix. 'I don't. But I plan to find out.'

Vin could tell that Keix was agitated, so she let her have a minute to gather herself.

'After the ritual,' said Keix after a long pause, 'when we were at Dace's house, I felt . . . lost. After Sector L, after everything that happened . . . it was as if my entire life had been a lie.'

Vin cast her eyes downwards. 'That's why you left,' she said softly. She knew that it wasn't easy for Keix to vocalize the complex feelings she was going through.

In their years of friendship, Keix had never spoken much about her family except to reveal her Kulcan heritage. And that was only after Vin kept bugging her about not being able to beat her in hand-to-hand combat despite training twice as hard and long. Vin's grouse was exaggerated, of course.

After that incident, Vin had taken care to never pry into Keix's personal affairs from her childhood. She knew that if her friend was ready to talk, she would.

The urge to look for a parent, a sense of direction in life, after what they had been through was understandable. Vin knew as much—which was why she couldn't fault Keix for wanting to hang on to this thread of hope, no matter how flimsy it was.

Vin wanted to let Keix know that she empathized, so she joked in an accusatory tone, 'Without telling anyone. Not even me.'

Keix had the cheek to look contrite. 'Why did you follow me?' she asked genuinely.

Vin sighed. 'I just . . . I know Pod and Zej had their reasons for letting the Ifarls go ahead with the ritual even though they knew that we were supposed to die—I'm not angry with them. Really. I just needed to get away.

'You were the only person in that house I could stand to be around. That's why when I saw you leaving, I panicked and went after you.'

Keix nodded. 'I'm sorry I didn't tell you. I needed to get away too.'

Vin sighed again. 'I know. That's why I didn't approach you right away. I just followed at a distance so you wouldn't notice.'

'Your tracking skills have improved. Either that or my senses have dulled,' said Keix, furrowing her brows and reaching for her third loaf of bread.

Vin gave her a mock-exasperated glare, picked up one of the loaves and sniffed. The bread had lost that delicious, sweet-salty aroma of its freshly baked counterparts, but it didn't smell stale either.

'Or you're undernourished,' reprimanded Vin. 'But if you're going to allow yourself to be poisoned by someone we barely know, I'd be there beside you every step of the way. What are friends for, right?'

Vin took a bite of the bread to prove her words, her teeth sinking into the still-crispy crust and soft, fluffy interior. She chewed the salty and dense bread. It was dry and a little hard to swallow, so Vin took a swig of the beverage that Keix had been drinking.

The beverage was surprisingly sweet and tangy, and it washed down the bread easily.

Vin looked at Keix. She thought back to the food that she had managed to get from the people she came across outside Atros. If only her friend hadn't been so stubborn and had asked for help like her . . .

'I'm coming with you, you know. You couldn't shake me off at the house. You can't shake me off now,' said Vin. 'Unless . . . you refuse to take a shower the next time you get a chance to do so.' She wrinkled her nose.

Keix waved her insult away. 'Can't smell. Turned off my sense of smell,' she said in an offhand manner.

Vin gave her friend the side-eye. 'Must be cool, being a Kulcan,' she muttered.

Keix punched Vin's arm good-humouredly.

'Ow! I see you have your energy back,' said Vin with a laugh. She took another bite of the food and spoke while she chewed. 'And speaking of Kulcans, yours must have sniffed you out miles away.' She jerked her chin in the direction of the hut.

'He's not mine,' protested Keix, looking a little embarrassed.

Even though Vin's joke was feeble, the two of them sniggered and then laughed out loud, their laughter pealing through the air.

The sound must have carried to the hut because Vin thought she saw Jūn turn his head towards them. Ignoring him, Vin and Keix continued to giggle uncontrollably.

For that split second, Vin imagined that they were back at the ATI, blissfully unaware of the web of lies that entrapped them. That was a such carefree time, because being witty and coming up tops in trooper tests were all there was to their lives.

When their spontaneous mirth eventually subsided, they caught their breaths and finished their meal in companionable silence.

The sun was beating down on them now and Vin welcomed the warmth of the sunshine as it melted away the vestiges of exhaustion—an exhaustion she hadn't noticed set in, having spent the most part of the past weeks under the canopy of the forest stalking Keix.

A niggling feeling at the back of Vin's mind made her turn to Keix just as the latter got to her feet.

Vin didn't know how else to phrase it, so she simply asked the question as it came to her mind. 'Why did you let yourself go so hungry?'

Gone from her voice was any trace of the gaiety from before, conveying her earnestness in understanding Keix's self-imposed fast.

'When I was following you,' continued Vin, 'I saw you avoid that first hut you came across. Why? The guy who lived there—and most of the people I came across subsequently—were cordial.

'They never said much to me, but I could sense that they had something against Atrossians. Even then, they were generous with their provisions, sharing them with me without questions asked.

'You wouldn't have starved if you'd asked for help from these people.' Vin couldn't help but chastise her friend. What had she been thinking?

Keix was stung into silence. She seemed to struggle with her emotions, and when the dam finally broke, she told Vin about what happened with Rold. He had been the first friend she made after Pod and Zej broke her out from PEER.

'He told me about the Ifarl's prophecy,' said Keix, 'and I just mocked him. And minutes after that, Seyfer arrived along with a bunch of hybrid soldiers and shot him with the sedative that is fatal to people with Ifarl blood.

'Seyfer wanted me. But Rold compelled me to stay hidden in the basement of the hut in which we had been lying low while I recuperated. Before he died, he spelled the hut to become invisible so that Seyfer wouldn't be able to find me,' said Keix.

'I was there. *Hiding* in the basement of the hut and I watched him die after he got shot! I couldn't do anything . . . and when Maii forced Rold's soul to . . .' Keix stopped to take a steadying breath.

Vin knew that she was talking about the hybridization process where a ghost was bound to a living person's body. She had been subjected to the same ordeal in PEER.

'When I became a hybrid,' continued Keix, 'I saw and felt what he really thought of me . . . He blamed me for his death.'

Vin almost couldn't nod. She recalled the extreme rage she had felt when she fused with the ghost of a man who wasn't able to survive the tortures that Atros had put them through.

'I just didn't want to see anyone else die because of me,' said Keix, her voice barely a whisper now.

Vin put her arm around Keix. She didn't know what she could say to comfort her friend.

'And there's something else you need to know.' Keix seemed to be gathering her courage. When she opened her mouth, the words came in a rush.

'Rold is your cousin. He's a descendant of Iv't too . . . I'm sorry, Vin. He died protecting me . . . I will never be able to forgive myself for that.'

Vin closed her eyes and tried to process what Keix had just said. She had an Ifarl cousin? And that person died protecting her best friend? She was shocked, yes. But was she supposed to be sad? She had never known Rold, so the only thing she felt upon hearing of his death was a deep sense of regret. And she knew better than anyone else why Keix was blaming no one else but herself.

As a hybrid, Vin had harboured so much resentment towards everyone and anyone she laid her eyes on. And when the portal was closed, what was ripped from her body other than the ghost who had been fused with her, was the pure hatred that fuelled the monster within.

In a way, Vin had been reborn. And she couldn't find the energy to be angry at anyone at all. Not Keix. Not Oron. Not Zej or Pod. Not even Atros.

But when it came to herself, the rebuke was stark. *Why did I allow myself to get captured by Atros? Why did I believe their lies? If I trusted the wrong people, how can I blame my friends for doing the same?*

After she calmed herself down, Vin patted Keix's shoulders and said, 'Perhaps one day we will learn to forgive ourselves, like how we forgave the others.'

6

Pod | The Light of Stars

Pod brushed his hand against his clammy nape, sweeping away the beads of perspiration gathered there. The humid night air grated against his skin and the acrid smell of smoke stung his nostrils every time he inhaled.

The air was still and heavy, yet he shuddered whenever he thought about how close Dace and Maii had come to getting blown up at *A*.

Zej had shown up at the lake house halfway through their mission and told Pod that they had to leave immediately. They then made their way to an apartment in an abandoned building in Sector B.

This district north of Atros's city centre was a sparsely populated residential Sector. There were standalone houses dotted along the boundary of the city centre and Sector B. These were reserved for high-ranking Atros officials who preferred quieter environments outside the bustling central. The taller buildings in this Sector were mostly derelict and scattered at the edges, in the opposite direction of the city centre.

Pod recalled reading about how these apartment blocks were home to families of Atros troopers. But this was way before the portal between the living and the dead had been opened—the big boom, as Pod liked to think of it. After that, too many people died. Too early. The population was eventually diminished, and these buildings, vacated and fell to disrepair.

The apartment to which Zej had brought Pod was located in one of these abandoned buildings strategically parked at the end of a narrow road. There were no other structures in its vicinity, and the unit had a window that provided a clear view of the road, so any movement along it could be easily seen.

This meant that it would be harder to ambush them. It also meant that they would probably have difficulties escaping from the building unnoticed if they were attacked.

Nonetheless, Pod was sure that Zej had an escape plan—one that likely involved wading through sewage water in the extensive underground pipe network. These massive tubes interlinked all the Sectors in Atros. Because of the way they weaved together, the number of escape routes were limitless. And Zej, for some inexplicable reason, knew them all like the back of his hand.

But the question was, where should they go from here? Their original 'Mission: Get Raye's fingerprints' had fallen apart faster than Pod could type Atros on his keyboard. Now, all of a sudden, Shin had cast towards them a 'please save Atros and the world' task.

Be it an Atrossian, who thought nothing of blowing up the landmark of their own city centre, or the group of ex-Atrossians that Shin called ExA, who supposedly wanted to reclaim the city, the threat that they were facing wasn't only dangerous and ruthless, it was unpredictable too.

Over the past two years, Pod thought he'd gotten used to shocking and unpleasant revelations of Atros preaching one thing and doing something else and nefarious behind their citizens' backs. But how they were spinning the explosion was another level of delusional.

'Authorities' preliminary investigation shows that the explosion at *A* was caused by a gas leak,' recited the female newscaster on Atros City News.

Standing at the ground floor entrance to the building, which was home to the prestigious club, in her signature white wrap dress, this newscaster personified calmness and trustworthiness. This was an image known and expected of her, and one that Atrossians were accustomed to, after two decades of her heading the news.

The broadcast was intercut with footages of thick, grey clouds of smoke billowing out of the top of the building. Anyone with eyes and half a brain would have seen that there was no way a gas leak could have caused entire floors to be blown right off the building.

Yet here was Atros City News, reporting the incident as if it were just a regular update on how Atros had managed to, yet again, reinforce the invisible, dome-like barriers that kept ghosts from entering the city and its Sectors—a frequent item in the news streams.

'Gas leak. Yeah, right,' muttered Pod as he put the news on mute.

He had set up the projector on a dusty coffee table facing an empty wall. The light from the image diffused throughout the living area of the apartment, casting an ominous glow on Zej, who was seated at the edge of a threadbare settee. His brows were snapped together, his tired eyes focused on the ticker on the screen.

GAS LEAK IN A CAUSES EXPLOSION
ESTIMATED 50 PEOPLE TRAPPED
CHANCES OF RETRIEVING SURVIVORS ARE LOW
TROOPERS HAVE BEEN SENT IN TO HELP

The tension rolling off Zej made Pod jittery. Despite having known Zej since they were eight, Pod had no idea what his friend was thinking about right now.

He wanted to ask Zej to whom the apartment belonged—did Dace's dad own this as well? Or was this another of Oka's safe houses?

But he'd sworn to himself that he was going to give his friend the silent treatment until Zej explained why he conspired behind his back to secretly plan for another exit strategy out of *A* with Dace.

It was hurtful, to say the least. Hadn't he proven himself to be reliable after all these years of friendship? When he had discovered that Zej joined Oka, he risked everything to become an undercover agent for the rebel group too. Granted, his main aim, which was to find and rescue Keix, who had disappeared after the ghost attack on Sector L, wasn't as virtuous as Zej's. Nonetheless, Pod felt he hadn't given Zej any reason to distrust him. So, he couldn't understand why Zej was always so reluctant to confide in him.

Pod swallowed the question that reached the tip of his tongue. Picking a spot in the apartment farthest from Zej, which happened to be a stool by the window, he slumped down.

In the distance, he could see the city centre-Sector B boundary, marked by clusters of buildings that grew increasingly taller as they neared the central district. Viewed from afar, Atros's city centre looked similar to a pyramid with staggered sides, with the skyscraper that housed *A* as its apex. An apex from which grey smoke was trailing into the sky now, like a tendril of truth escaping through a crack in Atros's façade of lies.

Pod puffed in frustration and glanced at the muted news again.

FIRE AT A PUT OUT BY TROOPERS
SEARCH FOR SURVIVORS ONGOING

The newscaster's lips were still furiously moving as she continued reporting from the scene, but Pod didn't turn up the volume. He wasn't interested in lies—Atros's, or anyone else's, including Maii and Dace.

The two of them had pretty much stopped conversing after they escaped from *A*, saying that they should not draw attention to themselves. Pod grew antsy with the lack of communication, and his frustration intensified with every passing second. Yet, all he could do was stare at the T-junction of the only road leading to the building as if he could summon Maii and Dace by sheer will.

* * *

After an eternity, during which Zej continued staring at the screen like a statue, Pod caught sight of a flicker of movement in the street.

Two figures were hurrying towards the building.

Dace was slouching a little, the smugness in his bearing toned down as he hung his head low. Maii, on the other hand, had her back straight and shoulders tensed, as if bracing for a confrontation.

'They're here.' Pod called to Zej in relief.

With the shattering of his self-imposed silence, the dam that Pod had constructed in his mind to hold back his questions broke. Was Dace's dad, one of the Atros council members, involved in the hybrid programme? What exactly did Zenchi instruct Maii to do? Was Maii really spying on them and reporting back to the Ifarls? Was she going to betray them again to further her elders' goals?

Pod felt a wave of despair at that last question as footsteps echoed through the corridor and approached the apartment. The front door creaked open and Maii and Dace stepped in, bringing with them a whiff of smoke tinged with alcohol.

In spite of Pod's earlier doubts, he rushed forward as soon as he saw how bedraggled Maii and Dace looked.

'Are you guys all right?' Pod gasped.

Maii waved in reply. Her evening gown was ripped on one side, all the way up to her thighs, revealing her black boots and an expanse of milky skin.

'Think I broke a rib,' groaned Dace. He looked to be in a worse shape compared to Maii, with his hair mussed up and singed in places. When he shrugged off his jacket, Pod saw a wet, dark patch on the front of his shirt.

'What happened to you?' Pod pointed to the stain.

Dace gritted his teeth in pain as he reached into his jacket's inner pocket, pulled out three large pieces of bloodstained glass and deposited them on the kitchen counter. The clinking of the glass against the stone counter sounded like claps of thunder reverberating through the house.

'See if you can still pull Raye's prints off it. Let's hope that only a handful of people touched that glass before it was served,' he said to Pod.

When Pod looked at Dace in confusion, the latter's eyes flashed with murder, his lips pressed into a thin line. 'What are you gaping at? Go on! Work your magic. Or am I the only one who remembers that the initial mission to go to *A* was to get Raye's fingerprints?' asked Dace.

Pod was stumped. He didn't think that anyone would have remembered their actual goal amidst all the game-changing revelations that had taken place at *A*. His admiration for Dace inched up and he hurried to his bag, thankful that he'd had the good sense to throw whatever devices he could get his hands on into his bag when he left the lake house.

He also fished out a clean T-shirt that he'd packed and passed it to Dace. 'Use this to clean and bandage your wound. There's no water or electricity here,' he said.

Dace didn't even mutter a word of thanks as he stripped off his shirt and dabbed at the lacerations on his chest caused by the broken glass.

'While Pod's at it,' said Dace, biting out his words, his face twisted in pain, 'why don't you'—he thrust his chin at Maii—'"explain everything", as Shin said? Preferably before Atros catches up to us again?'

Pod's hands stilled. He wanted to take Maii's side and ask Dace to quit using that tone with her. But after what happened at *A*, Pod wanted answers too. He could tell that Maii was rattled now. Her brows were snapped together, and her shoulders, squared and tensed. The vulnerability that he'd sensed in her from the first time they met was finally surfacing above the cool composure that she had carefully cultivated.

Maii took a long, deep breath. 'Where do you want me to start?'

Zej, who had been silent all this while, spoke first in a measured tone. 'What do the Ifarls want?'

Before Maii could answer, Dace asked impatiently, 'How about you start from the note that Shin passed to you? What does it say?'

'Note? What note?' asked Pod, frowning. He had reassembled the glass pieces and set it in the centre of the coffee table in front of Zej. From Pod's experience, it would be challenging to pull a proper print off broken glass stained with blood. He could only hope for the best as he placed the palm-sized scanner beside it and pushed a button to let the device do its job. The machine whirred softly, circling the glass on its two tiny wheels, analysing the surface.

'The light of stars shows the path,' recited Maii, retrieving the note in question from an envelope stuffed down her boot. She held out the piece of crumpled paper for the rest to see. 'That's what the note says.' Her melodious voice, together with the broad, cursive, indecipherable script on the crumpled piece of paper, sent a shiver down Pod's back.

'Well, that's helpful,' chimed Dace. His usual sarcasm was blunted by the pain in his voice this time around.

'Another Ifarl prophecy?' asked Zej.

Maii drew an impatient breath. 'Ifarls believe that all knowledge in the world is held in the stars. When they veer from their usual path, or when they become dimmer or brighter, it means there are changes afoot. This is Zenchi's handwriting.' She looked down at the piece of paper in her hand.

'Let me get this straight,' said Dace. 'You Ifarls stare at the skies every night, see a star or two *behaving abnormally*, and you conclude that you need to send us off on an errand to ask the Kulcans for help? Of all people—us, who have no idea where the Kulcans live. Intriguing. Is that why you followed us back to Atros, instead of heading back home with your Ifarl elders after the portal was closed?'

Maii's eyes shot icicles at Dace. 'Zenchi told me to keep an eye on Vin because . . . because the Ifarls who were involved in the ritual—including me—lost all our powers.'

Pod heard the shame in her voice. 'Why didn't you tell us?'

'What could you have done?' Maii's tone was bitter.

'Why Vin?' interrupted Zej.

'Because she's the descendant of that Ifarl who landed us in this fiasco in the first place. Right? Iv't, his name?' said Dace.

When Pod looked at him in amazement, Dace said irritably, 'Well, I listen instead of getting enamoured with the Ifarl.'

Pod's cheeks heated up. He didn't think that his crush on Maii was that obvious . . . ? Thankfully, he was spared the need to come up with a retort as Maii explained the Ifarl lore that was conveyed by the duo of rhymes, 'The Night of Legends' and 'The Act of Repentance'.

From what he gathered, even if the powerful Ifarl, Iv't, hadn't opened the living-dead gateway, he would have done something else drastic, like put the entire civilization in some sort of trance or something—or so the Ifarls believed. No matter what he did, they would have to 'right the wrong', to 'restore balance' in the world, just like what Zenchi had told Keix before the ritual.

'But what has this got to do with what Shin said Atros was facing?' asked Pod.

Zej nodded, as if Pod had voiced his thoughts.

Dace's eyes were narrowed, and Pod hazarded a guess that he was thinking about the repercussions of the portal-closing ritual.

'What do you know about how Atros—the current one—was formed?' asked Maii.

'The current one?'

'Why are we getting quizzed on Atros history?'

Zej and Dace asked their questions simultaneously.

Pod dug through memories of his lessons back in school. Thinking back, he realized that the textbooks always skirted around the formation and foundation of Atros.

Even as troopers, the main aim of their classes was to either train them in combat or drill into them the importance of maintaining the 'integrity' of Atros, of protecting the people residing within the Sector borders. It had always been hinted that if Atros should fall, the people would have nowhere to go, or that they would suffer. But the specifics were glossed over. Perhaps the fear of a bad outcome stopped everyone from asking the real questions.

The message was simple: These are the rules. Follow them. Never venture out of the protective sphere that Atros has cast over you. Atrossians' safety is the organization's main mission, they were taught. That was why Atros's emphasis was always on training the troopers, investing time and people to strengthen the barriers that kept the ghosts at bay. Because that was the only thing that kept life 'normal'.

'Without knowledge of where you came from, you'll be directionless when it comes to where you should head to,' said Maii. Her sage reply to Dace's question made his jaws drop. On the other hand, the furrow between Zej's brows deepened as he considered her words.

Pod didn't know what to make of the statement. He could hear the Sector rousing to a new day as a rustling sound flitted in through the open window. The back of his neck still prickled. Was he ready to confront another one of Atros's lies, the one that Maii seemed set to unravel?

But Maii didn't give Pod a chance to sort out his feelings. She continued, 'As Shin said, the current Atros government was formed after expelling the previous administration—the ex-Atrossians, or ExA in short. Before the current organization came into power, the people here were living a very different life.'

'So . . . you mean that the Atros officials—and all those high-and-mighty members of the current council—were rebels in the past?' Dace finally looked intrigued by Maii's story.

Maii tilted her head in response. 'That's one way of putting it.'

'But what do you mean by "a very different life"?' added Dace as an afterthought.

'The previous Atros leaders subscribed to a school of thought that said that if your life's not getting better, it's because you're not working hard enough, or you're not capable enough,' elaborated Maii.

'That's pretty elitist,' interjected Pod.

Zej looked increasingly troubled, but he remained silent.

'Anyone who was observant would know that this wasn't true,' continued Maii. 'The Atros leaders' lives seemed to be getting more and more comfortable, while the living conditions of the citizens kept worsening. They weren't starving, but they were working themselves to the bone just to keep Atros running. Yet, their homes were falling into disrepair and when they fell sick, they couldn't get proper medical care. It felt like ExA didn't care if they died. The leaders just wanted more—more weapons, more buildings, more everything. There was no concrete reason given for this excess.

'Eventually, some citizens banded together and chased out the very small group of people who were ruling Atros. Then, the rebels took charge over everything—weapons and material manufacture, the factories, and more. There was very little resistance once the ExA leaders were exiled because everyone felt oppressed by the ex-regime.'

Pod was listening with such rapt attention that he almost didn't notice when the scanner beeped twice, indicating an error. He tore his eyes away from Maii and restarted the device.

If, by some miracle, he could pull a couple of fingerprints off the glass, he might be able to access deeper into the system and find evidence supporting Maii's story. Of course, he was going to make locating Dace's dad and Lana his priority. But even if he did manage to uncover their whereabouts, he wasn't sure if they would be able to mount a rescue mission for them after the debacle at *A*.

To be frank, he wasn't even sure if they would be able to leave Atros to look for Keix, as Shin had asked them to do. What was ExA's ultimate aim? Revenge? Or did they simply wish to reclaim their city?

'And how is it that you know all this while none of us who's lived and grown up in Atros has heard of this before? Because you read it in the stars?' asked Dace, ever the sceptic.

Maii ignored the taunt. 'Because we observe and we take notes. And the Ifarls pass down the knowledge from generation to generation.'

Dace coughed. '*Riiight*. Because history is written by those who observe and take notes—not by the victors.'

'Well, it would be written by the victors, *if* they actually bothered to write it.' Maii sounded like she thought it was blasphemous that anyone would even consider not recording history.

'What happened to the people who lived through the rebellion? Why have they not spoken about it? Wouldn't rumours have spread—either in the form of urban legends or by word of mouth?' asked Zej.

'Not if everything has been systematically erased and replaced with a preferred version of history,' replied Maii.

'Erased?' interjected Pod. Considering how everything was recorded in the overall system, it might be possible to overwrite these information . . . But a person's memories too? Unless . . . An image of Atrossians lining up to be compelled by Ifarls to get their memories altered flew into Pod's mind and he felt a sudden wave of nausea.

Were Ifarls able to do that? He remembered Zenchi saying that Ifarls couldn't use their powers to harm people. But did scrubbing a person's memory count? He couldn't help but steal a glance at Maii and wonder if she'd be able to do that to him, if she still had her powers.

'Why are ExA attacking Atros now? Or rather, why does Atros suspect that it's them only now? How about the rebels? Why can't it be them?' asked Zej, determined to get the whole story.

Maii shook her head disapprovingly. 'ExA was complacent, so they didn't see the takeover coming. They were chased out of Atros with nothing but the clothes on their backs. So, they had to regroup.

'Ifarl intelligence says that they settled down in a piece of land a couple of months' trek from here, and they tried to source for raw materials to recreate the weapons that they needed to take back Atros.

'Yes, Dace,' said Maii, giving Dace an irritated look because of the look of disbelief that he made. 'They still had the knowledge to build the weapons, but they had to do so from scratch. And because they didn't have the numbers, they had to formulate another strategy to get back at those who revolted against them. So, they decided to turn themselves into weapons.'

Dace coughed and paused in the act of ripping the T-shirt that Pod had passed to him into strips. 'What do you mean "they decided to turn themselves into weapons"?' he asked.

'They tried to fuse with the machines,' replied Maii.

'They tried to *fuse* with the machines?' repeated Zej.

Somehow, this statement made Pod feel even sicker than the thought of Atros altering their citizens' memories. '"Fuse" as in build machine parts into their flesh?' His voice was a tad higher pitched than usual.

Maii half-shook her head. 'The specifics are unclear. But what we do know is that around the same time, Iv't opened the portal between the living and the dead.'

Pod didn't even bother to disguise the look of horror on his face. Even Dace's incredulity was wiped off his face. Everyone present knew that machines broke down, sometimes in destructive ways, when ghosts were around. If these people managed to 'fuse' with the machine, like Maii said, and they came near supernatural beings . . .

'All of them died?' Zej's voice was strained.

'Even if they didn't, they would have been affected adversely by the paranormal energy if they had machine parts built into their bodies.'

'Which meant that they wouldn't have been able to mount a full-scale attack on Atros . . . ?' The reality of the situation dawned on Pod. If Iv't hadn't opened the portal between the living and the dead, the Atros he had come to know might have ceased to exist decades ago.

He tried to imagine what his life would have been like had he been born into the old world order. He looked at Zej and Dace. Would they have met if their circumstances had been different? Would he have met Maii?

'That's why the Ifarls suspect that ExA are behind the recent attacks. Because now that the portal is closed, the long-overdue revenge is coming,' concluded Zej.

'Why did the Ifarls have to go and close the portal then?' asked Dace, as if coexisting with ghosts hadn't been such a bad thing after all.

'It's an anomaly that shouldn't have happened. And mistakes like that need to be righted,' said Maii.

Pod glanced at Maii. He thought that she lacked conviction when she uttered the last sentence.

'You can't simply *undo* "mistakes like these",' drawled a disapproving voice from the darkened corridor of the apartment.

Pod grabbed the screen, its news commentary still running, and directed its light at the hallway. All of them had been so engrossed in Maii's story they hadn't heard this intruder approach.

Despite the shock that they'd been discovered, everyone leaped into action.

Zej had his gun unholstered and pointed at the passageway in a split second.

Dace, whose wound was now bound by a makeshift bandage that used to be Pod's T-shirt, also had a gun trained at the corridor. Meantime, because Maii didn't have a proper weapon, she had her fists clenched in front of her, ready to fight.

Pod and Zej had done a sweep of the entire apartment when they first arrived to make sure that it was empty. There was no way that this guy was hiding in the apartment the whole time. Then, Pod recalled the rustling sound from before. It must have been made by this newcomer when he slipped into one of the two empty rooms here.

As the intruder stepped into the projector's beam, holding both hands up in mock surrender, Pod realized why the voice sounded familiar. The person's name came to mind easily.

Seyfer.

The last time Pod saw him, Seyfer had been in a cage together with Keix as the Ifarls prepared to close the portal. Everyone in the vicinity, including Pod, Zej and Dace, had been knocked out when the chanting reached a crescendo. When they woke up, Seyfer was nowhere to be seen.

The rest of the gang must have recognized him too. After all, it's hard to forget someone who had tried to kill you or turn you into a raging, possessed monster.

'Why are you here?'

'How did you find us?'

'What do you want?'

The questions came all at once from Pod's group.

Seyfer smiled, amused. His dark eyes flickered to the coffee table, and he pointed to the broken glass which Dace had smuggled out of *A*, as if he had been part of the conversation all along. 'Can you fix the glass?

To the way it was before?' he asked mockingly. 'If you can't fix something as small and insignificant as this, how can you fix the massive rip between two dimensions?'

Seyfer's voice sounded a little deeper than Pod remembered, but his habit of extending his S's when he spoke remained.

'That's a bad analogy and a lousy attempt to sidetrack us,' said Pod. He tried to ignore Seyfer's implication that the ritual to close the portal between the living and the dead had not been as successful as the Ifarls said it was. As if speaking to a child, he repeated the questions his group asked and added two more of his. 'Are you alone? Did Atros send you?'

Seyfer shrugged. 'I can take you to Tilsor, Keix and Vin, and the Kulcans.'

Dace faked a laugh. 'Sure. We'll get going as soon as you bring us to my father and Lana.'

Seyfer tutted, shaking his head. 'Not that unconcerned, I see. Estranged father and ex-girlfriend, you say? But don't worry. They're safe. For now.' He made a show of considering his next words. 'They'll remain safe if you guys help us.'

'Gosh! Do we look like an Atros helpline? Or perhaps mercenaries like Odats, but smarter? And do you really think that we'll trust anything you say, after everything? After what happened at *A*?' asked Dace with an exaggerated roll of his eyes.

'It's precisely after what happened at *A* that you should consider trusting what I say.' Seyfer gestured to the projector's image cast on his body—a distorted version of the building and the newscaster. 'This isn't Atros's doing.'

'Elaborate, Seyfer,' said Zej, his voice low and dangerous.

'We face a common enemy; the previous occupants of Atros. Or ExA, as the Ifarl'—he pointed to Maii—'calls them. They are the ones who blew up *A*. If they take over Atros, they'll have the means to manufacture even more weapons. And their priority won't be protecting Atrossians.' Seyfer's tone contained no trace of the self-importance he'd shown just seconds ago.

Dace snorted and Seyfer turned to face him.

'To strip a person of power,' began Seyfer in an even grimmer tone, 'after they've held it in their hands, and to deprive them of it for such a long time . . . It's not hard to imagine the lengths to which they would go to take it back. Not to mention, what they would do with that power when that happens.'

Pod couldn't be sure, but he thought he saw a flicker of fear flash in Seyfer's eyes.

'Say we believe this nonsense you're spouting. What kind of—Dace injected twice the amount of his usual sarcasm into the next word—'*help* do you want from us? Also, thanks for offering to be our guide, but we don't travel with people who have tried to kill us.'

When Seyfer glanced in Maii's direction, Dace added, 'Maii's not included. One, because she also knows the way to Tilsor, and two, because Pod—'

Pod hissed to interrupt Dace.

'—because that's none of your business,' said Dace, changing tack in an instant.

Seyfer laughed. There was something about the high-pitched sound that unsettled Pod.

'That's unfortunate,' said Seyfer. 'But don't you want to hear the deal that I have to offer?'

'Nope,' countered Dace. 'Had enough of those for today.'

Zej held up a hand in Dace's direction. 'We're listening,' he said to Seyfer.

'The Ifarl called Zenchi is withholding information from you,' said Seyfer with a smug smile. He paused for effect.

At the mention of her elder, the blood drained from Maii's already-pale face. Pod saw hints of guilt, anger and helplessness in her widened eyes.

'You'll need the Kulcan's help to take down ExA, that is true. But there's another person we need to speak to, and he's in Tilsor. If you let me join you and help me get to that person, Dace's father and Lana will remain safe.'

'Who's the person you're seeking?' asked Zej.

'All I can tell you right now is that he's a powerful Ifarl,' replied Seyfer.

Maii frowned at his words. She shook her head slightly when the rest looked at her, as if this was information that she truly wasn't aware of.

'And if we don't?' asked Dace.

'Then, when ExA invades, your dad and Lana, who are imprisoned, will not be evacuated with the rest of the innocent civilians,' said Seyfer. 'But if you accept my terms, Atros will make sure that they stay safe until your return.'

Zej stepped in front of Dace to stop him from charging at Seyfer. 'Why exactly do you need us? You could very well go alone and leave us to our own devices.'

Seyfer's smile was slow and deliberate. 'I'll need the help of at least three more people to get to the person with whom I want to speak.'

'Then round up your Atros buddies to go with you! Or get the Odats,' spat Dace from behind Zej.

'We can't afford to spare more *elite* troopers for this task. We may . . . not succeed,' said Seyfer without a trace of arrogance, even though Dace snorted when he uttered the word 'elite'.

'How do we know that Dace's father and Lana are indeed with you?' pressed Zej.

'I can give you my fingerprint to access the system, and the computer whiz here'—Seyfer gestured to Pod—'can go through the surveillance feeds.'

Seyfer cast a glance at the fingerprint scanner which had started beeping again.

'I doubt you'll be able to pull any prints off that broken glass. Though I've got to admit, targeting Raye was a smart move . . . if only you hadn't gone to *A*, one of the most surveilled spots in Atros,' continued Seyfer with a smirk.

Pod exchanged a look with Zej, who gave him a small nod.

After Pod took Seyfer's fingerprints and put them into the system, Atros's security locks came away easily. The tapping of Pod's keyboard intensified as he tried to double- and triple-check everything to make sure that they wouldn't be falling into another trap. As Seyfer claimed, Lana was held in a small, sparsely furnished room with a middle-aged man (Pod presumed this was Dace's dad; they shared the same facial bone structure). The video's timestamp indicated that this was a real-time feed. But there was no indication of where they were held.

As soon as Pod pulled up the stream on the projection screen, all the blood drained from Dace's face.

The air in the room came to a standstill as everyone contemplated their next move.

Pod wasn't sure whether Maii would tag along if they agreed to help Seyfer, although their goal of stopping ExA seemed to coincide, or at least overlap. His eyes flitted over to Zej, who had lowered his gun and moved towards Seyfer.

Of course, Zej would agree to Seyfer's terms. This was Zej. The person who had stepped in front of a group of bullies when Pod was mocked on the first day of school and then proceeded to assume the role of his protector. The person who had fired a black-hole bullet at his own teammates in order to stop ghosts from getting into Atros. And the person who had sacrificed the life of the girl for whom he spent two years searching because he thought it would bring an end to the suffering of thousands of other people—even though he knew that he would carry the burden of guilt for the rest of his life.

No matter how unfathomable Pod found his best friend's decisions, there was one thing consistent about Zej—which was that he'd always persevere on the road that he thought was the correct one.

And Pod didn't know if he should pity or admire his friend's steadfastness.

7

Keix | Moving Pieces

Keix returned to the hut feeling infinitely better. She'd had the most satisfying meal in weeks, and the desolation she felt was nothing more than a faint memory now that Vin was back by her side.

Ever since Zej broke her out from ATI, her days had been nothing more than a mindless search for answers. Answers to questions she couldn't even determine.

She wanted to set adrift into oblivion.

She wanted an anchor.

What she didn't anticipate was the isolation that set into her bones like a persistent chill when she'd left Dace's lake house. And for the past few days, the thought of starving to death outside Atros, searching for something or someone that didn't exist, had even struck her as poetic.

But now, having savoured the last crumb of the bread and downed the beverage Jūn had brought for her, she felt more alive than she'd been in ages. Even though she knew she looked dreadful with her puffy eyes, she gave the Kulcan a small, thankful smile.

Jūn, who was watching her with an odd look, returned her smile.

'Ready to go?' he asked.

'Where are we headed?'

'Tilsor.' Casting a glance at the sky, he added, 'We should be there by nightfall if we leave now.'

'Is that where my father is?'

Jūn shook his head. 'It's a town that we'll have to cross to get to Yurkordu, where we live.'

'Yurkordu . . .' Keix tested the word on her tongue. She wondered what it would be like. Up till now, the only thing she knew about the place where the Kulcans lived was that it was cold.

'You'd best not have any tricks up your sleeves,' warned Vin. 'Otherwise, I'll skin you alive.'

Jūn looked vaguely entertained at the threat but didn't say anything. Instead, he gave a nod and set off in the direction he had come from.

His pace was brisk and Keix and Vin followed close behind, taking three steps for every two that the long-legged Kulcan took.

A length of time after the sky had darkened, Jūn finally stopped and announced, 'We're here.'

A huge shadow with jagged edges that spanned the entire horizon came into view. The fog that obscured it seemed to disperse as the name of the place appeared in Keix's mind.

Tilsor.

Jūn hadn't spoken much throughout the journey. When Keix asked him what Tilsor was like, he just said, 'You'll see for yourself' and left it at that.

Considering the sight in front of her, Keix decided that even if Jūn had tried to describe the place, nothing he said could've come close to the real deal. To someone like her, who had spent her entire life in Atros, Tilsor evoked a sense of mystifying oddness.

While Atros had fences in abundance—between the Sectors and encircling the entire city—as a form of security measure, Tilsor had nary a picket around what Keix assumed were its boundaries. The buildings, of all shapes and sizes, as far as Keix could see, just stopped at a certain point, as if an invisible line had been drawn to indicate the borders of this place.

As Keix stepped past the threshold, she felt a strange energy surround her, making her hair stand on end. In a reflexive move, she reached up to touch her pendant.

Her sudden reaction caught Jūn's attention. He turned to her and said, 'Don't worry. You're safe with me.'

'That remains to be proven,' said Vin, giving him the side-eye.

Keix gave Jūn an embarrassed look. Like Vin, she had her reservations about him. But nothing he'd done so far gave her a concrete reason to believe that he was going to harm her or Vin.

Then, because she had her hand around her pendant, it suddenly occurred to her that she hadn't had the chance to return Jūn's necklace. After he'd left the hut, she had looped his chain around her neck because she couldn't find a safer place to stash it. She didn't think it was appropriate to keep wearing his accessory, but returning it now, under Vin's simmering scrutiny, didn't seem like a good idea either.

Misreading her discomfort for fatigue, Jūn said, 'I've reserved two rooms at an inn where we can get cleaned up and have a good rest. Just keep up so you don't get lost.'

With that, he turned on his heel and headed up the cobbled pathway.

The streets were deserted at this time of the night. It was cloudy, and the feeble candlelight from the widely spaced streetlamps lengthened and shortened their shadows as they passed beneath them. The weather in Tilsor was decidedly cooler than what Keix and Vin had been used to back at Atros, and they huddled closer to each other for warmth.

Keix fixed her eyes on Jūn's back and tried to sort out her conflicting emotions. On the one hand, she felt apologetic that he had to bear the brunt of Vin's hostility; on the other, she understood that her best friend was just looking out for her.

As the thought crossed Keix's mind, she squeezed Vin's shoulder to show appreciation for her friend's presence.

Surprised by the gesture, Vin looked a little mollified. She looped her arm through Keix's and grumbled under her breath, 'Would it kill him to walk a little slower?'

The next second, Jūn called over his shoulder as he approached an archway. 'Keep up,' he said. 'Don't want you guys to get lost here.'

Keix pointed to her ears and mouthed, 'Kulcan.'

'I did it on purpose,' Vin mouthed back. The two of them burst out giggling as they hurried after the subject of their secret conversation.

Jūn's pace was brisk but every so often, whenever he reached a fork in the road, he would hesitate as if he wasn't sure which way to go.

Vin's cheeks were flushed from keeping up with his strides, and she would stand there, huffing, glaring at his back whenever he paused.

Having recovered her strength after the meal, Keix wasn't as bothered as Vin with the punishing pace Jūn set. The cool and fresh air invigorated her, but she couldn't shake off the feeling that they were circling back to some of the streets they had already passed.

Atros's roads were always brightly lit, and the lack of adequate and regular lighting in Tilsor threw Keix off. Just as she opened her mouth to ask Jūn if they were lost, he stopped in front of a squarish building.

'We're here,' he said, ushering them through the main door of a two-storeyed house. Two skinny wooden columns stood on either side of the door frame, supporting a small awning. A single lamp hanging from the shelter cast a soft, welcoming glow on the establishment.

The moment they entered the inn, a middle-aged man in a grey robe stepped out from behind a counter to the right of the door and said, 'This way.'

Jūn inclined his head. Keix and Vin did the same.

The tavern was cosy. Along the border of the entrance hall were a handful of doors that Keix assumed led to rooms for rent.

The man directed them up a narrow flight of stairs into a short corridor which had only two doors that stood side by side.

'Which is the bigger room?' asked Jūn.

The man gestured to the door on the right, gave a curt bow and descended the stairs to return to his original spot behind the counter.

'This is your room. Have a good rest and I'll bring you out to buy some supplies tomorrow,' said Jūn, disappearing through the archway on the left.

Vin shrugged at Keix and entered their room, where two baths in makeshift wooden tubs had been drawn. The water was tepid and appeared to have been prepared a while ago, but Keix and Vin relished in scrubbing the grime off their skin anyway.

When they were done, they saw that a change of clothes, similar in style to Jūn's outfit, had been laid out for them. Each set came with three layers of full-length robes and a sash, and Keix opted for the royal blue ensemble while Vin went for the maroon one. By the time they figured out the sequence of the layers and how to secure the waist belt, Keix's eyelids were as heavy as lead.

Even though she wanted to talk to Vin, there were two things preventing her from doing so. The first was that she didn't know if Jūn could hear them from the adjacent room, and the other was that she didn't know what to say.

Vin didn't seem keen on chit-chatting either. She'd lain down on a raised rectangular surface in the room, which Keix assumed was the bed. Vin was staring at the ceiling blankly while she fiddled with her hair, trying to tease the tresses dry.

After blowing out the candles in the room, Keix made herself comfortable next to Vin. The thought of revisiting the nightmare filled her with dread. But the sturdy bed felt like heaven after weeks of falling asleep leaning against tree trunks. Soon, the tension left her body and she surrendered to the exhaustion, letting it lull her into the deepest slumber she had had since she left Atros.

* * *

When Keix awoke from a dreamless sleep, it was already afternoon. Vin, who looked to be in a better mood, was seated cross-legged on the bed, munching on some biscuits.

She pushed a plate of them over to Keix, as well as a cup of milk. 'Your Kulcan sent these up this morning,' she teased.

'He's not mine,' reiterated Keix. She stuffed a biscuit into her mouth and threw her friend an exasperated look.

Vin clapped smugly and said, 'What I said. I told him you already have Zej back in Atros.'

Keix choked and started coughing violently.

Patting Keix's back, Vin continued, 'And he acted as if he hadn't heard me and asked me to not wake you up because you needed the rest.'

'You what?' gasped Keix when her coughing abated. At the mention of Zej, Keix's memory of the kiss that she'd tried to avoid thinking about came rushing back. It was her fault that she hadn't considered thoughtfully enough the implications of leaving Atros after taking that first step with Zej.

Was he worried when he found out that she had left the lake house? Would he come after her? But how could he, when he didn't know where she'd gone?

'Told him you have a boyfriend,' repeated Vin. 'I saw Zej coming out from your room the night you left Atros . . . You mean you didn't tell him you were leaving?'

Keix resisted the urge to slap her forehead. Who else *hadn't* seen Zej leaving her room that night?

'It's . . . complicated,' she stuttered.

Understanding dawned on Vin and she awkwardly added, 'I guess it's hard to reconcile yourself to what he did, considering how long you've had a crush on him.'

Keix didn't know how to answer her friend.

Back in ATI, Vin and Zej behaved like squabbling siblings. More accurately put, Vin was like the younger sister who loved making fun of her brother, and Zej was the older brother figure who let her get her way most of the time.

Vin must have complicated feelings about Zej's betrayal too, thought Keix. She sighed and hurried to wash up. Having one good night's sleep wasn't enough to restore sufficient functioning in her brain cells to think about Zej. She pushed him to the back of her mind and resolved to revisit these thoughts later, when she was less frazzled.

Besides, hearing that Jūn had waited an entire morning for her made her uneasy. She didn't want to feel more indebted to the Kulcan than she already did.

When they stepped out of the room, Jūn was outside, leaning against the parapet. He looked much younger, having shaved and changed into a midnight blue robe. In addition to the sword, he also had a cloth bundle strapped to his back now.

He straightened up as they walked out and smiled in greeting. 'Let's get going,' he said, leading them out of the inn and into the streets again.

In the daylight, Keix could finally see how eclectic Tilsor was. She had found the architecture here a little odd last night. Now, she felt disorientated by the strange-looking structures flanking the street.

In Atros, buildings were, more often than not, rectangular in shape. Be it low-lying houses or high-rises, they were always neatly arranged in rows to make the best use of the land. The houses here were not only haphazardly arranged, they were creatively constructed too. Keix's gaze fell on a small cylindrical structure which had a single, almost-opaque window on its side. She wondered if it served a special purpose, because its exteriors looked much cleaner than other buildings around it.

Along the street, there were also squarish blocks with pyramid-like roofs, oval-shaped structures, as well as buildings topped with spheres and bent cylindrical extensions, among others. Some of them looked abandoned, while others would sometimes have people going in and out of them.

The more Keix walked on, the more she realized one thing. Tilsor was sprawling.

The pathways forked at odd angles and without any discernible pattern. The texture of the narrow pavements varied from gravelly coloured pebbles to stone setts—a world of difference from Atros's neat, tarred roads, and right-angled crossroads and T-junctions.

'Haven't we walked past this place before?' asked Vin.

Keix squinted at the ochre building that Vin was pointing to. It looked vaguely familiar.

Jūn gave Vin an appraising glance. 'You're right. We've walked past this Section before.'

Vin frowned at him. 'So, you're lost?'

'No. I'm just finding my way.'

'Isn't that the same as being lost?' Vin looked incredulous.

'No,' insisted Jūn. 'How do I put this . . . ? Tilsor is made up of groups of countless Sections. Every dawn and nightfall, these Sections . . . rearrange themselves.'

He gestured to the two archways on his right. 'Go down the path on the right now and later tonight, after the sun sets, and you'll likely end up in different Sections.'

'Then how do you know where you're going?' asked Vin.

'You'll almost always be able to identify a pattern if you pay enough attention,' explained Jūn. 'The Sections seem to be grouped together, and they usually only rearrange themselves within their groups. So, the first step is to memorize the buildings on the sides of the roads. The differences between Sections may be subtle, but you'll be able to spot them if you're familiar with Tilsor.

'Take this Section, for example. Brown roof'—Jūn pointed to his left—'Green roof. Cylindrical building. Red, red, grey roofs and so on. And if you take a fork and it leads you back to somewhere you've been before, you'll want to take the other path when you come back to the same Section again.'

Keix's eyes almost popped out of their sockets when she asked, 'Did you memorize the entire map of Tilsor? And where each path leads to?'

Jūn gave a short, embarrassed laugh. 'Not as well as I would have liked. See that building with a flag hanging from its window? That's an inn. You'll find more of these along the roads near Squares.'

'Squares?' asked Vin.

Keix could hear the cogs turning in her friend's head. Vin relished puzzles—the more challenging, the better. Keix's head was hurting just trying to visualize what it would be like if Atros's Sectors moved around or rearranged themselves, like these areas in Tilsor.

Jūn nodded in reply to Vin. 'We call these smaller areas "Sections", and the bigger ones "Squares". The Squares are where people gather to trade and mingle, and there are sixty-four of them in Tilsor. You'll see the difference for yourself once we come to it. We should be at one of them soon.'

True enough, with each turn they took, Keix noticed that there were more and more people in the streets. Four turns later, the three of them emerged into a massive and bustling courtyard.

The overhead sun beat down on the open space, lending a cheery and welcoming vibe to the Square. Bordered by low-lying buildings on all four sides, the most prominent feature in this area was a rectangular tower emblazoned with the number fifty-eight.

Figures clad in all sorts of get-ups were milling around. Most of them wore simple, layered robes like Jūn. The Atrossian style of dressing didn't seem to be popular in Tilsor.

Perhaps it isn't suitable for the weather here, thought Keix, as she was reminded of how cold it was last night when she was still wearing her favourite jeans and T-shirt. The layers of her current get-up, coupled with the loose sleeves and pants, helped keep her warm and let her move around much more freely as she explored the Square.

Pushcarts that ran the gamut from wooden makeshift to welded metal ones lined up end to end, in no particular order, snaking around the open space and turning it into a maze. These hawked a host of weapons, odds and ends, and other items Keix had never seen in her life.

She turned up her sense of smell and was able to make out the aroma of freshly baked bread. Mingling in the air were also the fragrances of spices, flowers and wood, as well as the salty tang of sweat and a host of other foreign scents.

Even though Keix had wolfed down all the biscuits before they left the inn, she found herself gravitating towards the pushcarts that emitted clouds of delicious-smelling steam and smoke.

In her excitement, she pulled Vin along, totally forgetting that they were supposed to be following Jūn. Some of the vendors displayed bowls of thin and translucent noodles while others were handing out icy treats to the people stopping by their stalls.

'Here you go.'

Keix tore her eyes away from the pushcarts at Jūn's voice and found him holding out two skewers she'd been eyeing just moments ago.

'Thank you,' she said, her mouth watering at the tantalizing savoury, spicy smell of the marinated meat. She handed one of the skewers to Vin and took a bite from hers. The burst of flavours took her by surprise and she couldn't help but let out a low groan of approval.

'Anything else you want to try?' asked Jūn, giving her a wide smile.

Keix suddenly felt self-conscious. She coughed and shook her head.

'Let's get going then,' said Jūn.

'Do the Squares move like the Sections?' asked Vin, who was now committed to figuring out the puzzle that was Tilsor's layout.

Jūn looked impressed by Vin's question. 'The Squares are the best places to reorientate yourself. Their exits always lead to the same Sections. So, if your destination is, say, west of Tilsor, you should keep heading in that direction at every Square you come across, and you'll find your way out of the town eventually.'

Vin nodded as she digested the information. 'Why don't people just go around Tilsor then, if it's so confusing to navigate?'

'People who know Tilsor well enough see it as a shortcut. You just need days or a couple of weeks to get to your destination if you go through here. But if you make a detour around it, the journey could take months. Of course, people who don't know their way around might get lost in Tilsor for years.'

Keix glanced at the people around her and wondered how many of them were stuck here against their will. She couldn't find an unhappy face in the crowd.

'Which direction are we headed?' asked Vin.

'Yurkordu's to the north of Tilsor,' answered Jūn.

Seemingly satisfied with his answers, Vin nodded and waved for him to continue on his way.

As they weaved through the lines of pushcarts, Keix caught sight of a young man standing on a makeshift platform speaking animatedly. A couple of handfuls of people were standing around him, and his raised voice carried over to them.

'. . . Taavar tournament . . .'

Keix's ears perked up. A tournament? She remembered the competitions that she used to participate in at ATI, and the fun and thrill of winning them. She tugged at Jūn's sleeve and pointed to the man, indicating that she wanted to get closer to listen to him.

Jūn threw a disapproving glance at the man.

'I'll be just a minute . . .' She knew that it was already late afternoon and Jūn needed to get some supplies, so he probably didn't welcome the delay, but her curiosity was getting the better of her.

Her earnestness earned a curt nod from Jūn. Keix flashed him a brilliant smile and pulled Vin towards the man. Up close, she could tell that he was younger than her, but his confidence hit her like a wave.

'Come one, come all,' the speaker said, his high-pitched, charismatic voice ringing in the air. 'Come one, come all!'

The vendors in his vicinity stole curious yet fearful glances at him, which piqued Keix's interest even more. A few of his audiences had walked off with expressions ranging from intrigued to disbelieving, but even more people were gathering around him now.

Once the lad was certain that he had the attention of the new joiners, he swept his arms in a dramatic arc towards them. 'Are *you* brave enough to join the Taavar tournament? The annual event where your true mettle will be tested!'

The crowd waited for him to continue, but his silence made it clear that the ball was no longer in his court.

'What's the tournament about?' one of the audience members said.

The young man rubbed his hands together in glee, as if he'd expected the question. 'That's the catch. No one knows.'

A murmur of dissent rippled through the crowd.

The man raised his palms as if to reassure them. 'But we know that there are three rounds. The first to test your physical abilities, the second to challenge your mind, and the third . . . is a mystery, like the tournament itself.'

'You said this tournament happens every year,' came another shout from the increasingly clamorous audience. 'What about those who've joined before? Don't *they* have stories to tell?'

The crowd bobbed their heads in agreement.

'Those who've joined the tournament . . . and lived to tell the tale'—he made another theatrical pause—'have nothing to tell! Because once you're in, there will be no backing out. You'll be put under oath to never speak of it within earshot of people who've not participated in it before.'

'Sounds like a bad deal!'

The audience burst out laughing at the bold assessment.

'Then what's the reward?' came another voice.

'Reward. Reward. Reward. Yes, that's important, isn't it? Well, the reward is that you'll get to speak to a powerful person who may grant you a wish as they deem fit.'

Keix shook her head. She had heard enough. A tournament in which you could die at any time, or couldn't speak about even if you were to get out alive, in exchange for a wish that might not even be granted? No one in their right mind would willingly enrol in this Taavar thing.

Vin, echoing her thoughts, muttered, 'What a load of rubbish. Let's go.'

Keix gave Jūn a small, embarrassed smile for having wasted his time, but he didn't seem to think much of it.

Just as they weaved out of the crowd, an elderly man in a loose, white, full-length tunic approached them. He had wise eyes and hair so translucent, he seemed to be wearing a halo on his head. 'Joining the tournament, I see?' he asked with a kindly smile.

'No,' replied Jūn without a second thought.

The man was taken aback by the direct rejection. He looked perplexed for a moment. Then, he said, 'Ah, I'm early, I guess.'

Jūn turned to Keix and Vin and said, 'We'd best get going.' He gave the elderly man, who had made no move to leave, a polite nod. 'Good day.'

The man inclined his head in reply. 'I'll see you again at Square twenty-eight.'

Keix wasn't sure how to respond, so she bobbed her head towards the old man and Vin followed suit as Jūn led them away.

Seconds later, when Keix turned back to get another look at the elder, she found that he had disappeared into the throng of people. Subconsciously, she reached up to rub her nape, trying to smooth out the goosebumps caused by the odd conversation that they had just had.

8

Zej | Reluctant Allies

'Almost done,' said Zej, extracting a shard of broken glass from Dace's wound with a sterilized pair of tweezers.

'I said'—Dace sucked in a sharp breath through gritted teeth and gripped the edge of his seat in pain as Zej pulled out another sliver of glass—'I can do it myself.'

Zej ignored Dace's protests and swept the fluorescent light across the mass of jagged gashes on his chest, checking to see if there were any more glass pieces embedded in the skin.

Dace's makeshift bandage had staunched the bleeding, but it also pushed tiny splinters of broken glass further into his wound, causing it to fester.

'Disinfect the wound again,' said Zej, holding out a bottle of liquid. He felt thankful that they had been able to grab some basic first-aid supplies from an unmanned guardhouse which they came across after they emerged from underground.

Taking the disinfectant from Zej, Dace picked up a ball of gauze and cleaned the area around the lacerations on his chest.

Zej had noticed Dace's face getting paler by the hour and knew that his wound was inflamed after wading through the underground sewage pipes to get out of Atros.

'Hold out your arms. I'll dress the wound for you,' said Zej, unrolling a length of dressing.

Dace looked down disdainfully at the bandage. 'How about one of those quick-healing rubber plasters?'

At Zej's stare, Dace snatched over the roll and said, 'I can do it myself.' His movements were still sluggish, but Zej let him have his way.

Without another word, Zej began packing up.

They were about a day's walk from Sector M and had stopped for the night at an abandoned hut. Seyfer was out 'making sure there was no one around' and Pod and Maii had tagged along to keep an eye on him.

No one bothered to hide their suspicions about Seyfer, and the Atros trooper didn't seem concerned at all. Zej hadn't expected him to be.

Since the very first time they met, when Seyfer approached him to ask if he knew anything about Oka, the soldier had exuded an air of efficiency and decisiveness. The hybrid version of Seyfer had been the same, just more intense and deadly.

So, when Seyfer said that they would take about two weeks to trek to Tilsor, everyone had taken him at his word. No one trusted him, yet somehow, everyone believed that he needed two things: to get to Tilsor quickly and their help.

Two weeks, thought Zej. Fourteen days and he might see Keix again . . . He kept replaying their kiss in his head. It was the first and only time he remembered giving in to his heart.

You had no right to do that after the way you offered her up as sacrifice. The reproachful voice in his head made him uncertain if he should be excited at the prospect of seeing Keix again or dreading the meeting. All he knew was that the lead-up to today's journey seemed inevitable. For the past few weeks, he had been searching for Keix.

His thoughts had flown into a frenzy the moment he discovered that she was missing. For the first time since his father died, doing the right thing, saving lives and putting Atros first to honour his memory no longer seemed as important.

The portal had been closed. There were no more ghosts in this world. His ambition to become the best researcher in Atros, to find or create something to contain the paranormal creatures, had become meaningless.

But now that his search had led him to learn that Atros was facing another older and possibly more formidable enemy, he found himself wondering whether these crossroads he was at were but two different routes that led to the same destination.

'Why did you agree to Seyfer's request?' asked Dace softly. The question came out of the blue, but it hit the true heart of the matter.

Why . . . Zej froze. He averted his eyes. 'Does it matter?' he asked, his voice tight. Until now, no one had questioned his decision to take up Seyfer's offer. Pod knew how stubborn he was, and Maii was preoccupied with her own demons.

'Maii knows the way to Tilsor. We didn't—don't—have to help Seyfer,' said Dace, with a hint of hesitation and gratitude.

Zej took a deep breath and released it slowly. He couldn't even sort out his motives himself. There was too much at stake, too much to consider. 'I owe you, Dace. I owe Lana,' he finally admitted.

It was only a fraction of the answer, but Zej felt like a weight had been lifted off his shoulders. He didn't think that he needed to apologize for firing that black-hole bullet to stop a swarm of ghosts when Lana was in the suction range. It was the right thing to do, but he'd wanted to express his regret for having to do so for the longest time. There was never a good opportunity and if Dace felt better hating him, there was no reason or need to try to change Dace's opinion of the matter.

Dace gave him an odd look. 'I . . .' he struggled before saying, 'Keix told me . . . that you knew about the black-hole bullet, and that you knew that Lana wouldn't die but get transported to somewhere else.'

Zej nodded. 'But I had no idea that she would . . .' Zej trailed off. He'd wanted to say he had no idea that Lana would be tortured and turned into a hybrid, but the words were just stuck in his throat.

'There's no point in saying all this now,' said Dace at Zej's hesitation. He sounded angry but resigned. 'We can't change the past.'

Dace is right. I have no excuse. I have to take responsibility for putting Lana into Atros's hands in the first place, thought Zej.

'We'll get Lana back safely. And your father too,' said Zej with steely resolve. He didn't know whether he was reassuring Dace or himself, but he felt a sudden pang of jealousy.

Be it with Lana or his father, Dace was in a far superior position compared to Zej to mend the relationships; Dace's father was still alive; and at the very least, with Lana, Dace had put up a fight to get her released before the portal-closing ritual officially started. Dace had proven that he cared for Lana, and that her life mattered more to him that saving the world. It was the complete opposite of what Zej had shown Keix.

Dace gave a hollow laugh. 'It hits differently, doesn't it? When the person whose life is on the line is someone so close to your heart.' He sighed and pulled his T-shirt back on before making for the door. The creak of the hinges snapped the temporary, albeit strained, truce between them like a dry twig.

And Zej agreed wholeheartedly with the words that Dace uttered before he stepped out of the hut.

Keix . . . You don't deserve her.

* * *

The next week and a half's journey to Tilsor was uneventful.

After leaving the vicinity of Atros, they caught sight of some Odats crawling around the Sector boundaries. Seyfer suggested that they make their way to their destination through the forest, and travel at night to keep a low profile.

'Running into anyone, be it Odats'—a look of disgust came over Seyfer—'Atros troopers or enemy forces will only slow us down. We've already lost at least a day because we had to stop to make sure he didn't die of sepsis,' Seyfer said, throwing a scathing glare at Dace.

Of course, Dace, who would never concede, made a rude gesture in response.

In the night, however, the trees transformed into shadowy figures that watched their every move beneath the illumination of the half-moon and the stars. With the exception of Seyfer, all of them found the atmosphere unsettling.

So, even though it sounded illogical that the Atros trooper would lure them all the way out here just for an ambush, Zej had insisted that they travel in the day and find a clearing, or if possible, an abandoned hut, to spend the night. As a compromise, no one complained about the breakneck pace Seyfer set.

The overcast sky had darkened exceptionally early this particular evening and Zej was glad to see the outline of a small, single-storeyed building.

This was the third such structure they had come across so far. Like the previous two, its exterior looked simple—wooden slats made up the squarish walls and triangular roof. But this one was clearly bigger and looked to be uninhabited.

Before this trip, Zej had only encountered these houses twice. More than a year ago, he had visited one of them on behalf of Oka to convey the bad news that the owner's sister had been captured and tortured to death by Atros.

That was when he belatedly found out that some Atrossians, who had moved out of the city of their own accord, built simple huts nearby in order to stay close to their loved ones who were still living in the Sectors.

Then, Oka had acquired a vacant one for him to keep Keix hidden while she recuperated after he broke her out of PEER. It was while they were there that he confessed to Keix about his involvement with the rebel group and how he had unknowingly been assigned to oversee one of her tortures during her captivity at Atros. He kept his distance after that to let her have some headspace, and everything went according to plan, until one day, when hybrid-Seyfer descended upon that safehouse and caused them to be on the run . . .

'Let's take shelter here for the night,' Zej called to the rest.

There was a foul smell that got stronger as he neared the hut and the slightly ajar door seemed to confirm his suspicions that this dwelling had been unoccupied for a while now.

But the moment Zej stepped into the house, the phantom cold draught that had been circulating around his nape dropped by a couple of degrees. He exchanged wary looks with Dace and Seyfer, who were right on his heels.

The room they entered was squarish and had obvious signs of a struggle. Two chairs were turned over on their sides, and the table that Zej assumed was part of the set was angled in an awkward position instead of being flush along the wall.

There was a threadbare couch against the opposite wall. The coffee table in front of it had been smashed into pieces.

In the corner, beside the main entrance, sat a stove with some pots and pans scattered around it.

'That stench . . .' whispered Pod as he stepped into the house with Maii.

Zej raised a hand to silence him, then stalked to the only other doorway in the room and poked his head through it.

It led to a bedroom, where there was a simple bed—a thin mattress placed atop a rectangular board with four legs. The bedsheets were crumpled and look slept in.

Zej took shallow breaths. The rotting smell was unbearable now. He pushed open the door to the en-suite bathroom and felt his stomach turn.

Sprawled in the dingy space was a man with the contents of his head splattered over every surface of the room in dark blotches. From the state of the body, Zej deduced that he had been dead for at least a couple of weeks now.

Dace, who had followed Zej into the bathroom, swore at the sight. And Pod, who had poked his head in, trailed off, 'What the . . .'

Seyfer's dark eyes were like bottomless pits. 'We should—' he began but was interrupted by snatches of conversation carried into the room through the open window.

A hush fell over the room.

'. . . foolish way to go,' came a high-pitched voice.

'Well, it's the only way of escaping our clutches, I guess,' joked another, rougher voice, earning a bout of laughter from their companions.

Whether they were Atros troopers or soldiers belonging to another organization, Zej couldn't tell. But it was clear that they weren't afraid of drawing attention to themselves.

Zej guessed that there were at least four in the group. It would be unwise to take them head on without knowing their abilities, even if his group outnumbered the one outside by five to four.

He exchanged glances with his teammates and shook his head to indicate that they should lie low and wait for the people outside to pass by. All of them nodded in silent assent.

But the wait that they were anticipating never came.

Without warning, the front door burst open. A figure clad from head to toe in black charged through it.

Maii, who was standing closest to the door, leapt forward and punched the intruder's shoulder. Instead of faltering, the svelte figure whipped around. They counterattacked by grabbing Maii by the shoulder and slammed her to the floor.

Pod was on Maii's attacker in an instant, aiming a kick at their torso. But the figure didn't budge an inch. With a snap of their fingers, a glowing, blue ball appeared in the palm of the intruder like a burning lighter.

Zej had never seen the like of it before. The sparking ball of electricity seemed to be a dangerous weapon that had been conjured out of thin air by the black-clad assailant!

'Look out!' shouted Zej and Dace in unison as the attacker extended the electric ball towards Maii.

Right before the punch landed, there was a loud thunk. Pod had whacked the figure on the head with one of the pans that he picked up from the floor.

'Are you all right, Maii?' he asked, helping her up.

The intruder staggered backwards, still holding the glowing, blue ball.

'Turn it back on them!' Seyfer's instructions rang through the dingy hut.

Three more figures filed into the room, holding identical crackling balls of blue.

At Seyfer's shout, Maii and Pod responded with impeccable coordination. They rushed forward to pin the first attacker to the floor, twisting their arm and directing the ball of blue electricity into its owner's chest.

But upon contact with the intruder's suit, the electricity dispersed like cracks on a wall, blue lines fizzling outwards, then seemingly getting reabsorbed into the outfit.

Zej watched as Seyfer adeptly dodged and grabbed hold of one of the other intruder's arms and twisted it up. He aimed the weapon at the exposed skin above the collar of the suit and grunted, 'On the skin!'

At the contact, the attacker convulsed and crumpled to the floor.

Following Seyfer's cue, Pod and Maii pushed the palm towards the exposed skin of the attacker's neck. The blue ball seemed to be shrinking, as if the owner was retracting it. But thanks to Pod and Maii's quick reflexes, the electric ball made contact with the attacker's skin before it disappeared altogether.

Two down, two to go.

The two other black-clad figures made snarling noises and turned off their electric balls after seeing the fate of their fallen comrades. Clicking sounds followed, and Zej was shocked to see blades extending out of their palms to replace the glowing balls.

Zej re-evaluated his opponents. The long weapons that the intruders were wielding were not made for fighting in a confined space; the odds might have just tilted in Zej and his teammates' favour.

However, the speed at which the intruders came at them left them no time to gloat.

Seyfer ran to engage one of the attackers.

Zej let his years of training as an Atros trooper kick in. He grabbed a pan on the floor and held it like a baton-cum-shield. As the assailant advanced on him, he darted and swung his makeshift weapon towards his opponent's knee.

A crack resounded at the contact, but the figure barely stumbled.

Dodge. Swing. Duck.

Zej continued to parry with his opponent as clanging sounds and grunts filled the air.

Dace, Pod and Maii were hanging back, looking for an opening. With two bodies now sprawled on the already-small floor space, an ill-timed stumble might spell defeat for them.

A crunch and ripping sound pierced the air as a glint of metal came at Zej.

'Duck!' warned Pod.

Zej whipped his head to his left and narrowly avoided having his cheek carved off. At that same second, he saw a sharp tip push its way out of the figure's head like a newly sprouted horn. The attacker's body slackened and fell to the ground.

Zej took a second to register the sight in front of him. The blade that had taken down his opponent was protruding from both the forehead and the back of the skull. On the latter end was an arm that Seyfer had ripped out of the second-to-last attacker he faced.

Everyone gaped at the elite Atros trooper with a renewed sense of cautiousness and reluctant respect.

When Zej was enrolled in ATI, he took his combat lessons seriously. But never had he seen anyone fight in such a deadly and ruthless way.

'Are they . . . ExA?' asked Pod.

Seyfer nodded. He bent down and started patting the bodies all over, searching for something.

'How did they know that we were in here?' Pod couldn't keep the worry out of his voice.

'Goggles that register heat signatures. Heightened sense of hearing. Pure luck. Any or a combination of those. Or none.'

'Have you fought them before?' Pod gawked at Seyfer.

'I have. But . . .' Seyfer considered for a second. 'But that was some time ago. Seems like they've made some breakthroughs in their weaponry,' he added, glancing to the blade.

'What are you searching for?' asked Maii.

'Communication devices, trackers, just about anything that could give us a clue as to where they're going or where they've come from.'

'If they are who you think they are, could all of those gadgets be embedded *in* their bodies and not carried *on* them?' wondered Dace.

'Fair point.' Seyfer straightened up. 'In that case, I suggest we continue to make haste. If we get to Tilsor, it'll be harder for them to track us down. We can be there in two days if we go through the forest at night. I know the way.'

Dace, Pod and Maii looked to Zej, who weighed their options.

Food wasn't an issue—they had enough to last them for at least another five days. But if they were to run into another group of these attackers, they might not get so lucky. They couldn't rely on Seyfer to defend them all the time.

The thought of finding Keix earlier and having a proper place to rest and wash up also crossed Zej's mind, so he finally agreed to go with Seyfer's proposal.

If the Atros trooper wanted to cause them harm, he had had plenty of time and opportunities to do so already, reasoned Zej.

With Seyfer in the lead, the five of them weaved through the trees in silence, each preoccupied with what had just happened. The events of the day seemed to have had a sobering effect on everyone, and the swaying shadows that had bothered them before were relegated to the backs of their minds.

Zej thought about what Seyfer had said about Atros trying to protect its citizens. He thought about the lengths the organization had gone to, to try to build that ghost army to fend off both ghosts and ExA. And he thought that maybe—just maybe—if they were able to truly eliminate ExA like how they had gotten rid of the ghost by closing the portal, there might be a chance that Atros would be able to get back on the right track once again.

Finally, near dawn, when the fatigue set in, they stopped at a clearing and sat down to take a breather.

Zej, who had been racking his brain about what he should say to Keix first, was surprised when Maii broke the silence.

What was even more shocking was that she addressed Seyfer when she spoke. 'What did you mean—back in Atros—when you said that we can't simply undo mistakes like this?' asked Maii. She sounded like she had been holding in the question for the longest time.

Even though Maii didn't state what 'mistakes' she was referring to, Seyfer knew what she was talking about immediately.

An unreadable expression crossed his face. 'Could you have fixed the broken glass?' countered Seyfer.

Zej couldn't quite follow the conversation. He could tell that Pod was almost as baffled as he was. They were talking about . . . a broken glass?

Then Zej recalled what Seyfer had said when he'd first approached them after the explosion at *A*; how he'd pointed to the crystalware that Pod had reassembled and insinuated that perhaps the Ifarls, contrary to what everybody believed, hadn't been able to fully close the gateway between the living and the dead. Zej felt a chill creep down his back.

'Are you saying that there are cracks in the portal and that ghosts could enter our world again?' interrupted Pod. 'But it can't be. After that night, none of us have encountered any paranormal activity at all.'

Maii opened her mouth, but no words emerged, so she shut it again. She looked as troubled as Zej had ever seen her. Pod kept casting worried glances at her.

'You guys should know that some of us volunteered to be transformed into hybrids,' said Seyfer after a long pause. 'And after we were turned back . . . things have been . . . different. There are those who have nightmares about their transformation, and there are those who have sworn that they've encountered ghosts again.

'That's why I need to go to Tilsor to find someone—someone who can help us make sure that the portal is indeed closed and stays that way. The Kulcans may be a match for ExA, but if the ghosts come back into the picture, we'll be fighting a battle we can't be certain we'd win.'

'Who's the person you're looking for?' Maii repeated the question that Zej had asked previously.

'A rogue Ifarl who's supposedly even more powerful than Zenchi. Before she lost her powers, of course,' elaborated Seyfer.

Zej wasn't sure if Seyfer was telling the truth. The trooper had kept mum about many things, but he hadn't outright lied about anything before.

'What are the chances that you'll turn back into a hybrid if the portal opens as much as a crack?' asked Dace. He had been silent throughout the conversation, staring at the ground with his head bowed.

Seyfer shrugged. 'It's anyone's guess.'

Zej saw trepidation and weariness flash in the trooper's usually indecipherable eyes, and he recalled the dossier that he had collated. There was too much redacted information on Seyfer in the hardcopy file that he found to let him get a proper read on this guy.

No one spoke for the rest of the way as they considered the gravity of the revelations.

When they finally arrived at Tilsor, these disclosures were chucked to the back of their mind. Because one moment, there was nothing on the horizon, and the next, the cityscape had appeared all at once. A smattering of buildings, assorted in colour, shape and size, spanned the entire range of their vision.

Zej let out a low whistle as he feasted his eyes on the view. Around him, the rest of his group—except Seyfer—did the same.

But as they approached the town, and eventually stepped into it, the wondrous scene that had greeted them faded into obscurity in his head. All he could see was the cobbled pathway and the buildings flanking it. With every step and turn they took, they entered both deeper into the city as well as into a situation of unpredictability.

9

Keix | Marked

It was evening by the time Jūn stopped in front of a trapezoidal structure. Even though Keix had seen some eccentric-looking buildings in Tilsor, the razor-sharp edges of this one still made her do a double take.

From certain angles, this three-storey-tall construction looked paper thin. Its exterior was made of a single block of sand-coloured stone, cut and smoothed to perfection. There were no signs, lamps, flags or any other distinguishing features so Keix couldn't tell what the building housed.

'We're here,' said Jūn. He hadn't spoken much since they left the Square, although he answered Vin's questions about Tilsor without holding back.

Keix could tell from his brisker-than-usual pace that he was in a hurry, so she didn't interrupt his focus with more questions. Besides, she was preoccupied with the mysterious elderly man in white they had met earlier today.

Jūn pushed open a rectangular door and waved Keix and Vin in. Except for the thin border which indicated that it had been cut from the same stone, the door blended seamlessly into its frame.

Stepping through the doorway, Keix's eyes widened. The space that she had just entered reminded her of the weapons room back in ATI, where her favourite combat training class was held. But instead of rows of guns and batons, there was a variety of bladed and blunt weapons hanging on the walls, reaching all the way up to the ceiling.

Even from this distance, Keix could tell that each of them was as elegantly made as the other, and polished to a shine to showcase their lethality.

The windowless space lit by dozens of candles felt neither hot nor stuffy. In fact, there was a comfortable, gentle breeze circulating around.

'You're late,' a masculine voice echoed through the spacious room. It belonged to a bald man who looked to be in his mid-forties. His deep-set eyes, squarish nose and non-existent lips gave him a forbidding aura and Keix instinctively drew closer to Jūn as he strode towards the counter behind which the man stood.

'My apologies. We got lost,' said Jūn.

Keix looked at Vin. *We did?*

Vin returned an annoyed look.

The man quirked an eyebrow at Jūn as if he didn't believe him, but he didn't say more.

'I sent word for a second weapon two days ago,' said Jūn.

Second weapon? Two days ago? Was it when he'd left her and Vin at the hut? Keix wondered.

The man grunted in acknowledgement. He reached below the counter, retrieved two long and narrow cloth-wrapped packages and placed them on the counter.

'That'd be eighteen gold marks,' said the man. 'And an additional six for the late notice on the second piece.'

If Jūn was buying weapons, he could have easily gotten one of the ready-made ones on display. Why did he have to send word beforehand—unless these two packages had to be custom-made?

Keix watched as Jūn nodded and fished out a ring with rectangular pieces of metal—bronze, silver and gold—threaded through and dangling from it. He counted twenty gold slats and twenty silver ones and deposited them into the seller's palm. Then he picked up the packages and passed the longer package to Keix and the shorter, bulkier one to Vin.

Wait . . . did he want them to carry the packages for him, or were these gifts? But what for?

Vin looked as surprised as Keix. Before they could utter a sound, the man had called out irritably. 'All right. Get out. I'm closing up,' he said.

Chased out of the weapon shop, Keix could no longer contain herself. 'What are these?' she asked Jūn.

'A gift for you,' he replied. Then turning to Vin, he added, 'You too.'

Astonished, Keix unwrapped her parcel at the foot of the building. She'd been wanting to get a sword of her own since she first saw Jūn's. Even though she had no idea how to use one, she swore she would put her heart into mastering it just because it looked impressive.

As soon as the covering came away, Keix's breath was stolen by the exquisiteness of the weapon. It *was* a sword, and it came with a matte-black scabbard etched with a pattern of delicate lines, making it not only glorious to look at, but also easy to grip. The hilt was also black and textured, although its pattern of tiny dots caused by criss-crosses was less fancy and more practical.

When Keix drew the weapon out of its sheath, the zing of metal brushing against metal rang through the air.

'It's beautiful,' whispered Keix, running her fingers along the shiny, double-edged blade. The sword was slender compared to Jūn's enormous broadsword. The width of the blade was about three-quarters the width of her palm, and its length, about half her height, tapering to a sharp, triangular point.

When she could finally bear to tear her eyes away from the shiny present, she saw Jūn watching her with an indulgent smile and she felt that same peculiar buzz from before.

Strictly speaking, she had only known Jūn for two days. She couldn't fight off the attackers and she couldn't make her way to her father without his help, so she shouldn't reject outright his well-intended gestures.

Nonetheless, disregarding how much she liked the sword, accepting it felt like she would be crossing some invisible line. Reluctantly, she put it back into its sheath, held the weapon out to Jūn and said, 'I can't—'

As if anticipating her rejection, Jūn waved in an off-handed manner and countered, 'Treat it as a gift from your father. I'm here at his behest, after all.'

Keix blinked. Jūn had said that he would take her to her father, but he had never said that he was here on his orders. Her father was looking for her?

Before she could probe further, Jūn had taken the sword from her and gently looped the strap over her head, securing the sword to her back. Adjusting the band, he added, 'I'll teach you how to use it once you're fully recovered.'

The sudden intimacy stunned Keix into silence and she grew conscious of his proximity. Jūn's warm, woody scent was almost close enough to envelop her. She found herself drawn into a pair of intense eyes, turned molten gold by the rays of the setting sun. When Vin cleared her throat, Keix almost jumped out of her skin.

'If Keix's sword is from her dad,' said Vin, failing miserably at trying to keep the self-consciousness out of her voice, 'then who's paying for these?' She had also unwrapped her package and was now holding a pair of curved, single-edge blades. They were shorter than Keix's sword—about the length of Vin's forearm—and not as intricately designed, but they were broader, sturdier and looked just as lethal.

'Me,' said Jūn, half teasingly. After the intense discussion of Tilsor they had had earlier today, the two of them seemed to have reached some kind of mutual understanding.

'Thanks, but no thanks,' said Vin, tossing the knives hilt-end towards Jūn.

He caught them easily and laughed. 'Just take it as a precaution. In case we get attacked again, you don't have to rely on me for protection.'

He held out the weapons to Vin, confident that his calculated provocation would have the effect he intended.

Sure enough, Vin snatched them back from him and buckled them on either side of her waist. 'I'll take them as a loan. For now,' she pretended to grumble.

The atmosphere felt considerably more amicable as they continued on their way.

Jūn suggested that they put up at the next inn they came across, but Vin wanted to get to another Square before the sun set. She reasoned that they would make better progress this way. From Keix's understanding of her best friend, she knew that the main goal of Vin's counterproposal was to check out what the Squares were like after dark. Keix was also curious, so she voted for Vin's idea and Jūn acquiesced.

Keix itched to take out her new sword to get a feel of it, but even with night falling and the number of people on the streets dwindling, it didn't seem like a good idea to be brandishing a weapon around. So, instead, she just concentrated on the cool, sturdy feel of it behind her back.

Thanks to Jūn's good sense of direction, they emerged into another Square before the sun set completely. This looked smaller compared to Square Fifty-eight, but had a similar tower which was numbered sixty. It was also lined with pushcarts, although many of the vendors were in the midst of packing up their wares.

Jūn bought a ton of food from those who were looking to sell off the remainder of the dishes that they had prepared for the day.

Keix watched in fascination as many of the vendors—young to elderly, men and women—bantered with him good-naturedly. Then, she moved to check out a pushcart selling bowls of colourful candies. Before she reached the makeshift stall, a shadow flew towards her.

In reflex, she turned to the threat and drew her sword. Because she wasn't familiar with the weapon, she couldn't unsheathe it properly. And when she tugged harder, she knocked the sword into the pushcart, sending candies exploding into the air like confetti.

The shadow burst through the colourful cloud.

Keix's blood froze as she got a proper look at the figure. She could have bet her life that this assailant belonged to the same group who had ambushed her outside of Atros less than a couple of days ago. The attacker had thrown on a long cape in order to blend in at Tilsor, but the cloak, now flapping behind as the figure ran towards her, exposed the very same style of uniform that she had seen then.

Keix tested the weight of the sword in her hands. She had fenced with wooden rods and batons when she trained in ATI, but wielding a bladed weapon was different.

She dropped her right shoulder as the figure neared and swung her weapon upwards to parry the pair of long, triangular blades aiming straight for her neck.

From this distance, Keix could see that the assailant wasn't *holding* the daggers—instead, the weapons were protruding out of their palms!

Because of her shock and lack of experience with the sword, she misjudged the angle and her blade only managed to lightly slap her attacker's weapon. Fortunately, her countermove was sufficient to steer her opponent's weapons off their intended course.

Keix felt the whisper of cool air on her neck as one of the daggers narrowly missed its mark by a hair's breadth. The figure barrelled into Keix, knocking the air out of her. Just as suddenly as they made contact, Jūn stepped up beside her, grabbed hold of the assailant and threw them into the pushcart.

Chaos erupted at the resounding crash. People in the Square scattered. The vendors who had finished packing up quickly hauled their stalls away from the commotion. Some others just fled the scene, leaving their possessions behind as the attacker, who had collided into the pushcart, stood up again.

Vin came up to them, her weapons drawn. But like Keix, her unfamiliarity with the blades was apparent. 'What do we do now? Fight?'

Keix's group backed away as figures in black approached them. There were at least fifteen of the caped adversaries clustered in groups of three. All of them had weapons drawn. Some had daggers and swords attached to their palms, like the one who just attacked Keix, while others held guns. One of them even held a whip in their hand.

'They have black-hole rounds,' whispered Keix. If these soldiers were to fire the bullets here, half of the Square would be directly transported back to Atros. But why were they hesitating?

'Those guns don't work here,' said Jūn, as if he could read Keix's thoughts. 'I'll explain later. We have to get out of here first. It's turned into a three-way fight. It'll get too messy.'

He jerked his head towards a corner of the Square.

Keix could make out a group of eight there. It was unlikely that this band belonged with the group of assailants; they were not dressed in a uniform manner, but they were armed too—with blades, axes, maces, even bows. They eyed Keix's group, as well as the black-caped figures, with suspicion and a wild hunger that caused an even more intense iciness to creep into her bloodstream.

These people were clearly outlaws and on no one's side but their own. They were standing apart from the main fight now, but Keix knew that they were more than ready to jump in to take advantage of whatever situation presented itself.

Jūn was right. This was going to be a messy fight the moment it started in earnest. Even though he had taken down the attackers easily when he had come to Keix's rescue outside of Atros, there was something different about the opponents that they were facing now. They were less agile and infinitely more aggressive in their manoeuvres.

The Square was also almost completely empty by now. Only a handful of bystanders remained, hanging around the fringes, like scavengers waiting for the worst to be over before swooping in to see what they could salvage.

'This way,' said Jūn, pointing Keix and Vin to one of the exits on their left. He rushed forward to engage the two nearest figures to get them out of the way. As before, Jūn's attacks were clean and efficient. But their opponents were closing in.

Keix and Vin ran in the direction that Jūn had indicated, and Keix thought she heard a crack in the air followed by a rush of air at the top of her head.

'Keep going,' Jūn called out. He was fighting against six figures and trying to keep up with Keix and Vin.

The attackers moved almost as quickly as Jūn. It was clear that their advantage lay in their numbers and coordinated attack strategy. Whenever one of them drew back, another one would take their comrade's place, forcing Jūn to almost always take a defensive stance.

Jūn was hot on Keix and Vin's heels as they ran out of the Square. They burst into an alleyway and a few curious onlookers turned in their direction.

'Take the right fork,' shouted Jūn from behind Keix. He should be leading the way, but he was still fending off the caped attackers who had followed them into the Section.

Left. Centre. Right.

Keix and Vin followed Jūn's directions, praying that they'd be able to shake off their pursuers. Unfortunately, three turns later, they ended up back in Square Sixty. The Sections had shifted because the sun had set.

Keix wanted to cry out in despair. They had not only lost any progress they made, they had also emerged back into the Square at the same corner where the outlaws were hanging out.

Time came to a standstill as Keix locked eyes with a balding, burly man dressed in a dirty, blue robe. Then, all of a sudden, he came at her, swinging a mace.

Keix didn't know if she should count herself lucky. On the one hand, the group of outlaws had shrunk in number from eight to two— one currently swinging his mace at her, and the other, a woman, rushing towards her with her sword raised. On the other, there was no other route that they could take except head back into the Section where the caped attackers were.

This was the three-way fight that they'd hoped to avoid.

'Go! I'll keep them off! Take the left fork!' directed Jūn as soon as they turned back into the Section.

The black-clad figures were also filing in from the right fork in the pathway. Keix and Vin pumped their legs as quickly as they could and headed towards the archway on the left. Jūn had stopped giving directions. It didn't matter where they were heading because their priority was to shake off the assailants tailing them, so Keix let Vin decide on their course.

Racing through yet another archway, Keix glanced over her shoulder. The two groups chasing them had become one, almost as if two predators had made a pact to take down their prey together. But they seemed to be losing steam too, their breaths laboured as they continued their pursuit.

Jūn knocked down one of the caped figures, causing those behind to slow down to avoid tripping over their fallen comrade.

If Keix, Vin and Jūn could maintain this pace and tire out their pursuers, the three of them might be able to elude the attackers soon. Just as the thought crossed her mind, Vin tripped and fell.

One of the caped figures saw the opening and leapt on to a teammate's shoulders, catapulting towards Vin. The split second before their sword slashed through the air, Jūn intercepted it and turned to hoist Vin to her feet.

Thanks to his lightning reflexes, the attacker's blade sliced through the air, right where Vin had fallen just moments ago. Before the assailant could even land, Jūn unleashed a counterattack that sent the figure flying backwards. The caped attackers, as well as the burly outlaw, fell.

The only one who remained standing was the sword-wielding female bandit. She had hung back before, but now, she moved nimbly past the mountain of bodies.

Jūn had already turned on his heel. He bellowed at Keix and Vin to continue running. 'To the right!' he called.

They turned the sharp corner and Jūn was right there beside them. But Keix noticed that his scabbard was no longer strapped to his back. Instead, he was using it to herd them through a narrow door that he had thrown open.

The door belonged to a building identical to one of the cylindrical-shaped structures that she had seen this morning. The entrance was tight and the instant the three of them entered the tube-like structure, Jūn slammed the door shut.

Once inside, Keix felt a gust of cold wind whirling around her. The interior was bare and white, and sounded surprisingly quiet. All she could hear was the thundering of her blood in her ears.

'What's this place?' Keix whispered to Jūn.

His eyes looked unfocused and his lips were turning blue. Before she could say another word, he'd pitched forward. Her first reaction was to reach out her arms to break his fall and steady him. But as she wrapped her arms around his torso, she felt something warm and thick trickle down his back.

Vin's gasp confirmed her worst suspicions. 'There's a huge gash on his back, Keix.'

'I'm fine,' rasped Jūn.

He did not sound fine, but Keix didn't want him to expend his energy on pointless arguments. 'Where are we? Will the attackers come in after us?'

The door of the building slid open, and Keix tensed for another assault even as Jūn moved out through the exit. When he turned around, Keix inhaled sharply. Vin wasn't exaggerating when she described the laceration as huge. It ran from Jūn's right shoulder diagonally down to his waist, marking the spot where his scabbard should have been. Keix couldn't tell how deep the wound was, but Jūn's robe was plastered to his back, no thanks to the blood pouring out of the long cut.

Keix hurried to his side, worried that he might stumble again.

'They won't. Not if we move fast. These devices are scattered all around Tilsor. When you step into one, it takes you to another part of the city randomly. Even if those guys were to step into it after us, they might not be transported to the same place that we are at now.'

'It's a teleportation device?' asked Vin in awe.

'In Atrossian terms, yes,' said Jūn, taking stock of the buildings around them.

After the ruckus at the Square, this Section seemed exceptionally quiet. Under the darkening sky, the only sound Keix could hear was the three of them huffing after their encounter.

'I think I know where we are,' said Jūn. 'Come, there's a place in this area where we can lie low first.'

10

Keix | Confusion

Warning bells were going off in Keix's head. The streets had been secluded since they left the teleportation pod, and she was pretty sure that they'd shaken off their pursuers.

Her worry now was Jūn. She could tell that he was struggling to stay conscious and tripping with every other step he took. Just five minutes ago, he'd been moving normally despite his injury.

Looping her arm around his as support, she glowered at him, as if daring him to reject her silent offer of help. What little colour he had in his cheeks had been completely drained from it. In spite of that, he mustered up a small smile and leaned on her. Because he was much taller, he had to hunch over and rest his head on top of hers to steady himself.

'We should be there soon,' he reassured them. Then, he added, 'There'll be people around and word will spread if anyone sees that I'm injured. Can one of you help me take out the robe from my bundle and put it over me?'

If Keix wasn't so distraught, she'd actually be impressed that Jūn managed to hang on to his bag throughout the fight. Because she was still supporting Jūn, Vin took the bundle from the Kulcan and made short work of the knots on it.

The robe that Jūn had mentioned was the one that he was wearing yesterday. Vin had to tiptoe to throw it over him even though he was doubled over.

'What are we looking for?' asked Vin tightly as she completed her task, wearing an expression of concern mixed with frustration and guilt.

'A safe place to hide for now,' said Jūn, his words starting to slur.

'What I meant was, what does the place look like?' clarified Vin.

'It's a private bathhouse. A seven-storeyed building. At least ten times bigger than the inn we stayed at last night. Red exterior, with a copper-coloured'—Jūn had to stop to catch his breath—'copper-coloured roof. There's a white signboard that says "Ma.erdene's". If my calculations are right, we should be there with two more turns. Or a maximum of . . .'

Jūn's sword dropped to the ground with a clank and Keix's heart plummeted.

'Jūn!' she called. His entire weight had suddenly collapsed on her; she would have lost her balance had Vin not reached out to help support Jūn.

'He's still breathing,' said Vin, panting and hoisting Jūn's other arm around her shoulders. She was shorter than Keix, so this seemed like the best position to hold him up.

Jūn's groan was almost inaudible as Keix did the same.

The two friends shared a look. They were on their own now.

'What do we do now?' asked Keix.

The only one in their group who could navigate Tilsor was down. Keix didn't even want to consider their chances of survival if the black-clad attackers or the bandits caught up with them.

'We keep going,' said Vin, her eyes sweeping across the buildings in this Section. 'Jūn said that we should be there in two turns. I think I can find our way there.'

Keix nodded at her friend. If there was anyone who could figure this out, it would be Vin. 'Let's go,' she said, nodding resolutely, picking up Jūn's sword from the ground without letting go of him.

'See that building over there?' Vin pointed to a tall cylindrical building with tiny windows. It was the one that was the most conspicuous in this Section. 'That's our first marker.'

Seventeen turns later, both of them panting from Jūn's added weight—and Keix, from Jūn's sword that was much heavier than it looked—they saw the building that Vin had designated as their first landmark yet again. This was the third time they had circled back to this Section.

Keix was on the verge of breaking down. She had a sinking feeling that if they didn't get help for Jūn soon, he would be dead by morning.

But Vin broke out in a smile and said, 'I've figured it out. We first took five right turns, then we ended back up here. Then we took a right turn, then left, then right, and we ended up in the same Section that we had been in when we took the right turns the first time round!'

Keix gaped at her.

'Never mind . . .' Vin winked at Keix and laughed. 'But Jūn was right. We're only two Sections away from where he wanted to bring us.'

'So . . . we take a left now?'

'Yes.'

'Then . . . ?'

'Left again.'

'Wish you'd gone left instead of right the first time,' mumbled Keix, drawing another laugh from Vin.

True enough, two left turns later, Keix spotted the building that Jūn had described. She sighed in relief.

'Do we go in through the front?' she asked, suddenly unsure of Tilsor's protocol about dragging unconscious people into a bathhouse.

A stout man walked out of the front entrance of the building, ushered by a middle-aged woman dressed in black. The woman's platinum blonde hair which was swept up into a topknot shone like a beacon, and Keix was reminded of the elderly man whom they had encountered in the Square.

As if she had sensed Keix's stare, the woman turned to face the trio. Her sharp eyes widened when she saw Jūn, and she hurried over, her loose blouse billowing.

'Come on in, come on in,' she called, with the enthusiasm of a proprietor clinching a new client.

Keix and Vin looked at each other. What do they do now?

'Here, this way,' urged the woman. When she saw that they weren't moving, her amiable expression switched to one of outrage.

She lowered her voice and said, 'One of you must be Keix. I have no idea who the other is, and I don't care. Because this unconscious young man whom you are dragging around is Jūn Gantulga. And every second that you waste, trying to decide if you can trust me, gets him an additional step closer to Death's door.'

Keix and Vin were taken aback at the woman's vehemence. To Keix's surprise, Vin was the one who moved first. Without protest, Keix followed.

The woman led them right through the entrance and into a spacious hall comprising three nested squares. The smallest one in the centre was a platform that looked like some sort of a stage; the one in the middle had short flights of stairs on each of its side that led to the outermost square.

Outlining the inner border of this biggest square were maroon columns with intricate carvings. While Keix couldn't tell what the designs were depicting, she could see that each one of them differed slightly from the others. These pillars also acted like an ornamental fence for the corridor that they were following the woman down.

Keix didn't know what they were supposed to do, or what they were getting themselves into. But her instinct told her that the woman's concern for Jūn was unlikely faked.

Even though there was no one else around, the woman made a show of treating them like actual customers, as if she hadn't given them a dressing down outside. With every turn that she made, she bowed low and said, 'This way, please.'

Keix was bewildered, but she played along, smiling awkwardly and returning the woman's bows with a bob of her head because she was still half-carrying an unconscious Jūn.

Just as Keix wondered if the lack of activity in the bathhouse was due to the lateness of the hour, a gridded panel slid back and she caught a whiff of an invigorating minty, floral fragrance.

A man in brown robes emerged from the room. Keix stiffened. But the woman didn't miss a beat. She bowed to the man in greeting before turning back to Keix and saying, '. . . made the right choice. We'll have a bath specially prepared to ease the effects of overindulging . . .'

Keix adjusted her grip on Jūn. He did look like he was drunk. After the man was out of earshot, she released her breath.

At the end of the corridor, they turned into a dimly lit and narrow hallway flanked by plain white walls. The woman dropped all pretence of servility and drew the robe off Jūn's back. She took in a sharp breath at the sight of the wound and asked, 'Were you followed?'

Her slippered feet made no sound as she padded across the lacquered wooden floor, while Keix's shoes and Vin's boots clunked after her.

'No. Not as far as we know,' answered Keix.

The woman nodded. 'Who were the ones who attacked you?'

'We don't know.'

'Describe them to me,' said the woman impatiently. 'Jūn is poisoned. I need to know who were the ones who did this to see what's the antidote, if there is any at all.'

Keix's breath hitched. There had been two groups of people in pursuit of them, and she didn't see who was the one who'd slashed Jūn. But right before they entered the teleportation structure, the female outlaw with the sword had been the closest to them.

Keix described her build, the way she carried herself and her weapon to the woman. Vin chipped in with extra details as they continued up several flights of stairs.

For good measure, Keix decided to tell the woman about the caped figures they had encountered outside Atros and at the Square too. The woman looked troubled, but nodded in acknowledgement.

As soon as they arrived at a landing in the stairwell, the woman ushered them down yet another corridor, stopped in front of a gridded panel and slid it open.

'I can't get away right now,' she said. 'One of you will have to go and get the things I need to prepare the antidote. The other has to clean the wound. The longer the poison remains in his body, the harder it will be for him to recover.'

'I'll head out,' said Vin without hesitation.

Keix opened her mouth to protest but Vin interrupted her. 'He's injured because of me. It's the least I can do. Besides, I think I've figured out how to get around Tilsor.'

'But what if you run into those people again?'

Keix was worried for Jūn, but she didn't know if sending her best friend out into the open again was the best, if not only, choice available to them.

'Don't worry. I'll be careful.'

The woman stepped in and said, 'I'll give her a list of possible routes. There's no time to argue.'

She directed Keix and Vin to set Jūn and his sword on a wooden platform that was on one side of the spacious room. Then, she drew Keix behind a paper screen partition which concealed a large squarish recess on the floor that was about as deep as half of Keix's height.

Keix wondered if every room had a private bath like the one in front of her. On the side of the pit nearest to the paper screen, there was a step half the depth of the recess, on which she supposed the patrons sat to enjoy their bath.

'Pull the lever over there'—the woman pointed to one of two switches on the wall—'to fill the bath. Clean his wound thoroughly to make sure it's clear of any discharge.

'You'll find towels there,' continued the woman, gesturing this time to the sideboard to the right of the bath.

'Drain the water by pulling that other lever. Then refill the bath and let him soak in it until the antidote is ready. This room is reserved for special guests only, and as long as the door panel is closed, no one will enter.'

Keix focused her attention on memorizing the rapid-fire instructions and nodded as both the woman and Vin turned to leave.

Before they shut the door, the woman said, 'Do not venture out. Your friend might not be back until daybreak. But the most important thing now is to get the poison out of Jūn's body.'

'I'll be fine,' reassured Vin. 'And I'll be back as soon as possible. You take good care of your Kulcan.'

Keix knew that Vin was joking to try to assuage her worries, but she felt her ears turning hot when the woman raised an eyebrow at her.

'Vin's just joking,' Keix hurried to explain.

'So, you're Keix,' said the woman. Then, she waved Keix back into the bathing room and added, 'Make sure that you wash off all the poison. If he regains consciousness, try to keep him awake.'

The moment the door slid shut, Keix set to work. She pulled the first lever that the woman had indicated. Steaming hot water gushed out of a faucet at the side of the recess. A pleasant piquant scent filled the room.

In no time, the bath was filled with clear water that had a yellow tint to it. Keix laid a few small towels by the pit before going to get Jūn.

She stared at the Kulcan for a moment, trying to determine the best way to get him into the bath. As she dragged him into an upright sitting position, she noticed him wincing with every movement.

'Sorry,' she murmured. In response to her apology, his eyelids only fluttered.

She undid the sash at his waist and eased off his clothes, layer by layer.

The outer and middle layers came off easily, but the innermost one was stuck to the long laceration, which was now surrounded by blisters of all shapes and sizes. Some of them looked yellowish, while the rest were in varying shades of red and orange. Even though Keix took great care to peel away the garment as delicately as she could, some of the blisters burst. Murky, sticky fluid from within oozed out, emitting a sharp, acrid smell that made Keix cough.

'Jūn . . . Can you stand?' whispered Keix in his ear.

Jūn's lips moved, but whatever he said—if he did mutter anything—was inaudible even in the eerily quiet room.

'All right. I'm going to have to move you to the bath. This might hurt,' she said, putting his arm around her neck and hauling him to his feet again.

Jūn produced an audible groan, but remained unconscious otherwise.

Tottering to the bath, Keix gently lowered him into the water, seating him on the low step of the bath pit. First, she tried washing his back while kneeling at the perimeter of the bath. But the depth of the pool, coupled with Jūn's height, made it difficult to clean his wound properly.

After craning her neck at an uncomfortable angle for several minutes, she rolled up the long sleeves of her robe and secured them to her shoulder before stepping into the bath. The water soaked into her robes and weighed her down, but she wasn't going to be caught dead wearing anything less in this easily misunderstood setting.

Relegating Vin's teasing words to the back of her mind, she worked at popping each and every blister with fastidious dedication.

By the time she was done, the water had turned murky. She drained and refilled the bath. Just to play safe, she cleaned Jūn's wound once more and then drained and refilled the pit again.

Through the clear, yellow-tinted water, Keix could tell that the assailant's blade had been razor-sharp. It had cut through Jūn's skin and muscle cleanly—and the gash was tapered at the ends and deepest in the middle.

Keix worried her lip thinking about whether or not Jūn's mobility would be affected, but as her eyes roved over his back, she became acutely aware of how broad and toned his shoulders were. His skin looked golden as a result of the coloured bathwater and the warm, low lighting in the room. When her gaze stopped at a hollow that traced his lumbar curve, she found her cheeks heating up.

'Get a grip, Keix,' she chided herself through clenched teeth. It wasn't like he was entirely naked—he still had on his pants—but her thoughts kept straying.

Keix had never been a prude. She just didn't have the same kind of interest in anyone that other people her age had for their crushes back in Atros.

Growing up with an absentee father had made her sceptical about romantic love. The only types of love that existed in her dictionary were the love that her mother had for her and the friendship that she had with Vin, Pod and Zej.

Sure, she had a small crush on Zej before, but her feelings had never grown intense enough for her to act on them. She had been comfortable with the status quo. Zej had been, too. That is, until after the Ifarl ritual, when he confessed that he had felt the same way about her—and kissed her.

Keix's thoughts grew even more jumbled. She found herself staring at Jūn's lips. His cupid's bow was perfectly defined, and his lower lip looked luscious.

Keix slapped her forehead. 'Okay, Keix, stop staring,' she muttered under her breath.

She tried to busy herself by stowing away the dirty towels to one corner of the room, and she let out a low shriek when Jūn called her name.

'How are you feeling?' she asked, hurrying over to his side.

The Kulcan was silent for a while. When Keix thought that she must have misheard, he slurred in a whisper, 'Sluggish.'

Keix laughed in surprise. The answer was apt, considering the pace of their conversation. 'Well, better than unconscious, I guess.'

There was another stretch of silence, then Jūn gave a feeble cough. 'Where are we?'

Keix sat down at the side of the recessed bath. She swung her legs into the water so they were parallel to Jūn's body and bent down to hear him better. 'Ma.erdene's,' she replied.

'You found it.'

'Vin found it. In case you haven't noticed, she's the brain, I'm the brawn.'

Jūn smiled after another beat. 'Ma.erdene?'

'Middle-aged woman, slim face, sharp eyes, platinum hair that glows, no-nonsense attitude?'

'Hm.'

Keix took that as a yes.

'Did you get a scolding?'

Keix thought for a moment. She didn't know if the woman's outburst at the entrance of the building could be considered a 'scolding'. Shrugging, she said, 'She was worried about you.'

'I bet.'

'She also said that you would be dead in no time if we didn't listen to her. But you look fine to me,' joked Keix.

Jūn chuckled. 'Kulcan's healing speed.'

'It's not looking that speedy right now,' murmured Keix.

'Hm?'

'Nothing. It's just . . . You've been poisoned.' Keix broke the news to him.

'I know. Poison slows you down. Organs fail. Death.'

'Vin's out to get the antidote. You'll be fine.'

There was another pause and then a murmur of assent from Jūn.

Keix hung her head and fought down the guilt that crashed into her. She had been the best fighter in her ATI batch, yet she was useless against the last two groups of people who had attacked them. The first time round, she had been starving and weak. This time, she couldn't even wield a sword properly; her hand-to-hand combat skills also seemed wholly inadequate against foot-long, metal blades.

Through the translucent windowpanes, she gauged that it would be daybreak soon. Vin had been gone for a couple of hours.

She remembered Ma.erdene's instructions to keep Jūn awake, so she tried to keep him talking.

'Tell me about Yurkordu.'

Jūn stirred, although he didn't open his eyes. Moments later, he said, 'Cold.'

'Anything else?' asked Keix with a laugh.

'Beautiful.'

'Anything else?'

Jūn took an even longer pause. 'You'll need the pendant to get in.'

The pendant? She reached her fingers to the spot on her chest where the charm rested. While, technically speaking, this accessory was from her Kulcan father, Keix had never considered it to be so. Her mother was the one who had handed it to her and made her promise to never take it off. Whenever she touched the stone, she felt a little closer to the most important person in her life whom she had lost.

She remembered Jūn passing his necklace to her at the hut and that he had said it was 'far more valuable' than his sword. So this was the reason why? Because they needed it to enter Yurkordu?

Retrieving Jūn's pendant from under her shirt, she compared the two stones. Her purple one was tinged with gold, and Jūn's black one was flecked with silver. While hers was flat, with jagged edges, his charm looked almost like a long, solid cuboid with one of its corners chipped off.

Without hesitation, she looped Jūn's necklace over his head.

'You shouldn't hand over something as precious as this to someone you barely know,' she scolded.

Jūn fidgeted at her reprimand and his shoulder touched her knee. 'I know you,' he insisted.

'I know. What I'm saying is, you *barely* know me,' she insisted.

Through the layers of her robe, she could feel Jūn's body heat. She touched his forehead and panicked when she felt his burning skin.

Ma.erdene had told her that Jūn needed to soak in the water until the antidote was ready. But the bath had run cold since the last time she refilled it. Did being submerged in cool water cause the fever? Perhaps she should drain the water and refill it with the heated bathwater again?

Just as Keix stood up, Jūn grabbed her wrist lightly.

'You were eleven . . .' he mumbled. 'I was fourteen . . .'

Keix couldn't follow Jūn's thread of thought. The fever must be making him delirious. But she decided to just go with the flow to keep him talking. 'I was eleven when you were fourteen? You're saying that you're three years older than me?'

That meant that he was twenty-one now.

'. . . when we met,' continued Jūn.

It took Keix a while to piece together what he was saying. 'We met when I was eleven? I don't remember meeting you,' she said, frowning.

'Hm. Your father sent me,' he said.

At the mention of her father, Keix's thoughts were thrown into disarray again. Her father had been sending Jūn to keep tabs on her since she was eleven? That was messed up. She didn't know if she should be happy or freaked out. All her life, she'd never had any reason to believe that her father wanted anything to do with her. And Jūn had been stalking her for so many years? Was that why she found his presence strangely familiar? It can't be . . .

A sudden thought struck Keix. 'Was that how you managed to find me on the night of the ritual?'

Jūn's head moved but Keix didn't know if he nodded or shook his head. 'You went missing for two years. I rushed over as soon as I received word that you'd resurfaced. But I was too late . . .' Jūn sounded crestfallen, as if he'd failed at an important task.

Keix felt a surge of indignation. 'What about my father? Why didn't he come himself? Why did he send you?'

'Couldn't get away,' replied Jūn.

Keix's anger dissipated when she saw Jūn's brows furrow in pain and self-reproach. It wasn't his fault that her father hadn't come to look for her himself. She sighed and asked, 'Why couldn't he get away?'

'General.'

'General?' Keix thought of Oron. 'As in the head trooper of the Kulcans?'

Once again, Jūn made a noise that sounded neither like a yes nor a no. 'What's he like?'

'You'll see.'

'Why can't you tell me?' Keix asked with a snort.

'Don't want . . . to affect your judgement.'

Keix frowned at the odd reasoning.

Jūn seemed to sense her uncertainty, so he elaborated, 'Atros tells. You do. They tell you how . . . what to think. You should learn.'

Even though his reply was slurred and delayed, Keix could tell that he was upset. The tangent at which this conversation had veered off was unexpected, but she supposed Jūn had a point.

Her life in Atros had always been about working for a bigger plan, the greater good, the sacrifice of self for the good of the organization. But she had never considered it an issue—it just felt right to choose and follow one of several well-worn paths that Atros mapped out for anyone who lived there.

Jūn's direct assessment about her lack of agency pierced through the calm and composed façade that she had so carefully constructed.

After she'd discovered Atros's plans to create a hybrid army, all the values that she believed in were turned on their head. The blame was on Atros—squarely and irrefutably. She had even forgiven her friends—Zej, in particular—who stood by as she was offered up as a sacrifice.

She told herself that she understood why Zej had done what he did. But had she truly forgiven him—and her other friends—in her heart? Was there a disconnect between the emotional and rational parts of her? Was that why she snuck out of Dace's lake house in the middle of the night without telling anyone—even Vin?

Jūn said she should learn. But . . .

'Learn what?' she asked, not bothering to keep the bitterness out of her voice.

'To think for yourself.'

A long time after Jūn muttered these words, when the bathwater had run cold, when the translucent panes of the windows were set aglow by the rising sun, Keix remained unmoving, filled with an emptiness and unwillingness to face up to the real question of whether the person she was searching for was her father or herself.

11

Vin | Illusion of Choice

Vin stepped out of Ma.erdene's and took a deep breath. The rich aroma of sweet bread, savoury soups and spices permeated the fresh morning air in Tilsor, and she felt, once again, a sense of amazement at how this magical city had grown on her.

The sun was making its ascent across the sky, sending the shadows from the assortment of buildings that stretched out to their neighbours in the night, whispering secrets that no one could catch, retreating. The melodic jingle of bells from hawkers setting up their stalls posed a merry accompaniment as sleep was coaxed out of the city's inhabitants.

It had been a few weeks since they were ambushed in the Square. Because of Jūn's injury, they had had to stay at the bathhouse to wait for him to recover before continuing their journey northwards.

Every daybreak, Vin ventured out to buy the fresh herbs required to concoct the antidote for the poison in Jūn's body. And every day, Tilsor's roads provided a new puzzle for her to solve. She relished the thrill of taking a turn and discovering a Section with alleys and shops she'd never come across.

Taking her usual right turn out of the bathhouse's Section, she emerged into a cobbled pathway flanked by a combination of dull green and brown buildings she had never seen before. She smiled, filed the pattern away in her head and picked up her pace. She would have to spend more time figuring out the route to her destination today. If she didn't want an earful from Ma.erdene, she'd better hurry.

The proprietor of the bathhouse had an impatient streak, but she was kind to Keix and Vin and made sure that they were well fed and cared for. With Jūn, she was like a strict parent, fussing over him, refusing to let him out of the bathhouse until the poison was completely eliminated from his body.

That, of course, meant that Keix had to be holed up in the room to take care of him. But Vin could tell that her friend didn't mind it one bit. Because when she was out, Keix would train with the Kulcan, her mind intent on mastering the use of her new sword because she seemed to blame herself for Jūn's injury.

Vin also felt guilty about the way she had treated Jūn when they had first met, so she tried to make up for her initial rudeness by making sure that he got his medication. She was also trying to treat him with less suspicion.

But wasn't it understandable? He did, after all, turn up out of the blue with the aim of whisking her best friend away to a foreign land. And after Atros, anyone who wanted to earn her trust would have to try infinitely harder. Taking a blade on her behalf was a good place to start, she supposed.

In the beginning, even though Jūn was mostly bedridden, he would make the effort to sit up and verbally instruct Keix on how to use the blade. After he regained most of his strength, he started sparring with her.

He also trained Vin in the use of the pair of curved blades he got for her, both of which now hung loosely on the sides of her hips. A few weeks of training wasn't about to make her an expert at wielding the weapons, but at least now she carried them with enough confidence to ward off opportunists looking for easy targets to pickpocket.

After four dozen turns and a fair bit of jogging, Vin breezed through a short and narrow door tucked in the corner of a street.

'Cutting it a little close today, huh?' a smoky voice greeted Vin's rather dramatic entrance.

Vin grinned at the petite woman who was seated in her usual spot behind a wooden counter. 'Morning, Mohgen. I unlocked two new Sections,' she replied, flushed and a little breathless.

Spotlighted by the rays streaming in through the high windows on her left, Mohgen radiated a youthful but commanding vibe. Her hair was slicked back into a taut ponytail, showcasing her piercing brown eyes and high cheekbones. 'Exciting,' breathed Mohgen, a corner of her mouth turning up in amusement. 'What are they like?'

As Vin described the Sections, she noticed that the deep red trimming on Mohgen's black robe matched her mahogany hair perfectly.

Mohgen's brows furrowed for a bit before she broke out in a smile. 'Ah, those,' she said. 'I know one of the inns there sells the best fritters in Tilsor. Take you there someday?'

Vin nodded enthusiastically.

Mohgen had an outgoing and playful streak. After their first encounter, when Vin had awoken her at the crack of dawn to acquire the herbs for Jūn's antidote, Mohgen had taken it upon herself to give Vin a tour of Tilsor.

Vin was wary about trusting people after what happened in Atros, but she knew that it wasn't practical to completely shut herself off to the world.

Tilsor had presented her with a chance to start anew. So had Mohgen's unexpected friendship. It was up to her to take the step forward, and now it had become a regular thing for Mohgen to drop by Ma.erdene's twice a week to take Vin out to try some delicious dish or explore the town with her.

'The herbs,' said Mohgen, tapping a package wrapped in brown paper. 'And'—she turned to the shelves behind her, packed from floor to ceiling with rows upon rows of unlabelled drawers, and retrieved a bunch of balls, some green, some blue—'these.'

Vin stared at the orbs. Ma.erdene hadn't said a word about getting anything other than Jūn's antidote from Mohgen.

'Oh,' said Mohgen, sensing Vin's confusion. 'It's just something I owe Ma.erdene. When you hand them over to her, remember to tell her, "blue burns, green turns".'

Vin raised an eyebrow at the rhyme.

'Easy, right?' Mohgen smirked.

'Blue burns, green turns,' recited Vin, nodding and retrieving the ring of steel coins, hooked hidden under a flap of her robe.

'Six marks, as usual,' said Mohgen. 'This should be the last dosage. I'll see you tomorrow evening then?'

Vin paused in the act of counting the rectangular coins. This was the last dose? Jūn had mentioned that they would be making their way to Yurkordu once he was fully recovered.

'We might be leaving Tilsor soon,' said Vin, the dejection in her voice surprising even herself. When she set out this morning, she hadn't expect this to be her last trip to the apothecary.

'Oh, well then. I'll see you when I see you.' Mohgen didn't seem all that concerned about not being able to see Vin again in the near future.

Vin picked up the brown package and hesitated, trying to find a reason to linger. She held up the blue and green balls and asked, 'What are they?'

Mohgen gave her a mischievous grin. She leaned over the counter, putting her weight on her elbow. 'This'—she pointed to the blue ball in Vin's palm—'contains a highly flammable fluid. Throw it hard at something you want to ignite and after the ball bursts, the slightest bit of friction will set the liquid within ablaze.

'The fluid in the green one corrodes anything it comes into contact with, turning it into smoke. Blue burns, green turns,' she said with a wink.

'Here,' she added, producing a container and gesturing for Vin to put the balls into it. 'They're quite fragile. You don't want them to burst accidentally. All right, get going. Ma.erdene's going to have a fit if you're too late.'

Since she'd run out of reasons to hang around, Vin left the shop.

The buoyant mood that had buzzed through her this morning evaporated as Vin made her way to the nearby Square Forty-nine.

She and Keix had fallen in love with a particular snack—a chunky, squarish pastry with a filling that was just the right balance of sweet and tart—sold by one of the vendors here.

Even though Vin had replenished their supply of the snack a couple of days ago, she decided to get more of the delicious titbit to hoard, in preparation for their imminent departure from Tilsor.

After paying for the pastries, Vin moved to hurry back to the bathhouse and prepared herself mentally for Ma.erdene's lecture. The old woman had a habit of admonishing them whenever they made her worry. But it was a worthwhile exchange—tasty food for a few hours of nagging.

Then, as she was exiting the Square, a flash of white caught her eye. She did a double take when she saw that it was the elderly man whom they had met on their first day in Tilsor, in Square Fifty-eight. He was wearing the same spotless white tunic.

In the weeks spent exploring the town, Vin had seen Tilsorians decked out in various colours—maroon, indigo, teal, and the occasional yellow and orange—although a good half of them seemed partial to black. There were spots of light grey and even ivory, but nothing came close to the unadulterated white that this man wore.

Vin's curiosity was piqued, but it was the surreptitious way in which the man moved that made her feel compelled to follow him. From where she stood, she saw him head through one of the exits opposite to the one he'd emerged from.

As if pulled by an invisible string of desire to unearth a secret that she wasn't even sure existed, Vin set off after the man. She recalled their short, but strange, conversation. The elderly man had assumed that they would join Taavar, some inane tournament that a young lad was babbling about in the Square that very same day? And when Jūn contradicted the old man outright, the latter had said that he was early. Early . . . for what?

Vin kept at a safe distance as she followed him, just close enough to see which forks he took.

A dozen turns later, Vin frowned at the somewhat familiar Sections that the man was leading her through. Was he leaving Tilsor . . . ? She couldn't be sure that these were the same Sections she'd traversed when she first stepped foot into the city. It had been night-time then, and there hadn't been adequate illumination for her to see the buildings clearly. She also hadn't been aware of the concept of the moving Sections in Tilsor then, so she didn't pay that much attention to her surroundings.

Just then, Vin saw an unassuming, squarish building with two wooden columns beside its door. It looked a little too similar to the inn at which they had spent their first night in Tilsor. As soon as she caught herself straying, Vin turned around to seek the man in white. But that fleeting moment of distraction had caused her to lose track of the person she was tailing.

Vin ran along the path to see if she could still catch sight of the old man, but there was no trace of him anywhere. He must have disappeared through one of the forks along the path! It would take a miracle for her to find him again.

Vin growled in frustration. She checked off the list of things that she'd done today to earn Ma.erdene's impending rebuke. Lingering at Mohgen's—worth it. Making a detour to buy her favourite snack—worth it. Following the man in white on a whim . . . then losing track of him— not worth it.

Well, at least it was two to one in terms of worthwhileness. Vin swung the pack of goodies over her shoulder and set off at a light jog back to the bathhouse.

A hesitant voice from behind her made her grind to a halt just as she was leaving the Section.

'Vin?'

Vin turned, as if in slow-motion, in the direction of the voice. Her jaw dropped. Standing in front of her was a group of five whom she'd, one, never thought she would see again so soon after she left Atros; and two, never imagined would travel together as a group.

The two tallest figures in the party were people she was least familiar with: Dace and Seyfer. The two shorter men—although they still stood a good head taller than her—were her friends from ATI, Pod and Zej. And the fifth person, the only woman among the lot and also the shortest, was Maii. All of them were staring slack-jawed at her.

Vin opened her mouth to form a question, but before she could speak, Pod asked, 'Where's Keix?'

* * *

On the way back to the bathhouse, the entire group was mostly silent. Pod asked Vin about when she and Keix arrived in Tilsor and how they planned to find out where the Kulcans stayed. But Vin didn't know how to summarize their journey, so she just told him to reserve his questions for Keix.

Vin's own queries hung unspoken, thick in the air. What made Zej and the rest come all the way to Tilsor? If Zej was here for Keix, why had he brought the rest along? Why was Seyfer with them? Where was Dace's girlfriend?

But Vin held her tongue. She knew that it was pointless to ask anything right now. Zej had made it clear that he wouldn't say a word unless Keix was around.

The six of them reached Ma.erdene's before the sun set because Vin had been noting down all the turns she took while tailing the suspicious-looking elderly man. Despite making the trip back in record time, Vin couldn't shake off the niggling feeling that they'd drawn too much attention to themselves.

Maybe it was due to their Atrossian get-ups, or Maii's bright pink Ifarl hair, people kept throwing more wary than curious glances their way. Vin ran her fingers through her hair self-consciously every time she sensed someone looking their way. She decided that it would be better to not parade the entire group through the main entrance of the bathhouse.

Circling to the rear of the bathhouse, Vin slid open the back door. It led to a multipurpose room where Ma.erdene was bent over a table preparing bath salts for the next batch of customers.

The middle-aged woman had her back to the door, so upon hearing the panel slide open, she started nagging, 'Where did you go gallivanting? I was worri—' She stopped mid-sentence, her hands paused in the act of wiping them on her robe, as she turned around and saw that Vin was not alone.

'These are my friends from Atros. I ran into them in one of the Sections,' Vin hurried to explain.

Ma.erdene assessed the lot in front of her from head to toe without a word. Her eyes were first drawn to Maii's bright pink hair and her lips curled disapprovingly. Pod bowed nervously as she scrutinized him, while Zej gave a polite incline of his head. Dace was the only one who flashed her a dazzling smile and said hi, as Seyfer just stood there, expressionless.

'All of you need a change of clothes,' said Ma.erdene. She instructed Vin to bring the group upstairs and stay there until she sent the clothes up.

'Keix and Jūn must be getting ready to go out to look for you.' Ma.erdene gave Vin a stern look. Spared a tongue-lashing, Vin handed over the package of herbs, as well as the green and blue balls she got from Mohgen's. Then, she quickly ushered the rest of them upstairs.

When Vin opened the door to the room she shared with Keix and Jūn, Keix's reaction was almost an exact replica of Ma.erdene's. A half-uttered scolding before the shock set in.

'Zej?' said Keix, her eyes widening. 'Why are you here?'

A muscle in Zej's jaw twitched.

'How could you leave us without a word?' Pod's voice cracked with worry. 'Did you know how long we searched for you? Dace and Maii even went to *A* and almost got blown up!'

'What?' Both Vin and Keix shouted at the same time.

Zej, who was obviously addressing Keix but refusing to meet her gaze, said, 'Let's sit down. We'll explain from the beginning.'

And so, minutes later, after they were all seated—with the exception of Jūn, who'd retreated to a corner of the room after Keix introduced him—Pod and Zej started filling them in with all that had happened after Keix left Atros. Dace threw in a few sarcastic comments at intervals, but Maii and Seyfer didn't speak throughout.

'So, you're telling me that the people who used to govern Atros—before it was "our" Atros—are back for revenge? And Atros, the Atros as we know it, need the'—Keix turned to glance at Jūn—'Kulcans' help to fight them off?'

Dace clapped and beamed at Keix. 'Succinctly put.'

Keix turned to Seyfer, her expression wary. 'What has any of this got to do with you? Why are you here?'

Vin could tell that her friend was trying to keep her emotions in check due to a mix of curiosity and magnanimity. There must be a convincing reason why Zej's group was travelling with Seyfer. Otherwise, why would they put up with the presence of someone who killed Rold and then had them locked up?

That said, Seyfer had committed all these offences when he was a hybrid, and Vin had done things she wasn't proud of when she was a hybrid too. She had been right there, beside Seyfer, when they captured Keix, Pod, Zej, Maii and Dace, on Atros's orders. The whole situation was just a delicate mess that no one wanted to touch with a ten-foot pole.

'He kidnapped my father and Lana,' said Dace, biting out his words.

'They are under our *protection*. As long as you help me get what I need,' said Seyfer, pressing his lips into a thin line.

'How are hostages considered "protected"?' shouted Dace.

'What do you need?' asked Keix. 'Besides the Kulcans' help?'

'The ExA, as your friends call them, are half-machine, half-human,' said Seyfer. 'With the closing of the portal, there's nothing stopping them from advancing towards Atros and taking over.

'But they won't stop there. If you think Atros is despicable, trying to build a hybrid army to protect its citizens, your blood will run cold if you learn what ExA is capable of. They won't be satisfied with merely reclaiming Atros. Eventually they will lay waste to whatever land they can reach. And you can bet that they are more than willing to kill and enslave people since they don't have to worry about dealing with ghosts now.

'Zenchi lost her powers on the night of the ritual, as did all the Ifarls who took part in it. We need someone with as strong, if not stronger, Ifarl magic to help us win this war. And that person is in Tilsor. Relying on the Kulcans' brute strength alone isn't enough.'

A voice, quiet but firm, spoke up. 'What if the Kulcans refuse to help?'

Vin could tell that Jūn was offended. If all the Kulcans fought like Jūn, the term 'brute strength' would be vastly inadequate and inaccurate to describe their skills. They were not Odats, after all.

Vin had trained with Jūn and seen his keen discipline and technique first-hand.

Seyfer let out a humourless laugh. 'We cannot beat ExA if we don't combine forces. Whatever protection we're offering to his'—he jerked his head in Dace's direction—'father and girlfriend, and the Atros citizens, we can only try our best to fulfil it if we have a fighting chance.'

Keix frowned as she considered what Seyfer said. 'I cannot make promises on behalf of the Kulcans. I don't even know them. But if I help you get to this person you're looking for, you must ensure the safety of Dace's father. As well as Lana,' demanded Keix.

Seyfer ground his teeth together.

'It's one against seven here. We could kill you right now and no one will be the wiser. Or we could trap you here and return to Atros to rescue Dace's dad and Lana. If you want our help, we want your promise,' said Keix.

Vin wasn't familiar with Dace, having met him only after she had been turned into a hybrid. Afterwards, they had interacted cordially during her short stay at his lake house. But she could tell that Keix had formed a tight friendship with this guy who never hesitated to put his sharp tongue to good use, criticizing people he didn't see eye to eye with—especially Zej.

'I knew you were naive, but not to this extent,' scoffed Seyfer. 'My life and safety are of no value to Atros. If I don't get back to Atros after a certain date, they will assume that I've failed my mission and whatever special arrangements Atros has in place for your loved ones will be withdrawn, and they will be left to fend for themselves.'

Keix had laid out her terms and made it clear that Seyfer could either take it or leave it. So, she chose to ignore Seyfer's warning.

Vin had only known hybrid-Seyfer. She'd seen the cold and ruthless side of his character, a trait that all of them shared as hybrids. She'd seen him work with an impeccable efficiency, befitting his status as leader of the hybrid army. But not once had she seen him cave to pressure.

The tension in the room stretched tauter and tauter with every passing second. Neither Keix nor Seyfer spoke. Even Dace and Pod remained quiet, knowing that the first to speak was the first to concede.

Finally, Seyfer said, 'If you help me, I'll do everything within my power to make sure that no harm comes to the two of them.'

Keix nodded at his concession. 'Who is this person and how do we get to him?'

'There's a tournament called Taavar in which we have to participate to get to him,' elaborated Seyfer.

Goosebumps dotted Vin's arm. She recalled what the showman had said about the winners of Taavar being granted a wish. Then she thought back to how the old man in white had approached them and made the assumption that they would join the competition . . . And today. . . The man had appeared out of nowhere, and as if he knew that she'd follow him, led her straight to Pod and the rest.

Had he orchestrated everything? Surely, it couldn't be coincidental that the person whom she'd bumped into today would be the very person who would issue an ultimatum to get them to join the tournament by holding Dace's loved ones hostage.

But how did the mysterious old man know that Zej and the rest were coming to Tilsor? Vin and Keix would have left the town long ago to head to Yurkordu with Jūn had he not been injured and poisoned. Unless . . . the man sent the figures in black and bandits after them?

Vin could tell that Keix was troubled by this turn of events too.

'There is very little information on Taavar. I only know that I must form a group of four in order to enrol,' elaborated Seyfer. 'And I want you on my team.'

'No,' interrupted Jūn.

Everyone turned to look at him with identical looks of shock.

His voice had taken on an edge, and Vin could see anger flash in his eyes.

'Taavar is a dangerous tournament. Everyone who has participated in it has either died or gone missing. Only fools will willingly give up their lives for a promise so vague,' said Jūn, looking only at Keix as he spoke.

An uncomfortable silence fell as everyone appraised the Kulcan. Vin had seen Zej regarding Jūn with mild curiosity when the Kulcan had been introduced to them by Keix. Because Jūn hadn't spoken a word since then, no one had paid much attention to him. Now, following his outburst, anyone with half a brain could sense his protectiveness towards Keix.

'It's her choice,' said Zej, the challenge in his eyes clear.

Five pairs of eyes swivelled between them before turning to Keix.

Keix cleared her throat at the scrutiny, but when she spoke, her voice was firm. 'As long as you keep your word, I will keep mine.'

Jūn's lips tightened into a disapproving line, but he said no more.

Vin understood Jūn's displeasure. She wanted to say that she couldn't believe that her friend had agreed to Seyfer's request. Keix hadn't even had time to think through or discuss the pros and cons of taking on the task!

However, Vin had known on some level that, from the moment Keix learnt that Dace's father and Lana were being held hostage, it was a foregone conclusion that Keix would agree to help Seyfer.

Keix was a person who valued friendship to the extreme.

If ExA were to retake Atros, it wouldn't just be Dace's father and Lana's lives at stake. Innocent Atrossians would also fall prey to this new and deadly threat.

Vin knew Keix too well to think that her friend would stand aside and watch all this happen without lifting a finger to stop ExA. Because their lives had been so inextricably tied to the organization, Vin couldn't help but wonder whether severing Atros's tentacles and releasing themselves completely from its vice-like grip had ever been an option at all.

12

Keix | Preparations

Keix could sense Zej's eyes boring into the back of her head when she doubled down on her decision to help Seyfer. And he'd continued staring at her openly, unblinkingly, until the end of the discussion.

The room, which had been nothing but spacious when it had just been her, Vin and Jūn, now seemed a little too small for comfort. Keix knew that she'd have to talk things through with Zej eventually, so rather than let the awkwardness fester, she bit the bullet and said to him, 'Can we have a word in private?'

Zej nodded and the two of them stood up to leave the room. But just as they approached the door, Ma.erdene slid it open and stepped in, holding the pot that held Jūn's antidote.

Out of force of habit, Keix hurried over and took the container from her. For the past month, after Ma.erdene had prepared the salve, Keix was the one who would help Jūn apply it.

Ma.erdene reminded her, 'This is the last dose of the antidote. Make sure that the paste covers every part of the wound.'

To the rest of the newcomers, Ma.erdene said, 'I've laid out clothes for you in a room downstairs. Come with me.'

Ma.erdene was really talented at pretending to be servile to the bathhouse's customers, but she always took an authoritative tone when she was speaking to Keix, Vin and Jūn. With Pod, Maii, Dace and Seyfer,

Ma.erdene defaulted to her no-nonsense self, so Keix wasn't surprised when the newcomers started to file out of the room at her words.

Zej was the only one who hung back. Keix was about to tell him to go with the others and wait for her to be done with her task, when there was a rustle of clothes. She turned around to see that Jūn had untied his sash and was in the process of removing his robe. Although she'd gotten used to seeing his torso, Keix still felt her cheeks heating up. Couldn't he have waited until everyone had left the room?

Vin coughed unnaturally and took her leave too. By the time Keix turned back to Zej, he was gone as well.

Keix sighed. She didn't know if she should be relieved or frustrated that *the* talk with Zej had been inadvertently postponed.

Because the poultice had to be applied while it was still warm, Keix walked over to Jūn, who had sat down on the platform bed, and started spreading the paste on his back. His wound had healed, leaving behind a permanent, long, reddish scar.

'Why did you agree to it? Don't you want to look for your father any more?' asked Jūn without preamble. He sounded more disappointed than angry.

Keix pretended that she hadn't heard his question. If what Jūn had said about the tournament being a one-way trip to her demise was true, she would've left Atros for nothing. She knew that she shouldn't allow herself to get sucked back into the organization's mess, but the repercussions sounded devastating. And Dace needed her help to rescue his father and Lana.

'You could head back to Yurkordu first . . .' she suggested. 'I'll look for you after the tournament ends and Seyfer finds the person he's looking for.'

At her words, Jūn whipped around to face her and she quickly hung her head and averted her eyes from his bare chest.

She heard him take in a deep breath and release it slowly. Then he repeated the action as if he were trying to calm himself down.

After a long silence, he said in an almost inaudible whisper, 'I won't leave you again.'

Keix's heart tightened at his promise. She recalled the night when he had gotten injured. He'd said that her father had sent him to check on her when she was eleven.

You went missing for two years. I rushed over as soon as I received word that you'd resurfaced. But I was too late . . .

Was that why he was adamant that he wanted to stay by her side? Out of a sense of duty to her father? Or because he felt guilty that he hadn't been able to protect her previously?

But Keix kept her questions to herself. She wasn't sure if she could handle the answers. For now, ignorance was bliss, so she decided to take the coward's way out and didn't say a word as Jūn turned away and she resumed applying the last bit of the medicine on to his scar.

* * *

Following Keix's decision to join the Taavar tournament, Ma.erdene filled them in with all the information she could gather about it—which wasn't a lot. As the charismatic youngster at the Square had said, the first round was a test of physical abilities and the second was a mental challenge.

The only other important piece of information that they found out was that the first trial was scheduled to take place in a week's time. There wasn't much time to prepare and since no one had any idea what the second trial entailed, they could only focus on physical training.

The eight of them split into two groups to practise hand-to-hand combat and learn to use the weapons that Jūn had acquired for them. Jūn took on the task of coaching Keix's group, while Seyfer took the other team under his wing. In terms of technique, the two of them were considered on par and way more advanced compared to the rest, although Keix felt that Jūn edged out Seyfer by a small margin.

At times, Keix found herself feeling envious of Seyfer's elite training at Atros, which seemed far superior to what she had been taught at ATI. Still, her skills had improved by leaps and bounds in the past month under Jūn's guidance. She was sure that she'd soon surpass Seyfer if she continued to throw herself into the training. Of course, Seyfer's height and strength gave him a natural advantage, but Jūn had taught her that she could use these traits against her opponents too.

The week flew by and on the day before the first trial, Pod, Keix and Zej were taking turns to spar with Jūn while the rest of them trained with Seyfer in the other room which Ma.erdene had arranged for them.

Pod was supposed to go first so he stepped up to the square area which they had designated as the arena. He twirled his stave—a long, thin, iron rod tipped with a horn-like, spiral-shaped club—in a flashy manner.

Jūn stood facing him, his brown eyes glinting in amusement, reflecting the morning rays diffusing through the windows.

'I was *so* close to knocking you down yesterday,' said Pod, adopting an attacking stance.

Keix, seated at the perimeter of the square, laughed. Pod was an agile fighter, but it would take a lot more than a week's training for him to even begin to stand a chance against Jūn.

Still, Keix had to give props to Pod's creativity. Most of the time when he unveiled a new trick, Jūn would be stumped, and that momentary delay would give Pod that split second of advantage. Nevertheless, Jūn usually recovered his composure in time to deflect Pod's attack.

'Keix disagrees,' replied Jūn with a smile. He was standing in a relaxed manner, his sword still undrawn, as if he were a spectator instead of a participant in this match.

'Pfft . . . What does Keix know about fighting?' asked Pod, lunging at Jūn before he finished his sentence.

Jūn laughed at Pod's outrageous insult and sidestepped the blow easily. He twisted his body and gave Pod a slight push on the back as he pitched forward, making him fall on his face with a shout of pain and frustration.

'More than you, definitely,' replied Jūn, still smirking.

As Pod picked himself up from the floor, he rubbed his cheek and glared at Jūn. He had lost this bout.

Keix picked up her sword and moved into position. 'Watch and learn,' she said to Pod, and he jokingly showed her a rude sign.

Holding up her sword, Keix bounced on the balls of her feet and focused her attention on Jūn, who had just drawn his sword.

Keix was more familiar with Jūn's rhythm since they had been sparring for the past several weeks, so she fared much better than Pod. But after a couple of minutes, Jūn managed to send her tumbling to the floor as well.

When it was Zej's turn, the temperature in the room dropped to freezing point. The two of them fought wordlessly, with laser-sharp focus and simmering hostility.

After Zej fell, Pod took his place and the training continued in a loop.

By the time they got to their last round, it was already late evening. Everyone was sweaty and tired, and ready to call it a day.

Pod had been thoroughly thrashed today. He hadn't even been able to land a finger on Jūn. Seeing that Maii had come over with the rest of her group after their own training session, Pod walked over and slumped down next to her, sulking.

Keix stepped into the square area once again, twirling her wrists.

'Let the sword become an extension of your arm. Don't wield it in the same way that you throw a punch. Keep your wrists loose,' reminded Jūn.

Keix growled in response to let out some of the frustration that had built up today. Jūn had been especially sharp, and she never managed to deliver a satisfactory blow.

With her sword-fighting skills at this standard, how was she going to complete the first trial tomorrow and help Seyfer and Dace? The thought filled her with dread and affected her focus as she lunged forward, and tripped.

Because of the unplanned manoeuvre, Keix's sword changed course and headed straight towards Jūn's belly. Just as she was sure that she'd skewer him, Jūn reacted with impeccable agility and knocked her sword aside with his own. Then he reached out his other arm and looped it around her waist to break her imminent fall. With a thud, they fell to the floor, Jūn twisting to make sure that he took the brunt of the impact.

As soon as Keix got over her shock, she pushed herself away from Jūn and stood up, embarrassed. Moving to the side of the room, she could see the mirth in Vin's and Dace's eyes. She decided to ignore them as Zej took his position opposite Jūn, holding his sword.

Without preamble, he leapt towards Jūn. Because the Kulcan had only just stood up, he had to take a couple of steps back to avoid Zej's thrusting blade.

Keix frowned as Zej pressed forward, unrelenting.

But Jūn had already regained his balance, and he deflected Zej's blows with his usual efficiency.

Just as Keix thought that Zej was going to lose the bout, he let out a cry and rushed forward, bringing his sword down in an arc. Once again, Jūn fended off the attack. But he had misjudged the intensity with which Zej was swinging the blade and Zej's sword grazed the back of Jūn's hand.

Zej's momentum also sent him crashing forward, and everyone was stunned into silence as his sword clattered to the floor.

'Are you all right?' Keix rushed towards Jūn the moment she saw a streak of red appear on his hand.

'I'm fine,' said Jūn.

Vin hurried over with a small towel and held it out to Jūn. He thanked her and pressed the cloth to the cut. 'The bleeding will stop in no time,' he reassured Keix.

When Keix looked up, she realized that Zej had left the room, so she hurried out to check on him. She knew that there was tension between Jūn and Zej but every time they sparred, their strokes had always been measured. Zej had never lost his cool—until now.

She flew down the stairs after Zej, but by the time she got to the street, he was already gone. Because she hadn't seen which fork he'd taken, there was no way for her to find him now.

Keix felt a surge of anger. Since that first night, when she hadn't managed to speak to Zej, he'd been avoiding her like the plague. His lips were always drawn thin whenever he saw her. No matter how many times she tried to get him alone, he would come up with an excuse and then vanish into thin air.

It was impossible to get him alone to . . . do what? Apologize for leaving Atros after their kiss? Figure out their relationship status? Ask him what he was going to do if Seyfer was able to find the person he was looking for?

Keix resisted the urge to stomp her feet as she made her way back to the room. She was going up the last flight of stairs to the top floor when she looked up to see Dace standing at the landing.

'Did you find him?' asked Dace.

Keix shook her head. She wasn't in the mood to talk about Zej, but Dace put a hand on her arm to stop her from heading towards the room.

'I . . . wanted to say thanks,' began Dace.

Keix blinked in confusion.

'For agreeing to help Seyfer,' elaborated Dace.

Keix pulled her thoughts back to the conversation. 'It's *you* I'm helping. Not Seyfer. I know how much Lana means to you.'

Dace looked down, his expression complicated. And just like the last time they were alone in the lake house, Keix accompanied him silently while he processed his inner turmoil. He had looked troubled since they met here, but Keix hadn't found the time to speak to him alone so far.

'My father . . . I've not spoken to him in years,' said Dace finally, giving Keix a crooked, humourless smile.

Sensing that Dace needed to get this off his chest, Keix said, 'We'll do our best to make sure that he's fine. He will be, as long as Seyfer gets what he wants. You'll get a chance to speak to him again.'

There was a conviction in Keix's voice that she didn't feel. She didn't want to lie to Dace, but she felt that, at this moment, this was what he needed to hear. Dace had only mentioned his father in passing once, when they had first set foot in his lake house. She didn't quite know what kind of relationship they had.

'He was never around when I was growing up. Everything was Atros. Atros. Atros,' said Dace with a bitter laugh. 'I haven't seen him in years, and I thought I'd be okay—never seeing him again . . . But when I found out that Atros was holding him prisoner, I . . .' Dace took a deep, shuddering breath. 'I hate him. Why do I care for someone I'm supposed to hate?'

Keix stared at Dace. He must have been holding back for a long time. She remembered how her emotions had broken through her tediously constructed composure when she'd had that heart-to-heart talk with Vin. If Lana was the only one who was being held hostage, perhaps Dace wouldn't be this affected.

Why should we care for someone we hate? That's a good question, thought Keix. Why should she care that Atros was in trouble after what they'd done to her? But she wasn't helping Atros. She was helping Dace. Which meant that she had to help Seyfer. So, she was indirectly helping Atros. But did it matter? Keix didn't want to think too deeply about the ramifications of her actions.

She patted Dace's shoulder awkwardly. 'It's okay. We'll get him back. Then you can tell him to his face how much you hate him,' she joked.

Dace cracked a smile at that. 'Thank you,' he said, the gratitude apparent in his eyes.

After a short pause, he teased, 'So . . . you and the Kulcan, huh?'

Keix swatted his hand which was reaching out to pat her head away. 'It's not what you think,' she said. 'He's supposed to take me to my father . . .'

'Is that why you left Atros?' asked Dace.

'That's . . . part of the reason, I guess,' admitted Keix. She didn't want to consider the possibility that she might lose her life during the Taavar tournament.

'Look at us, bonding over our absentee fathers,' said Dace jokingly.

Keix gave him a half-smile, half-grimace. 'Anyway, there's nothing between me and Jūn. So don't go around talking nonsense, okay?'

Dace laughed and flicked her forehead. 'Are you dense? He's giving Zej a run for his money!'

Keix opened her mouth to protest but she heard footsteps coming down the corridor. Dace's frame was so tall he blocked her entire view, so she couldn't see who it was.

'Keix?' She heard Jūn call.

Dace gave her a I-told-you-so look and said, 'I'll head back to the room for dinner. Thanks for lending a listening ear.'

He turned on his heel and inclined his head towards Jūn, before he made his way towards the room without another word.

After what Dace had just said—about how Jūn might be harbouring romantic feelings for her—Keix felt panic setting in at the thought of being alone with him.

'Let's go too,' said Keix, moving to catch up with Dace. But Jūn planted himself in her path.

Great, thought Keix. She was being approached by people left, right and centre to share confidences. Yet, the one person she needed to speak to the most was giving her a wide berth.

Keix tried to hide her uneasiness by asking Jūn the first thing that came to her mind. 'How's your hand?'

'It's just a graze. Don't worry about it,' replied Jūn.

Keix nodded. 'Shall we go?' she repeated.

But Jūn stood rooted to the spot. 'I'll join the tournament with you tomorrow,' he said.

'What? No!' exclaimed Keix. Jūn's sudden request chased away her nervousness. 'This isn't your fight,' she added. The image of the haagi she'd picked up outside Atros resurfaced in her mind and her back stiffened in fear. She wasn't cut out to save people, so why did she agree to Seyfer's request? But what was done was done. She couldn't drag Jūn into this mess in which she had landed herself.

'You will stand a better chance of winning the tournament if you have me on your team,' said Jūn, trying to sound practical. 'You need four people, so it'll be you, me, Seyfer and Vin. The rest are not ready. If they join, they'll only be courting death.'

'But—' Keix had barely uttered the word when Jūn interrupted her.

'Listen. We need to approach this strategically. This is Seyfer's mission, so there's no way he would sit this out. And I don't think you would either. Anyway, other than me, you and Seyfer are the best fighters in the group, so it doesn't make sense to keep you guys at Ma.erdene's.

'Now, for the last spot on the team,' continued Jūn, 'we need someone who can think on their feet. The best candidate is Vin. She's been at Tilsor longer than the rest, and I'm sure her knack for navigating around this town will come in handy.'

'Pod's smart too,' said Keix, attempting to poke holes in his proposal.

'I didn't say he wasn't. But he's not as streetwise as Vin. *Tilsor-streetwise*.'

'How about Maii?'

Jūn shook his head. 'Too unpredictable and she's not in the right frame of mind right now.'

Keix was surprised that he had made this assessment even though he didn't know Maii at all. Maii, although as stony-faced as before, did seem less self-assured with the loss of her Ifarl powers.

'Dace too,' added Jūn, predicting her next nomination. 'Too temperamental. And his reflexes are sometimes delayed. I think he got injured and hasn't recovered fully.'

'Then Zej? How about him? He's the most rational person I know,' said Keix as convincingly as she could.

Jūn gave her a look and her gaze flicked to the cut on his hand.

However, instead of rehashing what had just happened, he said, 'If Seyfer and Zej both join Taavar and neither of them make it out alive, who's going to handle Atros? And who's going to lead the team here? I'll only take responsibility for you, and Vin, by extension.'

Keix tsked. Jūn made complete sense. Still, she protested. 'But—'

'I said I won't leave you again,' said Jūn, agitation seeping into his voice. 'And that includes leaving you to fend for yourself during Taavar. I won't do it.'

'Why?' The question slipped out before Keix she could stop herself.

'I never make promises lightly. I said I'd take you to your father, and I will make sure I do everything in my power to make that happen.'

'But what if you . . .' Keix felt a chill creep into her heart at the thought of Jūn dying. But she also heaved an inward sigh of relief. Her assumption that he was looking out for her out of a sense of duty was right.

She wanted to throttle Dace for planting in her mind the seed that Jūn was romantically interested in her. She hadn't even spoken to Zej, which meant that she had no emotional bandwidth to deal with another relationship.

Sure, she was attracted to Jūn. Otherwise, her eyes wouldn't be wandering to him whenever they were in the same room, and her heart wouldn't race when he smiled at her. But there were more important things on hand—for example, surviving Taavar.

'I won't. We won't,' replied Jūn. Even though her question was incomplete, he knew exactly what she meant.

Keix couldn't help but wonder if Jūn was comforting her with platitudes just as she had reassured Dace a few moments ago. She sighed in resignation. 'We should discuss this with the rest. The first trial is tomorrow,' she said, taking a step forward.

Still, Jūn refused to budge. He looked like he was struggling to come to some decision. Finally, he asked, 'Do you need me to help you look for Zej?'

Keix thought back to the time when Zej had approached her at Dace's lake house after the ritual, and the path forward suddenly became clear. She was done chasing after him. Yes, she owed him an explanation. But if he didn't want it, she sure as hell wasn't going to waste her time begging him to listen to it.

'It's okay. He'll come back soon,' she said. *And if he wants to speak to me, he knows where to find me.* 'Let's go formulate a plan with the rest.'

13

Keix | Precision and Strength

Keix squinted against the glaring sun.

Square Twenty-eight turned out to be larger than the other Squares she had come across in Tilsor. The number tower here stood in a corner, and right in the Square's centre was an elevated platform.

There seemed to be some unspoken rule about going on to the stage, as the crowds milled around, packed shoulder to shoulder, creating an arrhythmic wave around the platform. Whether these people were here as participants or spectators, it was too early to tell.

With some difficulty, Keix's group of eight moved towards the platform. All of them were armed, like most of the people around them, but Keix hoped that only the four of them joining the tournament—Jūn, Vin, Seyfer and herself—would draw their weapons today.

'It's starting,' said Pod from behind her.

Keix could tell that he was still upset at having to sit out the tournament. But after a heated discussion last night, everyone, grudgingly or otherwise, decided to go with the plan that Jūn had outlined to her in the corridor. Zej floated the idea of their forming two groups to join Taavar, but he himself knew that it was a foolish suggestion. Putting all their eggs in one basket was unwise, to say the least, when the fate of the world was supposedly at stake. Not to mention, they needed to have a back-up plan to save Dace's father and Lana.

In spite of her complicated feelings towards Zej, Keix felt like a huge weight had been lifted off her chest when he agreed to hold the fort outside. She requested that Seyfer write a note to his team in Atros to ensure the safety of the two hostages in case he met his demise during the tournament. Shockingly, Seyfer agreed to it without argument.

Keix questioned inwardly whether his loyalties lay with Atros or if he had, and was concealing, some other agenda of his own. She couldn't tell. He was too quiet, always observing and deep in thought. But perhaps it was because he had always assumed a leadership role, he never minced his words whenever he had to advise on areas that they could improve on.

Keix gave the note to Dace for safekeeping. However, all of them knew that whether or not the instructions in the note were heeded wasn't up to anyone but Atros. Still, she appreciated the gesture, which was why her feelings towards Seyfer were more amicable today.

They were technically on the same team now, after all. Every bit of harmony would only help their cause.

After waiting for more than ten minutes, the crowd's murmurs faded as a figure strode on to the platform.

Keix's eyes widened when she saw that it was the same young man whom they had met before, the one who had been spreading word about the tournament when they had first arrived in Tilsor. As before, his charisma carried through the crowd. But today, aided by his outfit—a blood red robe that flowed as he walked, and his matching red hair combed skywards to mimic a flame burning atop alabaster skin—his presence was even more arresting.

'Welcome!' The young man's voice echoed around the Square, clear as the sky today. 'Those who wish to participate in the trials of Taavar, step up on to the platform with your group.'

Keix's group exchanged glances and nodded. As her gaze fell on Dace, he said, 'Don't die on me, Keix.' His voice was teasing but the gravitas in his eyes gave Keix pause.

She nodded resolutely. 'We'll take care. But remember, if we fail, you and Zej will head back to Atros to save your dad and Lana, and Pod and Maii will take my pendant and Jūn's, and head to Yurkordu to ask the Kulcans for help.'

This was the 'prepare for the worst and hope for the best' plan that they had come up with last night, with Jūn even divulging the information that Yurkordu's entrance was enchanted to ensure that only people who had the special stones—Kulcans and those welcomed by them—would be able to enter the place.

Pod snorted at her reminder. 'Don't jinx yourself. It's just the first trial.'

When Keix's eyes landed on Maii, the Ifarl jerked a thumb towards Dace and Pod and muttered, 'What they said.'

Zej looked tongue-tied, so he just gave a curt nod. Last night, a couple of hours after he left the bathhouse in a huff, he'd returned to find the group in the middle of drawing up their plans. He had refused to look Keix in the eye. Other than openly staring at him to get his attention—which he ignored—Keix didn't say anything else to press the matter. He was stubborn. She'd give him that. A dark thought crossed her mind then: if she were to die in the first trial, the regret would be his to bear.

Turning away from Zej, Keix hoisted herself on to the platform. Seyfer, Vin and Jūn followed suit.

If it weren't for the fact that she had promised to help Dace, Keix wouldn't have been caught dead anywhere near this rubbish tournament. Still, there were people making their way up the stage, greedy for a seemingly unattainable reward that they believed would change their lives.

Besides Keix's team, there were over twenty other groups of four. All of them, including Keix and her gang, were dressed in robes of varying styles and colours, mostly blue, black and maroon. Even though swords seemed to be the weapon of choice—Keix, Jūn and Seyfer were each holding their own, while Vin had her pair of curved blades with her—Keix spotted some participants holding maces and even bows.

As soon as the crowd settled down and it was clear that there were no more people coming on to the stage, the host's voice boomed through the Square again.

'Welcome to the first trial of the Taavar tournament, in which the participants will be tested on their physical abilities. There are three simple rules.

'One, those who wish to participate in Taavar will have to form a group of four.' He looked around the platform. 'I see that everyone is clear on this. Very well,' he added with a laugh.

'The second rule: Participants are bound to the tournament once it starts. You'll not be able to talk about the tournament outside of it, and the only way to leave is if you win it, or if you die.'

A murmur of unease pulsed through the crowd at the host's words.

'And lastly,' continued the young man, 'if your teammate dies, you're not allowed to replace them with someone else. You'll have to continue with the tournament with the remaining number of people that you have in your team.

'I trust that all is clear,' he said with a bow. When he straightened up, he clapped his hands and a handful of petite figures in identical white robes appeared seemingly out of nowhere and weaved through the crowd of participants on the stage, approaching each party with a small item and pressing it lightly to each contestant's hand.

As they neared Keix's group, she saw that the item was cylindrical and used as a stamp of sorts. The four of them in the group were also marked on the back of their hands with the device. The emblem, a circle enclosing an irregular pattern of squares and triangles, glowed blue for a few seconds, transmitting a cool, tingling sensation to the tips of her fingers, before dissipating.

This must be the binding contract of this tournament. Keix touched the spot on her hand where the mark had disappeared, feeling a little apprehensive.

When the simple ritual ended, the host raised his hand to get the attention of everyone. Then, he intoned, 'And the riddle of this trial is: Judge not the weak forces, for their resilience may surprise you. Fear not immense strength, for their fragility may but be hidden in plain sight. May the light of stars guide your way.'

Following his pronouncement, he disappeared through an archway which had magically appeared at the back of the platform and the figures in white followed him through it. The second the last figure went through the arch, the air vibrated and the sides of the platform glowed. The strange phenomenon elicited shouts as a ripple of surprise and awe thrummed through the audience.

Keix could tell that her friends shared her amazement as she caught sight of them, eyes widened, breaths held, near the edge of the stage.

'Keep your eyes peeled. Anytime now.' Jūn's warning, a whisper brushing past her ear, rang like a siren.

Keix thought about the riddle the host had posed.

Judge not the weak forces,
for their resilience may surprise you.
Fear not immense strength,
for their fragility may but be hidden in plain sight.

What did it all mean? But before Keix had time to analyse it, the glowing light around the stage shot into the sky, leaving an almost-transparent veil of shimmer in its wake, making the spectators disappear and shutting out their cheers and chatter.

The air was now filled with the foreboding song of imminent destruction which the participants' weapons sang as they left their sheaths.

Keix drew her sword too and tested her grip. This was the moment of truth. Was she as good a fighter as she thought she was? Had she trained hard enough to ensure that she would get out of this alive, together with Vin, Jūn and even Seyfer?

She looked at Vin, who caught her eye and winked at her. The memory of their last interaction in Sector L before they were attacked by ghosts resurfaced in her mind. Keix forced the unpleasant reminder out of her head. Both of them would be getting out of this alive, and in one complete piece, she promised herself.

However, when their first opponent appeared, Keix wondered if history would repeat itself and she would fail to protect her friends and herself.

A swarm of metallic balls, scattered around the perimeter of the now-enclosed platform, hovered in the air, as if suspended by invisible strings.

But because they didn't move, a murmur rippled through the participants as they held their ground, unsure of what was in store for them.

It was as if a stalemate had occurred even before the fight had begun.

The scene must have reminded Seyfer of his elite trooper training because, out of nowhere and as if he was lecturing them, he said, 'The first to charge into a fight with an unknown enemy is either not thinking or thinks too highly of themselves.'

Huh? Keix glanced at him, unsure if he was joking or being serious. She gripped her sword tighter. *That was all very well, but if you don't fight, you'll never know who you're facing*, she thought.

As she was about to take a step forward, Jūn touched her elbow. She barely caught him shaking his head when a battle cry sounded from a corner of the platform.

Keix whipped her head around just in time to see one of the participants—an average-sized man with a paunch—swing the axe he was holding and charge at a group of metal balls closest to him. He raised his weapon and brought it down in an arc on one of the orbs. Even though his target was stationary, he missed his mark and the blade of the axe only managed to brush against the metal ball.

'Not thinking, then,' mocked Seyfer. But he didn't have time to gloat, because the touch awakened the rest of the balls and they started buzzing in mid-air. Two of them flew towards the man from opposite directions. The balls, which were about the size of Keix's fists, made contact with the sides of the man's head at the exact same time and Keix heard a loud thud. The next moment, it was as if a jolt of electricity had shot through the man. His body stiffened and crumpled to the ground.

Fear rippled through the participants. Some of them started attacking the floating orbs near them, while others ran towards the door through which the host had disappeared, only to find themselves slamming into an invisible wall.

Pandemonium broke out.

Balls spun towards them from all directions.

Keix stole a glance at the man who had been rendered unconscious by the metal balls. Was he dead? She tried to ignore the sour taste in her mouth and backed up into the crowd of participants who had been driven into a tight circle as the hovering balls herded them together.

Jūn, who was standing in front of her, swung his sword upwards and split one of the metal balls just as he had split the black-hole bullet at their first encounter. The halves fell to the ground and lay there, unmoving.

When Keix tried to replicate Jūn's move with another orb that was flying towards her, she realized that hitting the fist-sized ball was harder than Jūn made it seem.

Physical strength is nothing if there is no precision, she remembered Jūn reprimanding her one afternoon, hours into their hand-to-hand combat training. She had seen an opening when Pod, even more verbose than usual, had struck up a commentary from the sidelines, asking Jūn all sorts of questions about the Kulcans. Keix knew that Jūn was gritting his teeth in frustration as he tried to focus on fending off her attacks.

Confident that she would be able to knock him off his feet, she had charged at him, barrelling towards his midriff. However, the Kulcan, with his lightning-quick reflexes, had managed to dodge her attack at the last possible second. But because she'd leaned too far forward in her haste, she lost her footing and stumbled forward.

Jūn had grabbed her arm to break her fall. Then he had said, 'Physical strength is nothing if there is no precision.'

Keix hadn't forgotten the embarrassing lesson, and now, she seared it into her head as she watched Jūn cleave apart another metal sphere.

'Gawping much?' said Vin with a laugh as she jumped into the fray.

Vin's words jolted Keix into action, and she fended off two orbs seeking to make her join the unconscious man who had wielded the axe. She couldn't halve the balls as Jūn had so effortlessly done and the orbs swerved at her with a vengeance after they bounced back off the ground where she had swept them.

Facing these wretched objects which were whirring even faster now and attacking with a stronger force, Keix finally understood the first half of the host's riddle.

Judge not the weak forces,
for their resilience may surprise you.

The relentless onslaught kept everyone on their toes. Soon, sweat was pouring down Keix's back and face. She had been knocked off her feet twice. Thankfully, she had managed to get up without help. Once in a while, Jūn and Seyfer would jump in front of her and Vin, to let them take a breather if they managed to gain some ground on their attacks.

Through the gaps between the balls flying towards her, Keix could see that only about half the participants were still standing. She took care to navigate around the fallen bodies while fending off the metal mob. The survivors were now aware that it was best to take down the balls at the first stroke, because those that hadn't been dispatched only grew more aggressive as they re-attacked.

Seyfer helped Vin knock down two incoming balls, and Keix edged towards her friend so they could band together. Like the old times, she found themselves moving to a familiar rhythm against a common enemy.

Keix didn't know how much time had passed, but when they finally cut down all the balls, she was panting and her arms were aching. About a quarter of the participants were left standing now. The rest were either dead or unconscious—Keix couldn't tell.

The figures in white who had imprinted the tournament's binding contract on the participants appeared through the archway and started carrying out the bodies scattered on the ground, as if to signal the end of the first trial.

Those who had survived the gruelling fight let their arms drop to their sides at the lull in action. Many of them were doubled over, trying to catch their breaths.

'Is that it?' asked Keix.

Jūn looked slightly winded. Just slightly, and Keix found a smile creeping on to her face as Seyfer came over to her and Vin, pushing his hair, damp with perspiration, out of his eyes. They had passed the first trial with their numbers intact.

'That wasn't that diff—'

Before Keix could complete her sentence, another whirring filled the air and the balls that they had taken down started humming again, emitting an electrifying vibe. The bodies had been cleared and the figures in white were nowhere to be seen.

'What's happening?' asked Vin.

Keix could hear the thread of panic in her friend's voice. Her heartbeat, which had just begun to ease back into their natural rhythm, started racing again.

As if in answer to Vin's question, the balls shot up back into the air and assembled into an irregular shape. That wasn't all. The scattered weapons on the ground which belonged to those who hadn't survived the round started vibrating, taking on a life of their own. After a couple of seconds, they shot upwards and towards the expanding mass.

The ground shook and the ear-splitting crunch of metal filled the air, intensifying the dangerous energy on the platform. Keix found her eyes riveted on the distorting shape in front of her, stretching out, then squeezing together, as if it were a piece of dough being moulded by a pair of invisible hands into its desired shape.

Everyone gaped as the mass quivered and moved, eventually settling into a life-like figure. The behemoth had a 'torso' in the shape of an inverted triangle that looked like dozens of hovercars stacked on top of one another. Metal plates formed by the discarded weapons from before were layered one over the other like the scales of a species of creatures called reptiles in Atrossian myths.

The armoured exterior glinted under the blazing sunlight and four rectangular chunks that could pass for its limbs protruded out of this triangular body. Two of these appendages anchored the machine to the ground.

'What the hell . . .' muttered Vin.

Just as Keix thought that the monstrous figure's transformation was complete, some of the metal plates on the centre of its torso reshuffled to reveal a bright, glowing light. And, as if to announce its presence, the metal beast let loose a screeching wail that almost burst Keix's eardrums.

The scream reanimated the participants who had been standing rooted to the ground, watching this petrifying metamorphosis. They scattered and fled in every direction as the machine stomped its way around the platform.

'Wasn't so easy after all,' said Seyfer. He seemed to relish the new challenge as he readied his sword once again, a determined gleam in his eyes.

Keix choked at Seyfer's blithe assessment of the situation. The swarming metal balls were just a warm-up, and yet it had taken out three-quarters of the participants. How on earth were they going to complete this first trial?

*   *   *

Looks could be deceiving. But in the case of the giant that rose from the remains of the pesky metal orbs, what Keix saw was exactly what she got.

Standing at four times Keix's height and at least twenty times as huge, the beast's 'shoulders' were so broad, they occupied a good chunk of Keix's vision whenever she looked at it. Every time it moved, the ground beneath them shook and strained under its weight.

For a fleeting moment, Keix wondered whether it would be possible for the machine to inadvertently stomp a hole through the platform and trip over itself, or fall flat on its face and knock itself out, saving all of them the trouble of having to take it down. But she knew it was beyond wishful thinking.

'Stay close now,' muttered Jūn under his breath.

Because of the bulk of the figure, everyone was backed up against the sides of the platform.

Keix didn't know if she should be relieved that she didn't need to watch her steps and avoid tripping over dead bodies, or troubled that the fallen participants had been hauled away so callously.

'How are we supposed to bring it down?' Vin's incredulity was apparent.

'You tell me. You're the smartest one here,' said Keix, half-jokingly.

The lines between Vin's brows deepened as she squeezed her eyes shut, thinking hard.

'Hold up . . . "Fear not immense strength, for their fragility may but be hidden in plain sight",' recited Vin.

'That's it!' jumped in Jūn. 'There must be spots of weakness we can exploit.' He scanned the giant from head to toe.

'Perhaps the joints?' provided Seyfer helpfully. Immediately after he spoke, he charged towards the metal mammoth and let loose a blow at a spot along the machine's 'leg' that could have passed off as the knee joint had it been a human.

'Well, he definitely thought before striking. Which means that he thinks highly of himself,' murmured Vin, referring to Seyfer's earlier statement.

Had the situation not been quite so tense, Keix would have laughed out loud.

Instead, her panic overrode the inappropriateness of the gibe as the metallic giant swung around and hit Seyfer on his side with its 'arm'. The blow caused Seyfer to fly backwards and hit the invisible wall along the side of the platform.

After it had dealt with Seyfer, the giant started stomping around the stage again. This time, it was bent over, sweeping its 'arms' in front of it and knocking down whoever did not manage to scramble out of its way. Where the metal ball swarm was graceful and elusive, and seemed to operate strategically, this figure blundered around, reminding Keix of the Odats she'd fought back in Atros, ready to tear apart the participants at the first chance. Yet, for all its clumsiness, there was an agility in the way it moved. Within a minute, it had gone one round around the platform.

Keix took stock of the situation. Most of the participants who had been knocked down had gotten back to their feet and were warily moving away from the giant instead of running around mindlessly like before.

Keix, Vin and Jūn had run towards Seyfer when he'd fallen, but luckily the most unwelcome member of their team proved to be hardy, getting back on his feet almost immediately.

'Not the joints then,' he even joked, as if he hadn't just been tossed ten feet into the air.

'What now?' asked Keix. Some of the participants were rushing forward to mob their gigantic opponent.

'Seyfer's right. We look for a spot of weakness,' said Jūn. With that, he ran towards the giant and tipped his sword into the ground, using the momentum and leverage to vault towards the behemoth.

Keix couldn't help but stare in awe at the graceful arc that Jūn's leap drew as he flew towards the giant's arm. Using the limb as a stepping stone—something Keix never thought was possible—Jūn went straight for the glow in the centre of the machine's body and slashed his blade against it.

The giant staggered back and emitted another deafening screech, as if it was in pain. Jūn's successful attack proved to be a courage booster for the rest of the participants as they charged towards it, eager to bring it down.

The giant narrowly missed striking Jūn as he jumped back down towards his teammates. Keix could have sworn that he winked at her the moment he landed on the ground beside her. But there was no time to celebrate because the next second, she found herself dodging the rapid blows that the giant was starting to rain on the ground.

Just as the metal balls had grown more aggressive after having been struck once, this machine picked up its attack pace. Its blows were twice as furious, but because it was relying solely on brute strength, it occasionally stumbled.

The remaining participants, who had rushed in to attack the machine after Jūn's successful blow, were now backing off. Some of them even tried their luck to see if they could run through the archway, but the arena remained locked down.

'Let's distract it so Jūn and Seyfer can continue attacking its body!' shouted Keix to Vin. From the way the giant screamed when Jūn hit the glaring light in the centre of its body, Keix deduced that it must be the weakness that they were looking for.

But the armour plates had rearranged themselves to conceal the light again, so Keix circled the giant, hacking at its ankles, and hoping for another opening.

Vin heeded her cue and did the same, but there was little damage they could deal to the machine.

Still, Keix noticed that the giant would turn in the direction of the attack every time it felt a blow land on its body, so that opened up small windows of opportunity for Jūn and Seyfer to attack its torso. After a couple of rounds, Keix saw a pattern emerging.

Every time Jūn or Seyfer hit its body, the machine would pause for a split second and the plates of the armour would ripple, as if shaking off the attacks. And from a particular angle, the glowing light would be exposed.

Fear not immense strength,
for their fragility may but be hidden in plain sight.

Jūn and Seyfer seemed to have made the same observation, and they started coordinating their strikes. Seyfer would slash the machine's back, and when it twisted its body and the armoured plates rippled, Jūn would jump in to land a blow on the half-concealed glowing centre of the torso. Then, they would switch roles. Jūn would distract the metal beast, and Seyfer would try to hit its weak spot. Because the angle at which they attacked had to be precise, there were more missed blows than accurate ones. But once in a while, when they struck their target, the machine would screech like before.

And even though it remained standing and continued attacking them, its movements grew more erratic and its blows landed heavier with every critical strike they made. Soon, it became more and more difficult to evade the giant's 'punches'. Keix and Vin found themselves getting knocked off their feet more frequently—yet, the end wasn't in sight.

Everyone was tired—even Jūn, and Keix realized belatedly that the rest of the participants weren't even bothering to fight. They were just hanging back, keeping out of the beast's reach and waiting for her team to take their opponent down.

In a final bid, Keix planned her attacks to lead the giant to a corner of the platform. Those who were standing only had two choices—fight or flight. Because of the bulkiness of the machine, it was hard to do the latter without running the risk of getting stomped on, so more of them joined the fray.

Just when Keix felt ready to throw in the towel, the giant stumbled and started toppling forward after Seyfer hit its back. As if in slow motion, Keix saw the opening that she was looking for—the armoured plates rippling in response to Seyfer's strike, the light in the centre of the torso, about to be exposed to her at the perfect angle and distance for her to strike.

She gripped the hilt of her sword as tightly as she could and ran in the direction of the opening armour plate, using the momentum to leap towards the bright light. From the corner of her eye, she saw a shadow, sword extended, aiming for the same target.

Jūn.

Together, their swords squeezed through the space under the armour plate, penetrating the core of the machine at the same time. Up close, the glow from the behemoth blinded her, and all she could feel was the force of the blow. Her sword vibrated so intensely that she thought the bones in her arm would shatter.

The next thing Keix knew, Vin was helping her up. She blinked away the halos of light obstructing her vision and saw a mound of metal on the ground.

'We did it, Keix,' said Vin. She was still panting from the exertion, and Keix could feel her arms trembling as she hugged her.

Keix wiped away the tears and perspiration streaming down her face with the back of her hand as exhaustion finally sunk in. Now that she didn't have to keep watching her back and dodging attacks, the images of the dead participants, some bloodied, some wide-eyed, rushed forth in her head. Before she knew it, her knees had given way and she found herself doubled over, expelling the contents of her stomach—a foul mixture of a half-digested breakfast and gastric juices—on to the ground.

* * *

Tentative chatter and laughter filled the air as the team tried to celebrate their victory in the first Taavar trial. The mood was odd because on the one hand, everyone was glad that Keix and the rest had passed the trial with minimal injuries. On the other, there was this untouchable blanket of gloom suffocating the four who had been involved in the tournament.

Keix knew that Zej was trying to catch her eye. He'd been stealing glances in her direction since Vin and Jūn made a fuss of her vomiting episode and insisted on half-carrying her back to Ma.erdene's. Perhaps Zej was worried about her. Or something had clicked in his mind while they'd been away, so he'd decided that he was ready to speak to her again. But today's fight had taken a toll on her. She was in no mood to have *the* talk, so she ignored him.

She headed out into the small, adjoining balcony of the room alone to take a breather. The cool air of the night wafted around her, but it did little to soothe her nerves that have been left raw by the rampage she had witnessed this morning.

Keix had never pegged herself as someone who was afraid of dying. Perhaps the unemotional way that Atros treated the lives of its troopers had been ingrained in her. But after surviving the ritual and today's trial, she suddenly felt that to treat her life so carelessly now just seemed . . . wrong.

She thought back to what the host had said before the trial started— something about letting the light of stars guide their way. Now, overhead, these celestial bodies sparkled, as if they were there to witness this faux celebratory moment. Lifting her head, Keix fixed her gaze on one of them and uttered a silent prayer for it to show her, as well as the others, the right path out of this mess. Then she repeated the gesture with every star that she could locate in the sky.

So absorbed was she in her task that she never sensed the eyes of her teammates roving over her silhouette, each pair imbued with their own sentiments. Of longing. Of guilt. Of trust. Of regret. Of kinship, grudging respect, and a cautious sense of hope.

14

Vin | Fractals

The first rays of the sun had chased away the revelry of the previous night, and Vin could sense the veil of bleakness looming over their group of eight as they made their way to Square Thirty-three, where the second trial of Taavar was supposed to take place.

Maii and Dace wore identical looks of indifference. And Zej's signature stoic expression was back after he kept stealing glances at Keix but got ignored the entire night. Vin didn't know what had gone wrong between the two of them. For the whole of the past week, Zej had been giving Keix the cold shoulder. Last night, the tables had been reversed. Vin sighed. She wondered when this mess would be resolved.

Only Pod seemed to be in a good mood. He was openly admiring and praising the genius of the layout of Tilsor—something Vin could relate to. But his usually infectious high spirits couldn't help her shake off the intensifying dread within her.

Because Pod hadn't witnessed the rampage at the first trial yesterday, he would never understand how it felt, seeing bodies stacked one on top of the other, not knowing if they were dead or unconscious. Neither would Maii, Dace and Zej. And Vin hoped that it would stay this way.

When they stepped into Square Thirty-three, apprehension crept through Vin, like a creature raking its long, sharp nails gently against her back. The location bore as many similarities as differences to Square Twenty-eight, where the first trial was held. This Square also had a platform in its centre, but the space was much smaller, as if whoever was hosting the tournament had expected the pool of participants to dwindle.

While the mood among those who had joined as spectators yesterday was anticipatory, albeit with an undercurrent of uneasiness, dread was written all over the participants' faces today. There were but a handful of groups with all their four members intact. The rest of the participants stood alone or huddled in twos and threes around the platform.

After a long wait, the host who had set the stage for the first trial appeared on the platform with an air of importance, as if he was right on schedule.

'Welcome to the second trial of Taavar. I trust that everyone is well rested,' he began. The smile he flashed didn't sit well with Vin.

'Participants of the trial, please approach,' he continued.

Vin felt a strange tugging sensation in the arm that had been 'branded' with the contract. She looked at the rest of her team and could tell from their expressions that they were just as bewildered, as they moved towards the stage.

Instead of the previous day's verbal exchanges, Vin's group simply looked at Zej's group and nodded solemnly before proceeding up the platform.

'The rules of the tournament announced yesterday stand. You're to stick to your original group of four . . . *if* the four of you are still standing,' the host said with a smirk. 'And the only way out of this tournament is that you either complete it or you die.'

'Well, don't mince your words,' mumbled Vin to no one in particular.

'We've resuscitated those who had been knocked out during yesterday's trial,' continued the man. 'You guys got lucky. If your teammates are not here, it's safe to assume that they are dead, and you won't be able to replace them. But who knows? Those who are alone might find this trial easier to complete.

'So, remember, for today's trial, the only rule is that the team needs to complete it together. And here's your riddle of the day: Four is all you need to pass,' said the host cryptically. 'May the light of stars guide your path.'

Vin rolled her eyes at the well-wishing.

The host took his leave, just as before, and the perimeter of the platform shimmered and the glowing lines shot up into the sky once more. Today, however, instead of just making the spectators disappear, the rest of the participants who didn't belong to their group vanished too.

'Wait . . . where did the rest go?' asked Vin, looking around the arena. She could tell that Keix, Jūn and Seyfer were equally bewildered.

'Okay . . . What now?' asked Keix.

Seyfer inclined his head in reply.

Vin followed his line of sight and saw that eight arches—two on each side of the platform—had appeared. They were not unlike the one that their host and his minions used to enter and exit the platform.

'It's . . . a puzzle?' Keix ventured a guess.

'"The team needs to complete it together. Four is all you need to pass." That's what the man said. But there are eight archways here.' Jūn frowned as he looked around the arena.

Dead silence followed.

Vin strode towards the arch nearest to where the four of them were standing. 'Let's assume that these archways aren't locked down like the one in the first trial . . .'

'. . . and that they are just like any of the other archways in Tilsor—meaning they should take us out of this place?' said Seyfer.

'So, we're supposed to figure out which one to step through?' Jūn squinted at the arch, as if he could find clues hidden in it.

'Guess there's only one way to find out,' said Vin. 'But what if we choose the wrong one? The host said that the team needs to complete the trial together. "Four is all you need to pass." Four people? What about those groups with one or more teammates down?'

'Let's just worry about ourselves first,' said Seyfer.

'So . . . we'll walk through one of these arches as a group? To see what happens?' Keix looked to her teammates in confirmation, her expression wary.

They nodded at each other and drew their weapons as a precaution.

'This one?' asked Vin, gesturing to the arch that she'd stopped in front of.

'I guess this is as good as the other seven,' said Seyfer, walking right up to Vin.

Together, they took a deep breath and stepped through the door frame. Vin felt a swooping sensation in her stomach, as if she had missed a step while walking down the stairs. But the next moment, her foot found firm ground. It took her a beat to realize that, in some bizarre plot twist, they had crossed back into the platform through one of the other seven arches. There was a surreal moment, just for a split second, when she saw everyone's back disappearing into the archway that the four of them had stepped through. She also thought that she saw the same door frame glowing blue. Before Vin had time to process the sight, a loud clang sounded. Vibrations reverberated throughout the space and Vin keeled over. Her head exploded with snippets of long-suppressed memories and she screamed. She barely heard herself over the echoes of the clang as she was transported back in time.

She was back in ATI. It was the day she had experienced what getting attacked by ghosts felt like. Pain engulfed her. It led her to the night when Sector L was attacked. The ghost of the girl who had attacked her was staring at her, a vicious smile on her pale face. *Shoot, then run.* She heard her own voice in her mind.

The memory shifted. Trial six hundred and sixty-four. She was plunged into freezing water. Liquid filled her nose. Her lungs. She was gasping for air. Her screams were nothing but gurgles, dissipating into the cold. The cold was a raging fire, burning from her very core. Another shift. The melodic chanting of the Ifarls sounded like shards of glass in her ears. She surrendered to the pain, letting it take over.

Then suddenly, there was a soft crunch of gravel and she found herself kneeling on sandy ground. It took her a moment to collect herself and get her bearings. She was back on the stage, right in the centre of the platform where she had started.

It was the second trial of Taavar and they had only stepped through an arch once. Was this the mental test that they had to go through? If so, why hadn't the host arrived and announced that they had passed it?

Teeth chattering, she looked to the rest of her teammates, each as pale as the other, eyes haunted. Keix and Seyfer looked like they had been swallowed by darkness, churned, digested and regurgitated. Jūn was the only one who looked more composed.

Vin suspected that Keix and Seyfer had relived the night of the ritual, just like she had, but she didn't voice out her conjecture. This was one of those things that people who had experienced it would never speak of—the horrors that they'd gone through—even if they were not bound by a contract.

'Do you suppose we need to cross through all eight arches to complete this trial?' Vin shuddered to think of having to relive the mental torture from moments ago.

'We'll never know until we try,' said Keix, a hardened glint in her eyes. 'But which doorway did we just go through?'

Vin looked around. Keix was right to ask that question. Because of the clanging that triggered their mental anguish, and the fact that they found themselves back in the centre of the platform, they had no way of knowing which doorway they had actually passed through. All the door frames looked identical.

'Let's try marking the doorway before we step through another one,' said Jūn, holding out his sword. He randomly chose an arch and swung his blade at it. But instead of cutting a notch on the it, his weapon passed right through it as if it were an illusion.

Keix exhaled loudly through her nose in frustration. 'How about this?' She pulled off her boot and set it right beside the archway.

Vin nodded at her friend and all of them took a deep breath before they stepped through the marked doorway.

Once again, the jarring clang rang out and the group went through another round of mental torture before finding themselves back at the centre of the platform again—along with Keix's boot.

'I guess one of the unsaid rules for this level is that no marking is allowed,' said Keix.

She sounded a bit more winded compared to before, and Vin knew why. The mental torture felt like it had lasted longer the second time round.

Their memories seemed to grow more vivid and longer with each subsequent time they passed the threshold.

On their sixth attempt, Vin could have sworn that the clanging was pulling her teeth from her gums. All four of them were panting, each consumed by the replay of their most agonizing moments.

Even Jūn, who looked the most put together among the four of them, was having trouble holding his back straight. 'There must be a way we can keep track of which doorway we've gone through. Otherwise, there's a one in eight chance that we're passing through the same one over and over again.' His eyes scanned the platform, searching for some irregularities that could help them tell the arches apart.

But Vin knew there was no way of knowing. The sun was hanging low in the sky now, tinting the arena with a tinge of dusty orange. The air still rang with a silence that reflected their lack of headway in this trial. It seemed possible that they could be stuck here forever.

'We keep going,' said Keix, her voice low.

'And hope for a breakthrough?' Seyfer's tone was on edge.

'Do you have a better idea then?' Keix didn't hold back her anger.

Everyone's nerves were scrubbed raw by now.

Vin saw Jūn look at her friend in concern, but he remained silent, his brow furrowed.

'This is pure stupidity. Going through them'—Seyfer gestured at the archways—'over and over again and expecting to turn up in another place other than this stupid platform, and experiencing that dratted ritual. Over and over again!'

'So, what? We just give up? If we don't complete this trial, we can't proceed to the next one, and you won't get to speak to that person whom you came here for in the first place. You're the one who brought us into this!' shouted Keix.

'*You're* the one who signed up for this,' countered Seyfer, matching Keix's tone. 'You could have left. Washed your hands of Atros and its problems.'

Jūn stepped in between Seyfer and Keix who were looking daggers at each other. 'This is not the time to attribute blame.'

Vin jumped in too. 'Keix, stop. Seyfer, please. Remember what this trial is about. A test of our mental strength. It's not just intelligence or logic skills we're talking about here. Clearly, they are messing with our heads. Otherwise, why would we be reliving these specific memories? You snap, you lose.' Vin had to stop herself from rolling her eyes. She couldn't believe that she, of all people, was being the voice of reason here.

Seyfer threw Jūn a dirty look and added, 'It's ironic really, the person who's been through the least hardship is the most able to withstand this trial.'

Despite Seyfer's provocation, all Jūn did was raise an eyebrow at the person who had insulted him.

Vin wondered how the Kulcan trained his patience.

After a long pause, Seyfer muttered with a sigh, 'Let's get this over and done with.'

Relieved that the squabble was over, Vin pointed to yet another archway she thought they should test, and braced herself for another round of mental torture. To her surprise, instead of the clang and the excruciating mental agony which she'd expected as she stepped through the doorway, a silvery bell chimed. And she didn't get swept to the centre of the platform either. The four of them remained standing in front of the archway through which they had just emerged. This door frame was directly opposite the one that they had just stepped through. Because they weren't disorientated by the 'punishment', each one of them clearly saw their group disappearing into the first doorway and the arch glowing green as they reappeared through another one.

Vin looked at the others, wide-eyed, her mood soaring. Had they just found the first correct doorway?

Jūn walked over to the opposite side of the arena and looked at the first and 'correct' archway. 'It glowed, right?'

Vin nodded but she stayed put. 'I thought my eyes were playing tricks on me the first time we stepped through that doorway and I saw it light up, right before the clang sounded! But, yes, it definitely glowed.'

Jūn frowned. 'I saw it too.'

'What colour was the glow the first time?' asked Keix.

'Bluish?' Vin looked to Jūn for confirmation.

Jūn nodded in reply.

'This time, it was green,' affirmed Keix.

And with that, the mood of the group shifted. This was the first clue that could help them advance in this trial. The rules were inexplicit—four steps to pass; the team must complete this together—they had been practically directionless.

Seyfer, who had been frowning at the first 'correct' archway, was now looking at his feet, deep in thought. 'Let me test out a theory.' He paced backwards and said, 'You guys stay where you are.'

'But the host said we have to complete this *together*,' protested Keix.

Seyfer frowned. 'Think about how the riddle is phrased. "Four is all you need to pass." What if it's not four people, but four *archways* that we have to get through in order to pass this trial? Obviously, we've exceeded that count going through all those "wrong" ones, but we've not been disqualified, seeing as we're still stuck here.

'So, perhaps the part about completing the trial *together* doesn't have to be interpreted as literally as we think. As long as we work together to figure out the puzzle, we're still conforming to the rules, no?'

'If you put it this way . . . it kind of makes sense?' said Keix, looking as perplexed as Vin had ever seen her.

Seyfer squared his shoulders. 'So, stay put, while I test my theory.' With that, he stepped through the arch that had given them the green light.

The second he disappeared through the archway, it glowed blue, and everyone heard the dreaded clang again. However, instead of affecting

Vin, Keix and Jūn like it had previously, Seyfer was the only one who was penalized. He shouted in anguish and doubled over in pain as he was teleported straight to the centre of the platform.

'Seyfer!' shouted Keix and she rushed to his side, with Jūn right on her heels.

But Vin stood her ground. Her brain went into overdrive. Why didn't it work the second time round? If their task was to endure mental torture to figure out the four archways that they should step through in order to pass this trial, there should have been a bell instead of the clang when Seyfer went through the arch. Unless his theory was wrong, and they had to go through the archways together.

But if that was so, why was Seyfer the only one who was affected by the clanging?

Vin racked her brains. One wrong move and they would have to start from scratch again . . . This development had blunted the fleeting optimism that had had them smiling just moments ago.

'Let *me* test out a theory,' she called to the rest of her team.

Seyfer was trying to get back on his feet, his face still scrunched in pain as he tried to shake off the assault.

'Let me do it,' volunteered Jūn, putting a hand on Seyfer's shoulder. He walked over to Vin. 'What do you need me to do?'

Vin looked at Jūn, surprised that he'd so readily agreed to do her bidding.

'I've never seen anyone take to Tilsor's streets like you did. If I had to pick someone who can lead us to pass this trial, I'll place my bets on you,' said Jūn with a smile.

Vin had to admit that Jūn's smile was cute. *But it's nowhere as dazzling as Mohgen's grin*, thought Vin. *And I feel zero attraction to him. Zilch. Unlike Keix . . .*

In any case, Vin pulled her thoughts back to the present and latched on to something that Jūn had said. Something that was sending a tickle down the back of her mind, as if it were a clue, sitting there in broad daylight, that all of them had overlooked. 'Tilsor!' she exclaimed. 'That could be it!'

'In layman terms, please,' chided Keix gently.

'Let me test out the theory first,' insisted Vin.

'All right,' said Keix, raising a hand at Vin. 'Please stop saying that. Look at how the "theory test" worked out for Seyfer.'

'Thanks for acknowledging my sacrifice,' muttered Seyfer. He was still leaning on Keix for support.

'Okay, look. Let's number these doorways, starting from the one behind me. This'—she pointed backwards—'is one. Then we go in an anticlockwise direction . . . Two, three, four, and so on.'

'We went through doorway six,' continued Vin, now pointing to the arch she was facing, 'and appeared through doorway one.' She gestured to the archway behind her. 'That was our first correct move. Then Seyfer stepped through doorway six again, but he got penalized. So, to test my theory, Jūn, I need you to step through doorway six again too,' said Vin.

'Wait, wh—' started Keix.

But before she could complete her question, Jūn had done as Vin had requested and reappeared through doorway one, a musical ding announcing his arrival back on the platform.

'That's unfair!' cried Seyfer.

Vin's grin was wide when she turned to Keix. 'Do you remember the day when Jūn was attacked? The first day we reached Tilsor?' she asked.

'What's that got to do with this?' Keix frowned, trying to connect the dots.

'Do you remember how we figured out how to get to Ma.erdene's?'

'After a whole lot of wrong right turns. We should have taken the left turn the first time round,' grumbled Keix.

'Yes, by elimination,' said Vin. She couldn't keep the excitement out of her voice. 'And I think that this trial is testing us with a simpler version of the same principle!'

'Simpler?' Keix looked doubtful.

'We need to find out the sequence of archways to go through in order to get out of this arena. Look, let's go back to the beginning again. When we first went through doorway six, it glowed green and we got a ding instead of an Atros-style mental torture, right?' repeated Vin just to make sure everyone was following. 'When Seyfer went through it again, his brain got "clanged"—'

Seyfer made a disapproving noise. 'But Jūn didn't get "clanged", as you put it. Why?'

'Precisely. So, these two experiments proved two things. One, that your'—Vin jerked her head at Seyfer—'theory, that we don't always have to step through the archways as a group, is right. And two, that *my* theory that the slate is reset after we go through the wrong archway is probably right too.'

'So, we'll just have to take turns to run through the doorways and bear with getting our brains "clanged", until we find the correct sequence to get us out of here?' asked Keix, finally grasping what Vin was saying.

Vin confirmed Keix's summarized assessment and gave her friend an apologetic look.

'Well, as Dace would say, "should be a breeze",' said Keix with a wry half-smile.

Jūn turned to Keix. 'You stay here with Vin to memorize the sequence. I'll do the running around,' he said.

'No, it'll be faster if the two of us do it,' insisted Keix.

'Three,' corrected Seyfer. 'Let's get out of this place as soon as possible.'

Within minutes, they had regrouped and started approaching the puzzle systematically. Keix, Jūn and Seyfer took turns to go through the doorways. Every time they met with a clang, they would restart from doorway six.

By the time they figured out the sequence—doorways six, eight, four, then two—it was almost the next morning and all Vin wanted to do was to get back to Ma.erdene's and try to sleep off the nightmares that this trial had resurrected.

As they stepped through the final sequence of archways together (since one person getting it right didn't seem to do the trick), Vin and the gang found themselves in a room facing the host who had welcomed them to the tournament.

'Congratulations on completing the second trial of Taavar,' he said. 'You're the second team to arrive at the third trial of Taavar, which begins immediately.'

15

Pod | Precipice

'How do you think they're faring?' Pod asked, breaking the suffocating silence in the room.

After the glimmering perimeter of the platform had shot up to the sky, transporting Keix and the rest into some secret location for the second trial of Taavar, he had returned to Ma.erdene's with Zej, Dace and Maii, a thick cloud of trepidation hanging over them.

Ever since Keix and the rest completed the first trial of Taavar, the uneasiness gnawing at him had been intensifying.

No matter how he tried to phrase his questions to find out what had happened at the first trial, the spell that bound Keix and the others to never speak of the tournament held fast. So, instead of harping on that, they had celebrated through the night, each as aware as the other of the fleetingness of the moment.

Right now, the mood in the room was downright gloomy.

Zej and Dace had planted themselves at opposite corners of the space, while Maii had moved a stool out into the balcony to sit in silence.

Pod caught her occasionally looking up at the sky, her brow furrowed, as he fiddled with the pieces of paper which he had scattered on the broad, rectangular platform couch. Each piece of paper had sketches and descriptions of the Sections that he had come across so far. And he kept rearranging them to see if there was a formula to predict how the Sections shifted every day. So far, he'd had no luck.

To say that Pod had been bored when he first arrived at Tilsor was an understatement. It was the first time in his life when there was literally nothing for him to do. No computers. No systems to crack. Nothing. The town was just so . . . primitive. They even needed candlelight at night, although if you were outdoors, the glittering stars provided just enough illumination to prevent you from walking into a wall. At times, the stark contrast between Atros and Tilsor made Pod feel like he had entered an inverted world—not just ideologically, but visually too, where the twinkling lights of the streets and buildings in the former were now reflected in the navy-blue sky of this enigmatic town.

Nevertheless, Pod found his fascination for the concept and layout of the town's streets growing with every day he spent here. Like Vin said, there was a new pattern waiting to be uncovered every dusk and dawn, and every new discovery made Pod feel like he was regaining control over his destiny—one that had been slipping out of his grasp ever since he joined Oka. Even if it were an illusion, it helped keep his mind off things that were really out of his control, such as the looming threat of ExA.

So, he had thrown himself into the task of mapping out Tilsor. Both Ma.erdene and Jūn, the Kulcan whom Keix seemed to trust implicitly, had informed him that it was a pointless exercise. Those who wanted to learn to navigate Tilsor simply familiarized themselves with the lay of the land by going around. They memorized unique characteristics of the Sections if they wanted to get around faster, but most people here seemed content to meander along on detours, as if they had all the time in the world—another thing that Pod, who grew up in the efficiency- and purpose-orientated culture of Atros, found peculiar.

'How do you think they're faring?' repeated Pod.

Lost in thought, Dace took a while to respond with a shrug.

'There's no knowing what the second trial of Taavar is, and how long they will need to pass it,' said Zej, as if laying out these facts was some sort of reassurance.

Pod wanted to scream at Zej, grab him by the shoulders and shake him—do anything possible to rattle his outwardly unflappable composure. It was clear that he was worried about Keix and Vin. It was even more obvious that he was jealous of Jūn. But knowing his friend, Pod could tell that he was holding back because he still felt guilty for allowing Keix to be sacrificed during the ritual. Thus, instead of shouting, *would it kill you to be less rational sometimes?* all he did was sigh at his friend's reply.

Deciding that he'd had enough of the tense silence, in a room full of people who were fully capable of holding proper conversations, Pod stood up and grabbed his staff. 'I'm going to take a breather,' he announced. The open air and continuing his quest to map out Tilsor would help take the edge off his worries for the moment, at the very least.

'I'll come with you,' said Maii, picking up the pair of short daggers that she'd been practising with for the past week.

'Ooh, a date,' teased Dace. He grinned when Maii threw him a scowl.

'Get lost,' murmured Pod, although he couldn't contain his smile.

'Make sure you do.' Dace smirked, his ringing laughter following Pod and Maii out of the room.

Making their way down the stairs and out of Ma.erdene's which, during this time of the day, was starting to get busy, Pod and Maii walked in companionable silence through a few Sections.

The night air hummed with a peaceful vibe, and Pod noticed, not for the first time, that the streets seemed particularly deserted at night even as pockets of activity, such as the influx of customers at Ma.erdene's, were prevalent.

'I'd always wondered what Tilsor looked like,' said Maii. Her melodious voice rang through the cool night air, adding another layer of etherealness to the magical streets.

'Does it live up to your expectations?'

'It's . . . a little grittier than I had imagined it to be.' Maii wrinkled her nose.

Pod laughed at her assessment. Under the soft moonlight, her eyelashes cast dramatic shadows against her cheekbones, softening the appearance of her scar. Pod often wondered how she acquired that scar, but he never had the courage to ask.

When Maii turned to him, her eyes smiling, Pod's heartbeat quickened. He belatedly realized that he hadn't had the chance to properly talk to her since the events at *A*. Before she could catch him staring, he cleared his throat and said, 'It's fascinating. To think that I never heard of this place growing up.'

They were approaching another junction now, one that forked into three different paths, and he slowed down to let Maii decide which turn to take. The last five Sections that they had passed had all been empty, and Pod was taking mental notes of the arrangements of the buildings, trying to get a sense of how the streets had shifted after sundown.

'It is. The way it's designed to evoke confusion if you're not paying enough attention. The way none of Atros's weapons work here,' said Maii, melancholic.

Pod wanted to comfort her, but he wasn't sure what to say, so he let the lull stretch on.

When they opted to walk through the pathway in the centre, they emerged into a Section that Pod had come across a couple of days ago. On a whim, he said, 'Let me show you something.' He led Maii to the tallest building in the area.

The structure was squarish and about eight storeys tall—twice the number of levels compared to Ma.erdene's, and it had a gently sloping roof. Like many buildings in Tilsor, it looked abandoned, and nothing except its height stood out. Yet, there was something about it that had intrigued Pod, so he had walked around its perimeter and discovered rungs on the side of the structure that allowed him to climb on to the rooftop.

He'd initially thought that he would be able to look into an adjoining Section from the higher vantage point, but the way the structures were arranged made it impossible to see farther than a couple of buildings away. So, instead, all he got was a scenic view that refused to reveal the secrets of Tilsor.

'What do you think?' asked Pod, helping Maii up on to the roof. 'Thought you'd enjoy the night view.'

On impulse, he decided to lie down on the roof and gaze at the night sky. He was pleasantly surprised when Maii sat next to him and did the same.

'I haven't had a chance to look up at the skies like that in so long. Atros was always too . . .'

'Busy? Bright?' ventured Pod.

Maii made a sound in agreement as she continued observing the sky.

Once again, silence reigned and Pod found his eyes straying to Maii. When he saw that she was frowning, he asked lightly, 'What's wrong? The view's not to your liking?'

'To be honest, the stars look a little out of place,' admitted Maii. 'It feels like they've been frozen in place.' At Pod's inquiring look, she continued, 'Stars move all the time, on a set path. We, Ifarls, believe that only when something momentous is about to happen will the stars veer from their usual path. And the way these stars are arranged—

they remind me of a night sky I saw in a book, ages ago, when I was a little girl.'

'Wow. You started reading the stars since young? And you actually remember how they are arranged in the skies?' Pod couldn't keep the awe out of his voice. When Maii didn't reply immediately, he said, 'Well, it figures, since you Ifarls have that "light of stars guiding the way" saying.'

Pod scratched his head. 'Come to think of it, did you feel a little strange, hearing the host say that before the trials started?'

'Perhaps. Though it could just be an old saying that got passed down,' said Maii after some consideration.

'I've never heard it before,' said Pod. He laced his fingers behind his head to make himself more comfortable. 'How old were you when you first started studying the stars?'

'Seven. We start school—similar to the institutions that you Atrossians attend—at that age,' said Maii. 'I've never seen this particular pattern of stars before, except in my textbooks.' She raised a hand and traced a series of random lines in the sky. 'It feels odd, like we've gone back in time.'

Pod wanted to ask Maii if she could go back in time, when would she choose to return to? But instead, he found himself asking, 'Do you think you'll ever get your powers back?' The question had made its way out of his mouth before he had a chance to consider whether it was appropriate.

Maii closed her eyes and took a slow, deep breath. For moments, there was only the sound of her breathing. 'I . . . I don't know.' She sucked in another lungful of air and continued, 'My powers returned for a split second when I was at A.'

'What?!'

Maii nodded. 'Just for that instant, since the ritual, my life was filled with colours again.'

Pod waited for her to elaborate, but she remained lost in her thoughts, the hurt spilling out of her glittering eyes. He knew that she was drawing on all her courage, perhaps more, to confide in him, so he didn't press her to say more.

Maii had always kept to herself, never revealing more than hints of what she felt. The way she would press her lips together to suppress a smile. The sparkle in her eyes when she was amused. The fiery look she reserved for times when she was annoyed. Her every micro expression captured his heart. So, he waited. Because he knew that she would come to terms with it in her own time. That, if he was patient, she would eventually open up to him.

'I'm sorry I used you. All of you. I believed that it was for the greater good.' Her voice was small. Then, as if the shame of admitting the selfishness of her race had finally eaten her up, she continued, 'For the Ifarls.'

Pod sighed and looked up at the inky sky. 'I joined Oka because I needed their help and resources to find Keix. It was thrilling at first, playing undercover. But as I uncovered more of Atros's secrets, the excitement turned to angst and then fear.

'I found myself constantly looking over my shoulder, wondering whom to trust. Is the person I'm crossing paths with someone who knew that I was hacking into Atros's systems to look for confidential files and information? What if the person sitting in my line of sight was on a stake out, just waiting for me to slip up?' said Pod. He didn't know why he was telling Maii all this. Perhaps he felt that if he confided more in her, she would do the same too.

'It was . . . a lot to bear. If it hadn't been for Keix, I might have gone AWOL altogether. Although I'm not sure where I would have gone. Now I know. Tilsor doesn't seem so bad,' he joked with a smile, trying to lighten the mood.

'Keix is lucky to have a friend like you. So is Zej.'

The mention of Zej made a lump appear in Pod's throat and his grin wavered. 'I guess what I'm saying is, you never quite know what something feels like until you experience it yourself.'

As the words left his lips, a bubble of anxiety and excitement rose from the pit of his stomach. It was then that he knew in his gut that he'd never get a chance like this to confess his feelings to Maii.

So beneath the blanket of stars, in the temporary absence of 'bigger picture' distractions, with only the sound of the rise and fall of their breaths that had somehow synced in this miraculous moment, he turned to Maii and said, 'After all this is done, will you work out a new path together with me?

'We can explore Tilsor. You can teach me the things you've learnt. We can do our own . . . I don't know . . . research'—Pod waved his hand awkwardly—'and find out about things on our own terms. No more getting force-fed narratives that we didn't ask for. No more talk of the greater good. Just . . . the two of us.'

On impulse, Pod reached out and covered Maii's hand with his. A warm, tingling sensation spread out from where their skin touched, and Pod's heart soared when Maii didn't snatch her hand away.

She nibbled her lips as she considered his words. After a long pause, she withdrew her hand gently and admitted, 'I've never felt that way towards anyone. I . . . don't know if I'll like you . . . in a romantic way. I've never thought about it . . . seriously.'

'So, the thought has crossed your mind before—just not in a serious way,' said Pod, his voice teasing, his impish smile filled with relief and joy.

Maii gave an imperceptible nod.

Pod sat up in excitement. He had to stop himself from jumping up in jubilation. Maii was aware of his feelings towards her now, and she would consider him. This was the best news he'd received in ages. But he was afraid of frightening her away if he appeared overenthusiastic, so he tried to keep his voice neutral as he asked, 'Will you think more about it, more seriously?'

'It sounds tempting . . . to find our own narrative,'

Maii's smile was small, but it held all the promise in the world for Pod.

'I'll take your word then.' Pod looked away, suddenly bashful, and grinned at the inky sky. He decided that it didn't matter whether or not the stars in Tilsor were on the right path or had strayed. The only thing that mattered was that they'd witnessed his confession. He tried to count them, to trace the arcs and shapes that Maii had shown him, but whatever message they held, it was clear that it was in a language as yet foreign to him.

As the moon moved through the sky, Pod thought he finally understood why Maii had said something was 'off' about the stars, about how they hadn't moved an inch. However, he didn't have time to analyse this anomaly because some movement at the corner of the Section caught his attention.

The two of them slid soundlessly to the edge of the roof and peered down at the street. A chill settled deep into Pod's bones when he saw figures in black, just like the ones they had encountered on their way to Tilsor, marching along the pathways.

'Do you have any idea where you're going?' one of the figures jeered.

'It looks like you're taking us around in circles,' quipped another.

'Shut up and just follow along,' said the soldier at the front of the group irritably. 'I've been here for a month. Even if I'm bringing you in circles, I still know the way better than any of you.'

His colleagues continued to grumble in low voices, but they did as he commanded.

Where were they going and why are there ExA soldiers in Tilsor? thought Pod. He turned to Maii and whispered, 'Do you remember the way back to Ma.erdene's?'

Maii nodded, gesturing to Pod that they should get back to the street level.

'Good. We'll split up. I'll follow them and see what they're up to. You get back to Ma.erdene's and warn the rest.' Pod shimmied down the building after Maii, who hesitated at his suggestion.

'Is that a good idea? To split up?' Maii landed silently on the pathway that the black-clad figures had just left.

Pod took a measured breath. 'It's almost dawn. The streets will move again soon, and we might not be able to warn the others in time if we don't split up now.'

'But if . . .' Maii's question hung in the air. It was easy to get lost in Tilsor, and they had no means of communicating with each other once they separated.

Pod felt warmth emanating from his heart at Maii's concern. 'Once I find out what they're up to, I'll get back as soon as possible,' he assured her.

Maii cast her eyes downwards, then nodded. 'Stay safe. I'll see you back at Ma.erdene's.'

Pod watched as she disappeared through the archway from which they had arrived. Then, he turned away to take the left fork down the path, stalking after the ExA group. He stepped through to the next Section just as the last silhouette disappeared through another arch.

When the sky lightened, Pod noticed that the leading soldier became more unsure of where he was going. A couple of times, the group circled back to the same Sections they had just recently passed by.

It was a testament to Pod's memory that he had every turn memorized in order to make a quick escape. But he couldn't shake off the feeling that someone was following him. He didn't know how far he'd gone into Tilsor, but he could hear the town awakening. Sounds of bustling activity resumed in the Squares, and the fragrant blend of savoury and sweet aromas permeated the air.

When the group finally slowed down, Pod gathered that they must have reached the outskirts of Tilsor.

He remembered the first time he stepped into the city. The sudden appearance of Tilsor as the name of the city came to mind. The sensation of having a blanket of vibrations coating him, clinging to his skin like an invisible veil before dissipating. In his peripheral vision, he had noticed a blurring out of the world outside of Tilsor. This very same hazy effect manifested in this particular Section.

There was only a handful of buildings in this Section, the largest one being a squarish, single-storeyed structure by the side of the street.

Pod was shocked to see dozens of ExA soldiers trooping in and out of it. What was ExA doing in Tilsor? Were they preparing to attack the town? What were they looking for? Had Atros truly fallen?

Pod's heart was in his throat. He needed to hurry back to the rest to let them know what he had seen.

In his haste to get out of this Section and back to Ma.erdene's, he tripped over a rock and sent it skittering down the path, and pitched forward. Several ExA soldiers, who had been hanging outside the building, turned in the direction of the noise.

Dread washed over Pod. He wasn't sure if he should pretend that he was passing by or pick up his feet and get the hell out of the Section. When he stood back up and saw a couple of the soldiers walking towards him, he panicked. And he ran, possessed with an urgency he had never felt before, as the troopers behind him shouted for him to stop.

Pod gauged the distance to the fork. A dozen more steps. Ten. Five. Two. He would have to outrun the soldiers if he were to stand a chance of shaking them off. Just as he was about to cross through the archway, a thick cord encircled his ankle and he found himself getting jerked back. He threw out his hands to break his fall and dropped his weapon. But because his reaction wasn't fast enough, he landed face down on the ground.

Pain shot through him. It felt like someone had rammed a brick into his nose, breaking it. Blood spurted out and trickled down his face into his mouth. He must have blacked out for a moment, because he suddenly couldn't see a thing. He felt a strong hand grip his collar and haul him up, and he heard a tsk tsk.

The next thing he knew, someone had gagged him and put a sack over his head. Both his arms were then secured in vice-like grips as his captors steered him towards an unknown destination.

Any trace of hope that Pod had had vanished in an instant. Even if he could escape from these people, it might take forever to find his way back to Ma.erdene's.

All he could do was pray that Maii had managed to get away unscathed to warn Zej and the rest of ExA's presence in Tilsor.

As his captors half-dragged, half-marched him around, he kept his ears peeled for any movement or snatches of conversation that could come of use later on. But there was nothing except for the shuffling of feet and the pounding of his heart as his captors went about their task without a word.

Eventually, Pod was shoved against something solid. His hands were then twisted behind him and it seemed like the ExA soldiers were tying him to a pillar to prevent him from escaping.

Engulfed in darkness, Pod focused on the only glimmer of light that he could see in his mind: the image of Maii's tentative smile and what she'd said about carving out their own narrative.

16

Keix | Replay

'Hell, no,' cursed Keix. She wondered if she ought to have said hell, yes? Because the moment the host disappeared in a flash of blinding light after his purported 'welcome address', the room had shifted into her personal purgatory. There was no warning, no stating of rules, nor a riddle to solve.

This was a setting that she had grown all too familiar with.

The complete darkness. The unmoving atmosphere. The ominous neutrality of it all.

It was the scene that had haunted her sleep for weeks.

But she wasn't asleep now—a fact of which she was certain.

She forced the rising anxiety back down her churning stomach and focused on analysing her current predicament.

Vin, Seyfer and Jūn were nowhere to be seen. Keix's best guess was that they had been transported into a dimension that was a manifestation of their worst nightmare. So, was the goal of the third trial of Taavar to overcome one's fears?

Worry gnawed at Keix. Did Vin and Jūn, like her, have time to prepare for the confrontation? Or had they been thrown into the thick of their trials, left to drown in distress?

Only when she tasted the tang of iron did she realize that she had been chewing the inside of her cheek. Gathering her wits, she nodded to herself. Her worry for her friends was pointless if she remained where she was. Just like the second trial, the only way to get out of this was through it.

She squared her shoulders and gripped the hilt of her sword. Eleven. It was always on the eleventh step that the spectre impersonating her mum would appear with the ghost troop.

Regardless of whether she needed it, she had that amount of time to mentally ready herself for the assault that would follow.

She lifted her right foot and took a tentative step. As expected, the echo was deafening against the silence. What she hadn't predicted, though, was an ethereal glow that appeared in her line of sight. And with the light came a familiar figure that Keix never thought she would see again. No. She'd seen this figure all too many times, in as many reincarnations as she could've imagined, and as terrifying as she had dared to envisage.

Except never in this way—clad in the clothes that Keix had last seen her in, kind eyes filled with affection and one corner of her mouth turned up in a smile that conveyed tolerance, adoration and amusement all at once. A smile that was reserved solely for Keix.

'Mother?' Keix's heart swelled even though she knew at the back of her mind that this was an illusion.

Her mother's smile widened, and she held out her arms.

Keix hesitated at the invitation. Her fingers, which had been scratching the hilt of her sword absentmindedly, reached up to touch the charm hanging around her neck only to remember that she'd left it with Zej and Dace. What was it that people said about hope? That it's something only fools cling to when all is lost?

But Jūn's words, when he had chided her for accepting too easily what she had been told, crossed her mind like a gentle reprimand; words which had been spoken under the haze of his pain, *You should learn . . . to think for yourself.*

Perhaps it was this reminder, the shock at seeing her mother, or the mental battering that she'd had to endure during the second trial. Or a cumulation of all three, that unlocked the memory of the day she was informed of her mother's death.

Keix remembered two Atros troopers turning up at her door that fateful day after she'd returned from school. They had stood outside her house, stiff and proper as troopers on duty were taught to be, and broken to her the news of her mother's death. They told her something about black-hole rounds and how Keix wouldn't be able to see her mother again—not even her body. Frozen with shock, Keix stood, stony-faced, oblivious to everything except the tightening of her throat, the ache at the back of her jaw and her shallow breathing, while every single coherent thought left her.

The troopers escorted her in a hovercar to an institution in the city centre for orphans. It was her first time on board such a vehicle, but instead of marvelling at the novelty of the experience, she had sat hunched, clutching her backpack which contained two sets of clothes. In her bag was also the only letter from her father that had come with the necklace— both of which her mother had passed on to her on her eleventh birthday, just days ago.

Anyone who had seen her that day might have deduced that she was in shock. But no one would have known that her heart was squeezed tightly, crumpled by an invisible hand.

'I miss you.' The words spilled out as she looked at the image of her mother, still standing with her arms outstretched. A tear fell from her eye. Then another. The flood of tears she'd wanted to shed but never came all at once.

If Keix were to be truthful with herself, she'd acknowledge that she never let herself feel true joy since she lost her mother. She'd laughed. She'd had fun. She'd felt bouts of sadness, annoyance and thrill. And she'd been rebellious too, just like all teenagers her age had been. Every passing second, hour and day had been but a gauze placed layer upon layer, burying the hope that her mum would appear before her someday. It was a mass of irrationality that she carried with her, never seen, but always felt.

As if her mother could read her thoughts, her smile faltered and she bit her lip, her eyes shining.

Before Keix realized it, she had thrown herself into her mother's arms even as she told herself, *It's just an illusion.* She should have run right through her mother—the projection, the hologram, the image, whatever you wanted to call it—and fallen flat on her face. But instead, a pair of arms encircled her, and she could almost smell the scent of freshly laundered clothes that she had always associated with her mum.

The temperature dipped. It wasn't the kind of chill that cut deep into one's bones; it felt like a cool breeze wafting across her skin, chasing the hot, suffocating air from her.

Keix lifted her face and saw that her mother was fading.

'No,' she pleaded.

Her mum smiled and said something. Even though Keix couldn't hear the words, she felt them form in her heart.

My girl.

The words coaxed the weight that Keix had been carrying away, and moulded it into the core of her being as her mother disappeared. In that moment, Keix knew that she no longer had to hold on to the grief as if it were a burden she couldn't bear. She had accepted that this sorrow was part of who she was—and that as long as she lived, it would never cease to exist.

* * *

A second may have passed. A minute. An hour. It didn't matter to Keix. All she knew was that she sat sobbing, letting the tears drain away the tension in her body.

'Keix?' A familiar voice called and Keix felt someone grasp her shoulders firmly. When she didn't answer, she was gathered into a gentle embrace.

Keix melted into the hug and let the person's warmth envelop her. She turned her head and rested her ear on his chest and let his solid heartbeat bring her back to the present.

When her sobs softened and subsided, she extracted herself from the person's arms and let him help her up. As her vision cleared, she saw Jūn staring at her unblinkingly, a mixture of worry, relief and concern in his eyes.

'Thank you,' she said, thinking back to how the memory of his words had given her the courage to acknowledge her true feelings in the nightmare that she had just conquered.

When Jūn remained silent, staring at her with an indecipherable expression, Keix suddenly felt self-conscious. She hastily brushed away the tear stains on her face and was about to ask him if he had seen anyone else when he raised his hands and cupped her face gingerly.

Keix's mind blanked as Jūn's dark eyes drew her in. In his irises, she could see a clear reflection of the full moon, which seemed to hold an unspoken promise.

Jūn's hands trembled slightly as he reached his thumbs to Keix's eyes. In reflex, she closed them and felt the pads of his fingers brush across her wet eyelashes, following the subtle arc of her eyelids, outwards from the inner corner. She surrendered to the hypnotic featherlight touches as Jūn repeated the motion, until he'd dried her tears.

When his thumbs finally came to rest at her temples, Keix couldn't tell if the heat she felt on her cheeks were from his palms or the other way around.

The air shifted as a touch of warm breath skimmed over her lips. She didn't have to open her eyes to know that Jūn had bent his head and that their faces were almost touching. At this proximity, she could feel his body heat. The day-old, piquant aroma of the bathwater she had grown accustomed to, tinged with the faint salty, musky smell of his sweat pervaded the air between them.

The memory of what Dace had said about Jūn's interest in her came to mind and Keix's heart raced when she realized his intentions. Was he going to kiss her? She stiffened. She knew that she ought to break the spell, but a part of her didn't know for sure if she wanted to.

The ticking seconds felt like an eternity to Keix, as she wondered whether Jūn would ever close the distance between them—if he placed his lips on hers, would she respond by sinking into it? Somehow, she knew that he was holding back, waiting for her to make the decision.

With great resolution, Keix pulled back and peeked at Jūn. When she saw disappointment flash in his eyes, she felt the urge to apologize.

But Jūn beat her to it. 'I'm . . . sorry,' he said, his voice husky with emotion as he let his arms fall to his sides. 'I couldn't control myself.'

Keix's eyes widened. She thought of how she'd left Atros on a whim, and all the impulsive decisions she'd made so far. If Jūn lacked self-control, then what did that make her?

'I'm a—all right now,' she stuttered and took a step back. The change in topic was graceless, but in her heart, she knew that if she couldn't identify her relationship with Zej, she had no business leading Jūn on.

Sensing the shift in the mood, Jūn ruffled her hair and patted her head.

'In your own time,' he said, with an understanding smile.

Keix returned a tentative and grateful smile. 'Have you seen the others?' she asked, trying to haul her focus back to the trial.

Jūn shook his head. 'Just you.'

Keix cleared her throat. Her question was stupid. If Jūn had seen Vin and Seyfer, the three of them would have been here together. She wiped her sweaty palms on her robe. 'Do you think they're . . .' *dead? disqualified? all right?* She didn't quite know how to complete her question.

'I think they'll be all right,' said Jūn. He hesitated before adding, 'I was fighting in the previous dimension, but when I awoke, I didn't have any wounds.'

'You were hurt? Where?' asked Keix, scanning him from head to toe to confirm his words. Her assumption that Jūn had been transported somewhere else before he arrived here was right. This could only mean that Vin and Seyfer were trapped in other dimensions, battling their own demons.

'I'm fine. Don't worry. Where do you think we are?' asked Jūn.

Keix didn't press him for details on his personal trial because she felt that it would be rude if Jūn shared his story and she didn't. The encounter with her mother had lifted a weight off her, but she wasn't sure if she was ready to talk about it.

She racked her mind to find an answer to Jūn's question. Hadn't both of them passed their tests, if the third trial of Taavar was for them to confront and overcome their worst fears? So why were they still stuck in this strange dimension?

She swept her eyes around, registering her surroundings for the first time. There were no standout features in the vicinity. The trees looked unremarkable—not too tall, not too thin, not too bare, nor too lush—and the ground was level, its terrain, uniform and boring.

'It looks like the woods outside Atros. The trees look so . . . similar, yet wrong. There seems to be a sepia cast over everything. And it's too quiet. Do you think we're still in the third trial?' asked Keix.

Jūn nodded.

'What do you think is the goal of this trial?'

Jūn shrugged. 'I have no idea. But let's walk?' he suggested. 'It's how I found you. Perhaps we might find Vin and Seyfer, or a way out.'

Keix nodded. They started meandering through the strange forest in silence, each absorbed in their own thoughts. Perhaps it was the unfamiliar environment, or the lack of ambient sounds and scents, but every element in this dimension felt off. Just like in her nightmare, everything was too still, too dissociated.

She couldn't shake off the unsettling feeling crawling on her skin. Her senses were on high alert, and she almost hit Jūn when he suddenly grabbed her elbow and steered her behind a thicket on the side of the path.

'What's wrong?' she whispered.

Jūn put a finger on his lips, then inclined his head and tapped his ear.

Keix stilled and listened. She could hear hurried footsteps heading towards them from a fair distance away. Minutes later, she saw a man who looked to be in his thirties making his way down the path. He was dressed in a plain white robe that hung loosely on his slight frame. His brow was furrowed and his hands kept gesticulating as he murmured to himself and kept looking up at the sky.

There was something about him that reminded Keix of the old man in white whom they had encountered in the Square on their first day in Tilsor. But the age was all wrong. And she had seen neither this man nor the elderly man at any of the trials. There was also this unnatural brownish cast enveloping him that made her deduce that he was a part of this dimension and a simulation.

Follow him? Keix mouthed to Jūn, who gave a quick nod.

The two of them moved soundlessly after the man and he soon led them to a hut in the middle of a clearing.

Keix and Jūn were still hiding behind the trees and they watched as the man entered the dwelling. Seconds later, a despairing howl rang out from the hut.

This was the first sound that Keix had heard in this dimension besides Jūn's voice. The raw emotion in the cry sent a chill into her bones.

She wanted to rush towards the hut but was forestalled by Jūn.

'Wait,' he said, his voice low, 'we don't know if it's a trap.'

Jūn could well be right. But Keix had a bad feeling about this. 'What if the goal of the third trial is to help him?' She gestured to the hut.

Jūn didn't loosen his grip on her elbow. 'There's another person heading this way too.'

Keix strained her ears again and could just about hear a faint flurry of footsteps. A pure Kulcan's hearing was sharp indeed.

'All the more reason that we should barge in right now. What if this new person gets to rescue the man before us? We'll lose the tournament!' She pushed Jūn's hand away and raced to the hut.

At that exact moment, the man in the white robe ran out of the door, his eyes ablaze and wild. He closed his eyes, tilted his head back and raised his hands. When his lips moved, Keix felt the air shudder. One second it was still, and the next, it was rushing towards him.

Keix watched, transfixed on the two vortexes forming above the man's upturned palms. As they grew in size, so did her sense of foreboding. Perhaps she should run and ram herself into the man to stop him from doing whatever it is he was doing. Perhaps she should grab Jūn and head in the opposite direction, away from where she was certain the tornado of chaos was going to hit.

But somehow, deep inside, she knew that there was nothing she could do to stop the chain of events. It was too late. And she could sense that Jūn knew it too, because he stood beside her, unmoving.

Both of them felt it—the second the vortexes reached their crescendos. The tension snapped and the air was sucked out of the atmosphere. Rushing into the vacuum were things that Keix never thought she would see again—glowing orbs of every colour. Ghosts.

In that moment, she realized why there had been a strange familiarity to the scene unfolding before her. It was a simulation of a story that she had heard not long ago. A story of deceit, destruction and decimation of the barrier between the world of the living and the one of the dead. And the man whom they had followed to this spot was Iv't, the Ifarl who had opened the portal and unleashed vengeful spirits into their dimension.

But the portal had been closed, reasoned Keix. This was nothing but a replication of the scene. Why—of all things, of all scenarios, why did the third trial of Taavar re-enact Iv't's story? More importantly, what was the goal of this trial? To stop Iv't? To defeat him? To help him? What has any of this got to do with stopping ExA?

Keix gasped when she finally put two and two together. The person whom Seyfer sought was Iv't! What had Seyfer said? An ally. An Ifarl with powers stronger than Zenchi's. A person who could grant the winner of the tournament a wish as they deemed fit . . .

How could Ifarls grant wishes? Using their powers of compulsion? And Iv't was dead, wasn't he?

Keix reorganized her thoughts. Come to think of it, Rold hadn't said anything about Iv't's fate after he opened the portal. Everyone assumed that he'd gone mad and died since he vanished after that.

But Keix didn't have the luxury of time to run through all the scenarios and possible explanations in her head. The globes were now floating towards her.

She turned to Jūn. She hadn't known him before the portal was closed, so while it seemed like yet another one of many stupid questions that she'd posed to him today, she had to ask, 'Have you fought ghosts before?'

Jūn raised an eyebrow and drew his sword. 'Of course.'

At his confident reply, Keix pulled out her weapon too. Then she froze. Wait. She had never fought ghosts with a sword before. Could Jūn's blade touch the paranormal beings?

Atros troopers were taught to avoid contact with ghosts at all costs because the spectres' touch debilitated them. Their modus operandi had always been to keep their distance, fire black-hole rounds and cast nets at their incorporeal opponents. She cursed her reliance on Atros's weapons.

The only time she could fight ghosts with her bare hands was after her escape from Atros, when Seyfer had sent them after her. She remembered how the spark of power at the back of her mind had been 'charged' by touching the spectres, and how she'd used this energy against the phantoms. However, since the closing of the portal, she no longer had that ability.

Keix glanced down at the sword that she was holding. If she couldn't fight the ghosts with it, would her powers come back if she touched these paranormal beings in this dimension?

She squared her shoulders for the confrontation, half-eager, half-apprehensive. Fighting was something that came to her naturally. It would take her mind off the amount of thinking that she'd had to do in recent days.

Nevertheless, as with all things in the Taavar dimension, Keix's prediction was way off base. She watched in horror as Jūn swung his sword at the first glowing orb that came within his reach—and missed.

Technically, he didn't miss. Jūn's precision with the blade was second to none. But instead of taking the ball of light out, the sword passed through it as if it were nothing but air.

Jūn's astonishment at the turn of events was written all over his face, and as the orb closed the distance between them, his eyes narrowed and he braced himself for the contact.

Keix was so focused on Jūn's fight that she didn't notice another ghostly globe approaching her.

'Keix, look out!' warned Jūn, ignoring the fact that he was also in danger.

Both of them braced for the mental anguish that they expected would follow at the wraith's touch, but it never came. Instead, in a flash of light, all the ghostly orbs disappeared. Keix and Jūn were still standing at the same spot, hidden behind the trees. From the corner of her eye, Keix saw someone hurrying towards the clearing—Seyfer. It must have been his footsteps that they had heard just now. Had he seen the ghosts too?

Keix was still contemplating whether to alert Seyfer to her and Jūn's presence or to remain hidden and quiet when something even more unexpected occurred. Iv't reappeared, hurrying into the hut like before and his howl of anguish resounded through the air again.

Déjà vu overcame Keix and she looked questioningly at Jūn, who returned her look of confusion.

What was going on?

* * *

After watching the person—phantom?—enter the hut for the third time, Keix, Jūn and Seyfer started to understand the 'rules' of this segment of the tournament: come into contact with the ghosts and the entire simulation would be reset to the part before Iv't entered the hut.

Jūn and Seyfer listened with rapt attention as Keix summarized the Ifarl legend that she had heard from Rold. She also shared with them her deduction that this man was likely Iv't.

What was worse: living in another man's nightmare or being in one's own private hell? Keix couldn't decide. But she was sure that if they didn't find a way out of this, they would be stuck in this never-ending loop forever. A shiver crept up her spine. Jūn had said that those who'd joined Taavar had either died or gone missing. How many people exactly were trapped in this dreamscape?

'How did you get out of the previous dimension? Mine kept . . . repeating until I . . . accepted and confronted my fears,' said Jūn.

Articulating this seemed to have the effect of lifting the lid of a mystery box that contained Seyfer and Keix's unvoiced thoughts.

'Me too,' said Seyfer. His tone was controlled, and his expression, dark.

'Me too,' echoed Keix. She was curious about Seyfer's worst fears. After all, if she could understand him a bit better, she might be able to find something to exploit should the situation come to a head. Still, she stopped herself from asking. Seyfer had been cooperative since the beginning. If they needed to get out of this alive, there were some lines that she shouldn't cross for now.

'So, should we try to convince him to accept the inevitable?' asked Keix.

Seyfer gave a small nod and Jūn said, 'We'll never know unless we try.'

So, when Iv't came into view again, Keix plucked up her courage and approached him.

'Sir?' she called.

The man paused in mid-step and turned to them. A flash of suspicion replaced the thoughtful look in his eyes.

'You are . . .' Keix found herself at a loss for words.

'You're stuck in a nightmare. The only way out of this is to confront your fears. To . . . accept them,' said Seyfer, stepping in.

Keix hadn't considered what Iv't's reaction to this direct approach would be, but the moment the words left Seyfer's lips, Iv't's polite, yet wary, demeanour was immediately replaced with hostility.

Iv't pushed past the three of them and ran towards the hut.

Keix and the guys were hot on the Ifarl's heels. The door to the dwelling burst open, and the three of them finally witnessed the sight that had driven Iv't mad.

The unassuming exterior of the humble hut belied the chaotic scene within. What Keix imagined used to be a small and cosy space was now a wreckage. Tables and chairs had been smashed and overturned. Ripped and destroyed décor and furnishings were strewn around. But the most chilling sight was the splatter of blood on the walls and every open surface. A body with long and deep gashes, limbs bent at odd angles, slumped over a couch.

'What have you done?' whispered Iv't, turning to them.

The horror, desolation, anger and disbelief mangling his features made Keix back away. As she crossed the threshold of the hut, she saw Iv't raise both his hands again.

Knowing that it was only a matter of time before the ghosts re-appeared to rush them, Keix, Seyfer and Jūn turned and ran from the Ifarl.

'What now?' asked Keix.

'We run,' replied Jūn, leading them away from the hut as air rushed towards the abode.

'Run?' Seyfer sounded unconvinced at Jūn's plan, even though he was following along.

Keix understood Seyfer's reservations. If they were touched by the ghosts, they could start on a clean slate and try another strategy like approach Iv't in a different manner or stop him from entering the hut. So why should they run?

'Run,' confirmed Jūn, 'Let's try to let the scenario play out and see what happens. Remember to avoid the ghosts at all costs. Otherwise, we might be stuck in the first few minutes of this rerun forever.'

What Jūn said seemed to make sense too, but because of their initial hesitation, they didn't manage to make it out of the clearing outside the hut before they heard pattering footsteps behind them.

Keix, who couldn't resist the urge to turn around to see how close Iv't had gotten to them, missed a step and found herself pitching forward. She threw out her hands to break her fall. By the time she got back to her feet, Iv't was barely a couple of steps away from her and getting closer. Dozens of glowing orbs floated behind and around him.

Keix's heart plummeted. It wasn't Iv't's proximity nor the ghostly orbs that made her freeze. It was the man's eyes. Gone was the bleakness that she'd seen previously. In its place was utter boredom and disdain, glinting in luminous yellow eyes that were blinding at this proximity.

Memories came rushing back. She could almost taste the intense anger and contempt that she'd had for the world and everything it held in that short duration when she was a hybrid.

It took a few moments for her brain to get up to speed simply because she couldn't believe what she was seeing. Was Iv't . . . the first hybrid?

17

Maii | Crumbling Fissures

'Pod's been caught by ExA!' shouted Maii as she burst into the room that Zej and Dace were in.

It had taken all her resolve to turn away after Pod had been caught by the ExA troops. Maii had promised him that she would return to Ma.erdene's directly, but she'd had a niggling feeling that something bad was about to happen. Thus, she'd turned back to stalk him at a distance. If she hadn't listened to her instincts . . .

'What?' Zej and Dace jumped up from where they were seated at opposite corners of the room and ran towards her.

'Where are they now?' asked Zej.

'I'm not sure,' said Maii. 'But I remember how to get to the building where they're keeping Pod. If we leave now, I think we can make it to him before the sun rises.'

The sky was lightening now. Maii wanted to help Pod with his little project of mapping out Tilsor, so she had been memorizing all the turns that they had taken once they left Ma.erdene's. Because of this, she had managed to make her way back to the bathhouse with little difficulty.

Dace picked up his sword and moved towards the door.

'Wait . . .' called Zej.

Maii and Dace whipped around.

'What are you waiting for?' demanded Dace, incredulous.

'How many of them are there?' Zej's brows were snapped together.

Maii did a quick count based on what she could recall of the scene. The soldier with the whip who captured Pod, two others who hauled him into the building, and . . .

'At least two dozen . . .' she said, realizing the reason for Zej's hesitation.

On their way to Tilsor, the five of them—Zej, Dace, Pod, Seyfer and herself—had had difficulties fighting off just four ExA soldiers. How could the three of them take on over twenty ExA troopers?

'We don't have to go head-to-head with them. But at the very least, shouldn't we try to make sure that Pod's all right?' Dace's agitation was clear from the way he raised his voice.

When Zej still seemed reluctant to rush headlong into a potentially dangerous situation, Dace looked even more incensed. He grabbed Maii's arm and said, 'Let's go.'

Just as they stepped out of the room, Zej picked up his sword and followed them to the door.

Ma.erdene, who had probably heard Maii tearing up the stairs, was standing just outside their room, arms crossed, looking stern but concerned. 'What's the matter?' she asked.

Maii and Dace exchanged glances. They were not familiar with the proprietor of the bathhouse despite having sheltered here for a week.

'Where's Pod?' asked Ma.erdene.

Maii knew that Ma.erdene could already guess what had happened. The woman's sharp eyes never missed a single detail.

'Describe them to me. And the place they're at,' commanded Ma.erdene.

Maii hesitated for a brief second before acceding to Ma.erdene's request.

'Go. But don't get yourselves caught too. Find out what you can, then come back. If Jūn and Keix get back before you do, I'll let them know,' said Ma.erdene. 'We'll need a plan, so don't be hasty.'

Maii knew that Ma.erdene's concerns, like Zej's, weren't unwarranted. It was why she had returned to find Zej and Dace instead of trying to rescue Pod on her own. They couldn't get backup, but at the very least, they needed someone to convey the news to Keix and the rest. As for the next step . . . they could only formulate a plan if they knew what they were up against.

Clenching her jaw in determination, Maii nodded to Ma.erdene and led Dace and Zej down the stairs. They raced through the streets, trying to outpace the fading moon.

No one uttered a word throughout the trip. Maii's heart sank when the Sections moved at dawn, but she kept her focus and they eventually managed to make their way to the Section where Pod was being held captive.

Passing through the archway, the three of them almost ran headlong into a group of soldiers who were standing by the wall of the building into which Maii had seen Pod being taken.

'—just the two of them?' asked one of the soldiers.

'Yes, they're in the compound with the one who was captured today,' replied another.

Maii's heart was pounding so hard she stayed deathly still. She feared that at any moment, the soldiers would discover them hiding in the narrow alley into which Dace had yanked them.

'Why are they here, anyway?' asked the first soldier whose voice was a little high-pitched.

'To make sure that those people stay honest,' replied the second soldier.

'Wha—'

A rough voice barked from the gate, interrupting their chit-chat. 'You lot! Stop slacking off. The next batch of soldiers will be here soon.'

The next batch? Maii replayed the conversation in her mind as she exchanged alarmed glances with Zej and Dace.

After the footsteps faded, Zej whispered, 'They're planning to attack Tilsor?'

'But how?' asked Maii. Tilsor's moving Sections were a nightmare to navigate, so it would be hard to plan a proper battle strategy. Plus, as far as she was aware, Tilsor wasn't ruled by any organization. Atros had an army of trained soldiers to protect its city; the Ifarls would give their lives to defend their homeland. Tilsor seemed to comprise of two types of people: those like Ma.erdene, who set up shop here to service the people passing through this stopover town, and the travellers themselves. If ExA were to mount an attack, would these people flee or stay and fight?

'ExA is amassing soldiers here, so it's not far-fetched to say that they want to conquer or take over Tilsor,' said Dace, shutting his eyes in concentration. 'They also said something about two people joining the one who was captured today. And I'm assuming this new prisoner is Pod . . . We should try to rescue them.'

'Are you thinking straight? We'll be dead if we're discovered!' hissed Zej.

'Then what should we do? We can't just—'

A shuffling noise interrupted Maii.

Together with Zej and Dace, Maii sank farther back into the alley until the three of them were leaning against the dead-end wall of the narrow cul-de-sac.

Maii held her breath. She watched as a group of soldiers walked past the alleyway with two civilian captives, a man and a woman, in tow. One trooper was leading the way, while the other four were dragging along their prisoners, who were either unconscious or heavily drugged, and had black fabric bags pulled over their heads. Something about the girl looked familiar, but before Maii could react, she heard Dace gasp and turned around to see him starting forward.

Maii cursed Dace's hot-headedness and her and Zej's delayed reaction. One of the soldiers had turned in their direction and was looking directly into her eyes.

The shadowy alley that had kept them hidden had revealed its secrets under the rapidly brightening skies. Even if none of them had inadvertently given away their hiding place, it would have only taken a tilt of any of the soldier's heads to discover them. There was only one thing left to do now. Making use of the split second of advantage from the soldier's surprise, Maii grabbed her daggers and charged at him.

Zej, who had come to the same conclusion, ran towards the soldiers flanking the man, swinging his sword. The soldiers' reflexes were as quick as the ones who had attacked Zej and his group outside Tilsor. Pushing aside their captive, whose hands were bound behind his back, the two men rushed at Zej, blades as long as their arms extending from their wrists.

Abrasive clangs rang through the air as Maii and Zej engaged the ExA soldiers.

Dace, who was the last to join the fray, sidestepped the action and rushed to yank the head coverings off the prisoners.

'Lana! Dad!' he shouted.

Dace's dad and Lana were here? What did it mean? Were these not ExA soldiers? Was this a trap laid by Seyfer? One of the soldiers had said that they had brought the two prisoners along 'to make sure *those people* stayed honest'—those people could only refer to their group!

Maii couldn't contain her shock and her lapse in focus proved costly as a sharp pain sliced through her arm. She looked down to see a bleeding gash on her forearm. Despite the injury, Maii knew she'd gotten lucky. Because the soldier had mounted their attack too hastily, the cut wasn't deep. However, she was beginning to feel the stinging pain every time she moved her injured arm.

Zej rushed to her side. He fended off another trooper and tried to drive back the remaining four. 'Are you okay?' he asked, his chest heaving with exertion.

Maii nodded, grimacing. 'We have to warn Keix and the rest,' she said. If everything that Seyfer had said in the beginning was a lie, and this was all an elaborate ruse to ensure that they cooperated, Keix, Vin and Jūn could be in big trouble at this very minute. But how were they going to get out of this mess?

Alerted by the scuffling noises, another group of soldiers rushed out of the compound towards them.

'Run!' shouted Maii to Dace. He was trying to support his father and Lana, both slumped over his shoulders, while dodging a soldier's attack.

Maii and Zej were facing four soldiers who'd cornered them. In a last-ditch attempt to secure an escape for one of them—preferably Zej—Maii prepared to leap into the air and launch herself at the soldiers. She angled her body to avoid the blades, but at the last moment, she felt a firm hand grab hold of her arm.

She turned to see Zej looking at her, his eyes filled with complex emotions at the futility of her actions. There was no escape. Even without the two semi-conscious prisoners they had attempted to rescue, the three of them would never be able to hold out against the soldiers swarming them.

Nevertheless, Maii put up a fierce struggle when the two soldiers nearest to her pinned her to the ground, took away her daggers and cuffed her hands behind her back. Dace and Zej were manhandled in the same way. Even as the former kicked and cursed at the soldiers, Zej remained impassive and allowed them to lead him away with little resistance.

When the three of them were dragged through the gates into the large courtyard of the building, she spotted a man tied to one of the columns flanking a corridor. He had a bag over his head, but Maii could tell it was Pod from his build and the clothes he was wearing.

The soldiers tied their new hostages to the columns dotted around the courtyard and discarded the weapons which the new inmates had been carrying into a corner. Maii couldn't help but wonder if perhaps they ought to have waited for Keix and the rest to get back before mounting this botched rescue mission.

Now that the four of them had been captured by the ExA, and Dace's father and Lana were also here . . . what could—would—happen next was anybody's guess.

* * *

Maii watched as night fell in Tilsor. For half a day now, she and her fellow prisoners had been exposed to the relentless sun beating down on them.

Dace's father and Lana had regained consciousness, but because they had been drugged and locked up back in Atros, they didn't have any useful updates about the situation over there.

Maii still couldn't determine if Seyfer had been double-crossing them all along, or if Atros had really fallen to ExA as Seyfer predicted.

The rapid departure of the sun's rays brought with them Maii's hopes of getting out of this convoluted situation alive. She didn't know if her description of the compound to Ma.erdene was detailed enough, if the proprietor of the bathhouse would be worried that they hadn't returned for the entire day, if she was able to locate Keix, Vin, Seyfer and Jūn, or if they'd be able to mount any form of rescue for those of them stuck here.

Just as she'd given up all hope, Maii found herself momentarily blinded by a burst of colours in her vision. Her gaze had been unknowingly fixed on the black bag covering Pod's head. All of a sudden, she saw a purple halo tinged with red and specks of yellow surround Pod. Maii translated the colours—anger, fear, with a touch of worry.

As shocked as she was, she pulled herself together. She'd fantasized about what she would do if she ever felt that spark of power again, playing out an endless number of scenarios in her head. How would she make sure that she got back her Ifarl abilities permanently? What would she give up in exchange? If she couldn't be whole again, would the loss be less devastating the second time?

Still, when it came to the crunch, she knew that all the what-ifs she'd considered were pointless. She knew exactly what she needed to do.

She focused on the thread of power—once a part of her, now just within reach—and she willed herself to pull at it. The touch scorched her, yet the pain was nothing but a second thought as the energy buzzed through her, cold, unyielding, resistant to her command.

It felt all wrong.

She hesitated, but only for a split second. There was no other time when she needed her powers more than at this very moment. So, she wrenched the energy from the atmosphere and felt something give way at long last.

Channelling the power that she'd garnered into a well within herself, she ignored the nausea building in the pit of her stomach. She moulded the energy in a way she had never done before, into a ball and pushed it through her larynx.

'Stop!' Her command rang loud and clear throughout the courtyard. Like the energy that infused a streak of magic into the word, it felt eerily out of tune.

But the moment the note hit the figures in black, they faltered and then ground to a stop.

'You. You. You.' Maii looked at the three black-clad figures standing nearest to her, her gaze shifting from one soldier to the other. 'Release us,' she commanded.

To the shock and amazement of the rest of her team, as well as to Dace's dad and Lana, their captors jumped to do her bidding.

'Hurry,' commanded Maii as the soldiers moved to work on Zej and Pod's knots. Dace, his father and Lana were free now.

Maii stood tall and got ready to project her voice. She could feel the power slipping from her grip and she tugged at the thread of energy in the atmosphere, hanging on to it for dear life. It was the only thing that could get them out of their current predicament.

Once Pod and Zej were released, they grabbed their weapons that the ExA soldiers had carelessly tossed aside. Maii projected her voice across the courtyard. 'Stay, and forget us!' she shouted, feeling the vibrations of the foreign energy escaping her. The pool of power within her was diminishing. Maii pulled at the thread of energy harder. She was going to need to wield more of that heady yet toxic power if they wanted to get out of this mess alive.

Just a little more. Just a little more to make sure that we have enough time to get to Keix and the rest, to formulate a plan to push these soldiers back, she promised herself even as she felt the euphoria and dread intensifying in equal parts within herself. This time, however, she felt the foreign energy slipping away from her. It was as if the cracks in the environment that had allowed the power through were mending themselves, stealing away that last bit of hope that they had at escape.

Maii grabbed a hold of the last vestiges of the power that was seeping away from her fingertips and pulled again, praying that the thread wouldn't give way as she tried to absorb the energy as quickly as possible. Just as they were heading out of the compound's front entrance, she encountered two guards.

Zej, Dace and Pod rushed to engage the two black-clad soldiers. Yet, all Maii could think of was that power. More. She needed more. And so, she yanked harder.

That was when she felt something break.

18

Keix | No Return

Keix was reaching for her sword when Iv't crashed into her, pinning her to the ground. The moment her head hit the soft, sandy earth, she thought she saw the dreamscape flicker.

It must be the impact, or a glitch, that was making everything slow to a crawl, she thought. Her reaction was too sluggish, like Jūn's when he had been poisoned. She could hear her teammates yelling her name in shock and concern, but their voices were also distorted beyond recognition, charged with static.

Yet inside her mind, questions were disappearing as quickly as they formed. She couldn't latch on to any one of them to make sense of her current situation.

Once more, Keix was struck by the disparity between how time was moving for her and how she thought time ought to move. Just as her fingers brushed the hilt of her sword, she sensed something snap and was momentarily blinded by a flash of white-hot light.

The weight lifted from her chest before she regained her sight, but she could smell the change in the air—layered aromas tainted with the stench of rotten eggs.

I'm back in Tilsor? The 'real' Tilsor? Disbelief was written all over Keix's face. She blinked away the orbs obstructing her vision and saw her shock reflected in Jūn and Seyfer's faces. She looked around and the tower emblazoned with the number thirty-three confirmed her suspicions.

They were back in the Square from which they had 'disappeared' for the second trial.

'Have we won?' asked Keix, her voice tentative because she knew it wasn't true. Her gut was telling her that something had gone horribly wrong.

Scattered around the platform were groups of people who looked equally stunned to see them. Keix quickly scanned their faces to see if there was anyone she could recognize, but just then, a blurry shadow flew towards her and enveloped her in a hug.

'Vin . . .' said Keix. The worry for her friend that she'd been suppressing finally turned to relief. *Vin was safe. Vin was safe now,* she told herself as she felt something wet and warm seep into her shirt just below her collarbone where Vin had buried her face.

Keix knew that the ordeal must have affected Vin worse than it had impacted the rest of them. Otherwise, her friend would have been able to walk out of her personal hell and met up with herself, Jūn and Seyfer in Iv't's nightmare. But this was neither the time nor the place to catch up. Keix placed her hands on Vin's shoulders and steadied her.

As Vin tried to get her emotions under control, Keix said, 'We have to get back to Ma.erdene's. I don't know what happened, but I'm pretty sure that we were either pulled out by an unknown force or kicked out of the tournament.'

Her teammates nodded in agreement. All of them had felt the snap that had ripped them out of the dimension in which they had been trapped.

As they moved to one of the Square's exits, Keix noticed other groups of contestants, all wearing the same mixture of excitement, relief, despair and disbelief on their faces, were making their way out of the arena. The instant she stepped past the threshold of Square Thirty-three, Keix's gut told her that something else had happened, or was happening, in Tilsor.

Moments ago, she had seen a group of three, each dressed in red, yellow and black robes respectively, stepping through another of the Square's exits. By Tilsor's logic, the chances of their bumping into each other again was less than zero. Yet, this group of people were now in the same Section as them. The bewilderment in everyone's faces were clear as they realized that the laws of Tilsor were warping right in front of them.

Keix and her friends hurried down the path and stepped through the fork on the left. The red-yellow-black team seemed to have also arrived at the same conclusion as Keix and her gang, so they went through the archway on the right.

Yet . . . both groups still ended up in the same Section.

'Here!' whispered Keix to her teammates. She'd spotted one of the cylindrical teleportation devices hiding in an unobtrusive corner of this Section. Perhaps it would whisk them away from the other contestants, into an emptier area in Tilsor . . .

'Are we going to hide here?' asked Seyfer, stepping into the tube-like structure and shutting the door behind him. 'I thought we're heading back to Ma.erdene's?'

Overcome with anxiety, Keix didn't answer Seyfer's questions immediately. She kept waiting for the gust of whirling wind that she'd experienced before to appear. But after a couple of seconds, she sighed in resignation. 'This is a teleportation device of sorts,' she explained. 'It's supposed to bring us to another random part of Tilsor. But it's not working.'

Vin and Jūn exchanged resolute nods as they stepped out of the building back into the Section. After making their way through two more Sections, it became clear that regardless of what they did and which turn they took, an unknown force was herding them towards a set destination. Without hesitation, Keix flew through the archways, one after another, as fast as her legs could carry her.

There was no point picking and choosing their paths when every one of them was going to lead them to the exact same spot. The only way out, was out.

* * *

After numerous turns, Keix and her team burst into another Square. For a split second, she thought that they had been routed back to Square Thirty-three, from where they came; the size of the current space, the buildings bordering it and the location of the exits were identical.

There were only two differences: the tower indicated that this was Square Thirty-two, and the mayhem that greeted them.

Scuffling noises, shouts and groans rang through the air, interspersed with the clanging and thudding of swords, axes, maces and more.

With her sense of smell turned up to the highest sensitivity, Keix could detect the tang of iron seeping into the open space, where a mass of bodies was engaged in fierce battle.

From where she stood, she saw dozens of black-clad figures with blades protruding from their hands. There were also some holding other types of weapons, such as guns and batons. Dotting this sea of black, which

Keix assumed were ExA soldiers, were fighters in dark-coloured robes of blue, maroon and green, who didn't look like they belonged to any troop or army. What was the reason for this clash? Had ExA invaded Tilsor? Did this mean that Atros had fallen into the hands of their previous leaders who had been exiled?

They hadn't helped Seyfer reach the powerful Ifarl whom he sought; were they too late now?

'What do we do now?' asked Vin.

Keix's first instinct was to fight their way out, but was this battle really something they should get involved in? She forced herself to calm down and think.

'We find a way back to Ma.erdene's,' she said firmly. They needed more information and to regroup if they were to take on ExA. Since no one in her team protested, Keix turned to leave through the archway they had just emerged from. Instead of stepping into the Section they had come from, however, she reappeared in Square Thirty-two through another exit on the other side of the area.

They were trapped. Just as in the second trial of Taavar, they were being routed back to the same spot. Did it mean that everyone else, including Zej and the rest, had been directed here as well? The thought made Keix pause and look around, and she saw unarmed people huddled along the border of the Square, trying to blend into the walls of the buildings because there was nowhere to hide.

A bald and stout figure moving with above-average speed and accuracy at the peripheral of her vision caught her attention. Upon closer look, she saw that it was the man from the weapon shop. He was brandishing two large blades skilfully, fighting off two of the black-clad figures facing him.

'We *need* to find Zej and the rest,' Keix told her teammates.

Jūn nodded. 'Seems like everyone's being driven into this Square.'

'Vin and I will go in a clockwise direction. You and Jūn head in the opposite direction,' said Seyfer. He had been looking troubled ever since they had been unceremoniously booted out of the Taavar tournament's dimension.

Keix couldn't blame him. After all, retrieving Iv't was his mission. Now that it seemed like he wouldn't be able to achieve his goal, what use were they to him?

An uneasy feeling crept up Keix's nape. If Seyfer took the chance to vanish, they would lose their only bargaining chip to get Dace's father and Lana back.

'No,' said Keix forcefully. The rest of her group were taken aback by her vehemence. 'We stick together. If we split up, it's going to be even harder to gather everyone.' She prayed that Zej would have the good sense to keep his group together too. Once she found them, they needed to get out of Tilsor immediately and figure out their next move. They'd be sending themselves into the jaws of hell if they faced ExA head-on when they were outnumbered.

The Square was getting more crowded and chaotic by the second.

Fighting down the rising panic within, Keix drew her sword and joined the fray. Behind her, Jūn, Vin and Seyfer did the same.

'Try to not let the non-ExA soldiers strike you; their weapons could be poisoned,' warned Keix. The image of Jūn's blistered wound was seared into her mind. If any one of them were to get slashed by a bandit . . . She refused to let herself follow this train of thought to its bleak conclusion.

Together, the four of them forged a path through the groups of combatants.

The first cluster they came across had eight Tilsorians going up against two black-clad figures. Even though the odds were four to one, the Tilsorians were clearly having trouble fending off the attacks.

Keix took two steps forward and flung herself at the nearest ExA soldier. Because she was standing just out of this trooper's line of sight, she managed to knock him off his feet. With a swift stroke, she brought the hilt of her sword down on the man's temple and knocked him out. By the time she stood up, Jūn and Seyfer had already dispatched the other ExA soldier.

As they continued fighting their way through the mob, Keix saw bodies everywhere—on the ground, pressing against her, knocking into her at every turn. She tried to force down the bile rising in her throat as images of the first trial resurfaced in her mind.

The stench of fresh blood grew thicker by the minute and Keix turned down her sense of smell to prevent herself from becoming nauseous.

She had no idea how big Tilsor was, or how many people lived here. But she was now surer than ever that their earlier deduction, about some force corralling everyone in the Square, had been spot on.

It wasn't just the number of Tilsorians that was growing, even as many of them collapsed to the ground; Keix and her gang were encountering more and more ExA soldiers as well. While she estimated that ExA soldiers were originally outnumbered five to one, the ratio seemed to have dropped to two to one, thanks to the astounding speed, skill and efficiency with which they were eliminating their opponents.

Keix was no longer weak with starvation and was also better trained now compared to when she had first encountered these soldiers. Yet, she found that she needed intense focus to parry and counter their attacks.

Strength and precision; these words, the basis of a great fighter that Jūn had drilled into her, kept her going each time she blocked an attack from an ExA soldier and felt a ringing pain that vibrated all the way down to her bones.

But Keix knew that their luck was running out. It was only a matter of time before the ExA forces overwhelmed them. Even now, they were herding those left standing and still fighting towards the centre of the Square, cutting off their escape routes. It was also hard to be on the lookout for Zej, Pod, Dace and Maii while she was trying to stay alive.

'Mohgen?' Vin yelled all of a sudden.

Keix slashed her sword in an arc towards the two ExA soldiers facing her. The move forced them backwards and she whipped around just in time to see Vin knocking away an ExA soldier's gun and kicking the assailant to the ground.

Taking advantage of whatever little time that manoeuvre bought, Vin ran towards a woman who was zigzagging through the crowd, parrying and counter-attacking those who came within her reach with a thin, curved sword.

That must be the owner of the apothecary from where Vin got the herbs for Jūn's antidote every day, Keix surmised.

'Vin!' panted Mohgen in exhaustion. She threw herself into Vin's arms.

Keix turned back to fend off three more soldiers who had appeared at her side. *I can't let this drag on. The longer we fight, the more tired we'll get, and the more easily we'll get caught or killed*, she thought.

As she thought hard to find a way out of this trap, she heard Mohgen say something that made her feel like someone had emptied a bucket of ice water over her.

'Ma.erdene said that your friend, Pod, had been captured!' came Mohgen's voice over the racket.

In her shock, Keix was almost skewered through her midriff by an ExA soldier charging at her. Luckily, she came to her senses at the last second and sidestepped the strike, countering it with a blow of her own. 'Pod?' Keix's question came out as a gasp as the soldier fell.

'Your friends—' began Mohgen, but she was immediately interrupted by a shout.

'Keix!'

Keix recognized the voice. Pod. Pod was all right. She felt some tension leave her shoulders as she took in the sight of the person she'd come to regard as her brother. Pod was sporting a blossoming bruise on his face, along with streaks of blood. His clothes were in disarray, and his hands holding his staff were bloodied.

On Pod's heels were three others—Dace, Zej and Maii—who looked to be in no better state than he was.

'Keix. Vin,' shouted Dace. 'We found Lana and my dad.'

Wait, what? How did that happen? thought Keix, registering Lana's presence, as well as a middle-aged man's, behind Dace. She didn't have time to voice her queries as another ExA soldier came at her. Before she could react, Jūn stepped in with a counterattack and the trooper crumpled to the ground.

'Concentrate, Keix!' shouted Jūn, his face flushed with exertion.

The swarm of bodies was getting tighter now, as the ExA soldiers gained the upper hand in the battle.

'What do we do now?' asked Pod.

Keix wondered if everyone had used up all the luck allocated to them for the rest of their lives. How was it possible that they were still standing among a group of fifty-odd people, barely injured, even as hundreds of bodies littered the ground in the Square.

'We—'

The moment Keix's mouth opened, she was interrupted by a cold voice which sliced through the air, halting every bit of activity in the Square.

'Hand over Iv't and we'll let you go.'

Keix couldn't tell who had spoken. The ExA soldiers looked like clones with their hoods pulled over their heads. Yet, even without any indication of whom the voice had been addressing, Keix could feel all eyes turning in the direction of her group.

No one spoke. How were they supposed to hand over someone whose whereabouts they didn't even know? If it had really been Iv't in the dimension of the third trial, could he have been pulled out of the dreamscape too? But she hadn't seen him in Square Thirty-three when they landed back there. He could still be stuck in his nightmare loop, or his existence might not even have been real . . .

As these thoughts raced through her mind, Keix saw, from the corner of her eye, a tiny movement between Mohgen and Vin. Before she could determine what was going on, she saw the two of them extend their arms and throw handfuls of green- and blue-coloured balls in the direction of the soldiers surrounding them.

The moment the balls made contact with the troopers, all hell broke loose again. Fire burst out on the bodies of some while others started clawing at parts of their bodies—faces, arms and legs—and falling forward. Screams of pain and the smell of burning flesh filled the air.

It took Keix a beat to realize that only the ExA soldiers were affected. She knew that there was no time to lose, so she didn't think much and just made a break for it. Shuffling noises told her that everyone who had been shepherded into the crowd were trying to escape too.

Taking care to avoid the writhing soldiers, Keix ran towards the nearest exit. When a strong hand closed around her neck, she knew she had yet again underestimated the ExA soldiers.

Yanked into the air, Keix saw that her teammates had been captured in the same way. Jūn was pinned to the ground by four soldiers. Seyfer too. But the elite Atros trooper was faring a little worse than the Kulcan. Blood was streaming down a huge gash on his forehead, yet he continued to struggle against his captors.

It was in that second that two realizations dawned on Keix. The first was that Seyfer had been telling them the truth about Atros and ExA all along. If he'd had any under-the-table dealings with the latter, it was unlikely that he would be brutalized in this manner right now. The second was that this group of ExA soldiers had clearly been instructed to not harm them, which partially explained why no one in their group had been crippled or killed until now.

But whatever Vin and Mohgen did must have provoked ExA and eviscerated any reservations that they used to have about not severely hurting them; or it could be the fact that they were in the hands of ExA now that the troopers decided there was no longer any need to handle their captives with care. Because to Keix's horror, she saw Lana being thrown into the air, and before anyone understood what was happening, a bloody blade was protruding out of her chest.

Lana looked down in disbelief. She reached a quivering hand to her wound. Before she could touch the spot, her hand fell away and she slumped forward.

'No!' Dace's cry was filled with anguish. He struggled against his captor and managed to land a kick in the soldier's belly. The soldier released his grip on Dace to clutch at his stomach. The very next second, two ExA soldiers had stepped in and wrenched Dace's hands behind his back, lifting his feet off the ground.

To drive their point home, the trooper holding Pod stuck his blade through his captive and twisted it before pushing Pod's staggering body away.

No! The word boomed in Keix's head as Pod lurched forward with his last breath. Keix felt like her soul had been ripped out of her body. Her hands dropped to her sides. She thought she heard Zej echoing her thoughts.

No. No, no, no, no, nonono . . .

'We'll kill one of you every time someone tries something funny,' came a voice. 'I'll ask again. Where is Iv't? Hand him over and some of you might be able to get out of this alive.'

Again, no one said a word. Keix didn't know how long the shocked silence stretched. It might have been milliseconds. It might have been minutes. But time refused to move for her until the air around her started vibrating to a fever pitch.

Keix thought she saw a glowing purple orb float up from within Pod's body and rush at the group of ExA soldiers holding them captive, felling them with a single touch.

As the orb attacked the soldiers, one by one, she also thought she saw a figure in white float through the air towards them. The person resembled the elderly man whom she had met on her first day in Tilsor, the one who had approached them after they stopped to listen to a young lad telling people about Taavar. Come to think of it, Keix could see traces of the young man in this white figure too. And now that she had come across Iv't in the dreamscape, she realized that all three of them shared an uncanny likeness. Were they one and the same?

At this moment, the man was chanting in a foreign language that sounded vaguely familiar. Then, snapping sounds echoed all around her and the ExA soldiers who were still standing dropped like marionettes whose strings had been severed.

Keix didn't know why, but the sudden thought that if she could go back in time, to when they'd been snatched out of the dimension that held Taavar's third trial, perhaps she might get another shot at saving Pod. Or, if she hadn't agreed to help Seyfer, perhaps Pod wouldn't have ended up here in the first place.

But she knew that she was grasping at straws.

There was no return, no replay, no starting over this time round.

19

Pod | Ghost

An out-of-body experience. There wasn't a description more apt to illustrate what Pod was feeling.

He remembered following Keix's cue and making a run for the archway out of the Square, his feet slamming against the ground—one, two, three—when a strong hand gripped his neck, and he was lifted into the air. He saw the ExA soldier who was holding Lana skewer her right through the heart. He heard Dace's scream and he saw Dace land a kick at the ExA soldier who was holding him captive.

The next thing he knew, there was a sharp, burning pain in his chest. Looking down, he saw a blade, bloodied, mocking, triumphant, protruding out of him. As quickly as the sword pierced through him, it was twisted and wrenched out, leaving in its wake the most excruciating and searing pain he had ever felt.

He remembered falling forward, his knees buckling. He was a mess. Literally and figuratively. Blood was gushing out of him even as he pressed his palm against his wound. The pain was causing him to hallucinate.

'Pod!' whispered Maii.

This can't be right, thought Pod. He couldn't have heard a voice as soft as this from this distance. And this level of bleakness . . . he'd never encountered it in Maii's voice before—even when she was talking about the loss of her powers. Moreover, he'd never seen her so emotional.

His vision blurred as his knees hit the ground. But when his cheek struck the same surface with a thud, he could no longer feel any pain.

A flare of anger and indignation at the person who'd plunged the sword into him started growing at a monstrous pace. Who was the one responsible? The dozens of black-clad figures teeming around the Square appeared identical.

No matter. He would chase them down one by one. And chase them down he did. He flitted past each of them, starting with the ones closest to him. With a mere touch, the figures convulsed and fell to the ground.

Just as a frantic energy filled him, Pod thought he heard Maii calling him again. Her voice was soft, desperate. It felt like she was whispering directly into his ear, yet there was a distant echo to the sound. When he whipped around, he thought he was staring into one of those screens in front of which he used to spend his time back in Atros—the monitor playing out a scene where Maii was hugging him, her eyes wild and shining.

All at once, the buzz fled, carving out an unfathomable void in his being.

He looked down. His body, his arms, his legs—they no longer existed. He floated, distorted, glowing purple and red, flickering. The reason for his emptiness became apparent all at once.

It was in this moment, between life and death, that he heard the phantom echo of Maii's musical laughter, playing an accompaniment to the words that had filled him with the kind of unbridled joy he had never before felt in his life . . . *tempting . . . our own narrative.*

Her subtle scent—fresh and green as always, with a hint of nectar— engulfed him, comforting him. Her tears fell on to the curve of his cheek, urging him, whispering, *stay.*

For a fleeting second, all felt right with the world.

In this moment between life and death, he felt his anguish dispelled by a foreign chant and replaced with a sense of immense calm and peace.

20

Keix | The Ifarl's Tale

Keix stared at the two mounds of pebbles they had stacked to mark Lana and Pod's resting places, the deadweight in her heart refusing to budge.

She had never commemorated anyone in this way before; Atros usually informed the deceased's next of kin, and that was it. So when Mohgen and Ma.erdene said that it was customary to bury the bodies of those who had passed on, the group had let the two Tilsorians choose a small rolling hill just outside of the town to lay to rest their two departed friends. The spot was peaceful, and the two markers lay beneath the single tree and its wide crown, sheltered from the natural elements.

A dim amber glow was just beginning to radiate across the horizon, and the five of them—Keix, Vin, Zej, Maii and Dace—stood in a row facing the cairns, still and silent as statues.

Jūn and Seyfer had hung back, paying their respects from a distance as they let those who were closer to Pod and Lana have their space to grieve.

The drizzle, falling like the tears in their hearts, had persisted throughout the night. Now, it cast a misty shroud over the peaceful funeral. Pod would probably have preferred his send-off to be a little more upbeat. The thought brought a poignant half-smile to Keix's face. This friend, whom she had known since she was fourteen, always brought good cheer to everyone with whom he came into contact. Still, try as she might, she couldn't muster the spirit to appear a bit livelier. Pod was gone, taking the optimism that had sustained everyone with him.

The silence stretched on until Dace cleared his throat. Everyone turned to him expectantly. His eyes were bloodshot, glistening with unshed tears. His lips moved as if he were preparing to speak. But he'd been emptied of his usual wit. Instead, he took deep, steadying breaths, his lips quivering, and walked towards Lana's marker.

Keix watched as he knelt down, placed a hand on the topmost pebble and closed his eyes. She fought the urge to step forward and comfort him because she knew he needed the space. He hadn't been himself since Lana's death, and Keix didn't know how close he was to his father; several times, she had caught Dace looking at his dad as if he had something to say, but eventually, he would always look away without uttering a single word.

After an extended silence, Dace stood up, repeated the gesture at Pod's marker—though he didn't stay long there—and then moved aside.

Keix followed his cue. When she touched Lana's marker, she could still feel Dace's leftover body heat on the stone. Even though she hadn't known Lana well enough, she spoke to Lana in her heart.

Wherever you are, please watch over Dace.

From her past interactions with Dace, Keix could only guess how much he had loved Lana.

When she knelt in front of Pod's marker, she found herself at a loss for words. So instead, she let the hot tears spill down her cheeks.

I'll miss you, Pod, she eventually thought. *Your voice, your exuberance . . . I miss you . . .*

Dace reached out to hold her hand when she moved to stand beside him, and she squeezed his hand wordlessly. Vin, who barely knew Lana, stepped up to her marker and bent her head for a brief moment. Then, she walked over to touch Pod's cairn.

Maii, whose eyes were as red-rimmed as Dace's, placed a hand on her chest and inclined her head at Lana's marker. Then, she bent down at the pebbles that marked Pod's resting place. She put both her hands on the marker before closing her eyes and bowing her head.

Keix knew that Pod had feelings for Maii, but she had never guessed that the Ifarl reciprocated them. For the longest time, Maii remained in the same position, but no one rushed her. After she stood up, it was Zej's turn to pay his respects. But instead of stepping forward, he stayed rooted to the spot, his eyes averted from the markers, filled with determination and sorrow.

When it became clear that Zej would not budge, the group prepared to return to Ma.erdene's, where Mohgen and Dace's father were waiting for them to discuss their next move. As they made their way down the hill, a figure in white approached them.

Even though the rising sun was behind him, casting a shadow across his face, Keix knew that this was Iv't.

Jūn stepped into Iv't's path as he neared the group.

'What do you want?' asked Jūn. He didn't draw his sword, but the lethality he exuded was enough to warn anyone approaching to keep their distance.

Nevertheless, Iv't walked straight up to him. 'I would like to speak to Maii, Vin and Keix alone,' he said without inflection.

Keix threw him a wary look and replied, 'Whatever you need to say, you can say it in front of all of us.'

'Keix is right,' said Vin.

Maii nodded, eyeing Iv't with a mixture of suspicion and curiosity.

Everyone knew that they couldn't let their guard down around Iv't because they'd witnessed first-hand how dangerous he was. He'd killed all the remaining ExA soldiers that Pod's ghost hadn't taken down without even lifting a finger. Well, technically, Iv't had muttered a chant, clenched his fist and then literally crushed all of the black-clad figures in Square Thirty-two.

Keix didn't have the energy to analyse his motives—not at this moment, when the loss of Pod was still so raw.

'I'm sorry for your loss. Your friend was a good soul,' said Iv't.

Keix inclined her head in acknowledgement. She couldn't believe that this man, who looked to be in his forties, with his grey-pink hair and eyes filled with wisdom and grief beyond his age, was Vin's great-great-grandfather. Now that she had gotten a good look at him, she realized that the young lad touting the tournament, the elderly man they'd met, and the dreamscape Iv't—they were all him, during his teenage, senior, and adult years, respectively.

Under Keix's scrutiny, Iv't said, 'Perhaps I should start at the beginning.' He didn't bother to keep the weariness out of his voice and continued, 'As you guys might have guessed, my name is Iv't.

'I . . . made a terrible mistake many years ago when some people, who were envious of my power and coveted it for their selfish ends, set a trap to capture my family.

'I wanted to take revenge, but I couldn't. Not when I was not myself. Grief consumed me. And I let my anger take over. I lost control over my actions. Yet, somehow, I knew deep down that what was I was doing was wrong. In one of my rare moments of clarity, I trapped that damaged part of me which held my Ifarl abilities in another dimension so I could no longer harm people,' explained Iv't.

Goosebumps dotted Keix's arms. Was the 'dimension' that Iv't was talking about the dreamscape to which she'd been transported during the Taavar tournament?

Interpreting the question in Keix's eyes accurately, Iv't replied, 'Yes, I was the one who created the dimensions in Taavar. I didn't want to merely contain that "evil" half of myself. I also wanted to punish greedy people. People who were willing to give up their lives for a vague promise.

'I wanted them to know that nothing good could come of coveting things that didn't belong to them. So, I trapped them in their worst nightmares. If they managed to get out of theirs, they would still be imprisoned in mine,' said Iv't, a manic gleam creeping into his eyes.

Keix thought about all the participants who had died for the 'vague promise'. Were they needless sacrifices in Iv't's convoluted vengeance plan? No matter how the Ifarl justified his actions, there was blood on his hands.

'To ensure stability, and to atone for my sins, I constructed Tilsor as a haven for those who didn't have protection against the ghosts.

'Atros was protected by a dome which the Ifarls had created, but I wanted nothing more to do with them. The Ifarls never accepted me as one of their own. To them, I was nothing but a riddle to be solved. So, I had to set out to create my own destiny.'

Keix couldn't help but empathize with Iv't. Hadn't she been the same? Wasn't her quest to look for her father nothing but a journey to find herself?

'If you are who you say you are, why haven't you aged? You should be dead by now,' said Keix. From her friends' sceptical looks, she could tell that they found it hard to believe this man too. Iv't opened the portal between the living and the dead more than seventy years ago. Yet, this man standing in front of her looked nary a day over fifty.

Iv't's lips twitched, but he didn't look like he was smiling at all. 'As long as a part of me is trapped in another dimension, I will never grow old.

'I was ready to be imprisoned for eternity, atoning for the chaos caused by my rash actions—until recently, when I sensed a change in the air. On the night that the Ifarls performed the ritual, I heard the chants and I followed them. I tried to stop them from closing the portal, but I was too late. If Zenchi had interpreted 'The Act of Repentance' correctly, this wouldn't have happened. Repentance is accepting that a mistake has been made, living with it, making amends. It's not about undoing the mistake. Because that can never happen.'

'It's like trying to put together a broken glass,' whispered Maii, glancing at Seyfer.

Keix wondered whether this was some secret code, because Zej and Dace's gazes also flicked to the elite Atros trooper.

Iv't nodded. 'I knew then that once the portal was closed, ExA would advance, and they would resume their quest to destroy the world in their pursuit of power, as they had done with my family.'

There was a sharp intake of breath all around at Iv't's words. Only Seyfer remained impassive, as if he had heard this story before.

Was it ExA who killed Iv't's wife? thought Keix.

'Yes,' replied Iv't, almost as if he had heard her unspoken question. 'ExA set a trap for me. They forged a note that said that the Ifarl elders needed me to attend a last-minute meeting. After I was lured away from my home, they attacked my family and killed my wife.'

Iv't's bitter laugh rang chillingly in the air. 'They had thought to kidnap my family to make me bow to their demands, but they didn't know that Mae was a fighter. She bundled up our daughter and let our pet oka drag our baby to safety while she faced down the kidnappers.'

Keix shuddered as she recalled the horrible scene she had witnessed in the dreamscape hut during the last trial of Taavar. She hadn't seen any oka around, though. Weren't okas extinct? How exactly did Iv't get this creature that only existed in myths as a pet? *Jūn has a shih, and you thought that species had ceases to exist too, right?* Her inner voice seemed set on reminding her of her ignorance at this inappropriate timing.

'ExA destroyed my family,' spat Iv't. His eyes shone with a terrifying intensity. 'They will pay.'

'Is that why you lured me to Zej's group? To ensure that we would join the tournament to help you break out the other half of your soul from a trap that you had created for yourself?' demanded Vin.

'Yes. When the portal was closed, the stars shifted. And I deduced somehow that I needed your group to join the tournament for me to regain my powers,' elaborated Iv't.

Keix tried to suppress the fury she felt at Iv't's words. Once again, they had been used as pawns. But she knew that she couldn't place the blame solely on Seyfer, Atros or Iv't. She was the one who agreed to Seyfer's terms to help Dace save his father and Lana. And, in a way, because of what they had gone through during the Taavar tournament and right after that, the Atros trooper became a grudging, albeit odd, addition to their team.

'Why are you telling us this?' asked Keix. They had already lost Pod and Lana because they got embroiled in Seyfer's mission. Why should they continue on this path and face the possibility of sacrificing yet more lives for a powerful Ifarl's personal vendetta?

'Because we must regroup and take down ExA,' said Iv't, echoing what Seyfer had told them. 'Otherwise, they will stop at nothing to conquer the world.'

'You crushed them by just chanting,' said Vin. 'Why do you need our help?'

'Because I can't do it alone. What I did back then will only delay their advancement. I tried to make sure that I killed every one of those monsters once I regained my powers. And I directed everyone into a Square to try to ensure that none of them slipped through the cracks.

'But I can't be absolutely certain that I managed to eliminate every last one of them. If any of the ExA soldiers escaped and is now on their way to bring the news of their defeat back to their leaders, ExA will re-strategize to launch another attack. If ExA doesn't hear back from their troops for a while, they will send a scout here. Either way, the information will eventually reach them.'

'And you need the Kulcans' help for this?' asked Jūn, who had remained characteristically taciturn all this while. He stood hovering beside Keix, casting a protective shield around her with his presence.

Iv't nodded. 'We don't know how big ExA's army is. You've seen them fight. There is strength in numbers, so we'll need all the help we can get to take ExA down.'

'What makes you so certain the Kulcans will help?' Keix thought that with Iv't's abilities, it would be a breeze to compel the Kulcans to bend to his will. 'Are you going to mind-control them into fighting this war?'

Iv't laughed again. This time, it sounded like he was genuinely tickled. 'You should know that Kulcans can resist Ifarl compulsion to a far greater extent than any other race, right? Besides, it'll be exhausting to get every one of them under my spell. It's also common sense to never go to war with soldiers who are unwilling to fight it for you.'

'How much time do we have before ExA attacks again? And how do we know where they'll target next?' asked Jūn.

'We can never be sure unless we manage to sneak a spy or two into Atros to find out how far ExA has progressed. They might have taken over Atros, for all we know,' replied Iv't. He glanced at Zej and Seyfer, as if he knew that the two of them, who hadn't spoken a word this entire time, were the most invested in Atros's survival.

Zej didn't look like he was paying attention to the conversation, but Keix knew that his brain was in overdrive. He must be seriously considering Iv't's implied suggestion of returning to Atros as an undercover agent again. Seyfer's face was devoid of emotions, but Keix thought she caught a hint of misgiving in his eyes.

'What do you stand to gain if you succeed in killing every last one of the ex-Atrossians? Your goal doesn't seem to be as simple as saving the world,' asked Dace.

Keix wanted to applaud him for voicing her thoughts. She'd had just about enough of megalomaniacs masquerading as saviours. Although she didn't know Iv't at all, she was sure that, unlike Zej, whose intentions had always been to do the right thing, the Ifarl's motives were not as pure.

With a sinister smile, Iv't replied, 'Revenge, of course.'

21

Zej | Predestined

'Can I have a word?' asked Zej as Keix stood up to leave the room.

Together with the rest of the team, they had spent three days and three nights plotting the various ways and means by which they could bring ExA down. It was decided that Zej, Seyfer and Dace would return to Atros to try to gather information on ExA, while Maii and Iv't would pay a visit to the Ifarls who had gone into hiding.

Vin wanted to stay behind in Tilsor with Ma.erdene and Mohgen. Iv't had restored the magical qualities of the town after the brutal battle, which meant that it still had the potential to impede the advancement of ExA troops unless they learnt how to navigate the Sections and Squares. Tilsor's location also made it the ideal spot to converge because the group was splitting up in different directions.

First thing tomorrow morning, Keix would set off with Jūn to Yurkordu to convince the Kulcans to join forces with them.

Zej knew that this was his only chance to speak to Keix and sort out their relationship. He regretted avoiding her when they'd met again in Tilsor. When he saw how protective Jūn had been with Keix, stepping in to stop her from joining the Taavar tournament, Zej had given in to his insecurities. Dace's words kept replaying in his head.

You don't deserve her.

Dace had hit the nail on the head because even Zej himself didn't know where Keix stood in his heart. It always seemed like he had to choose between her and the right thing to do.

As everyone filed out of the room in Ma.erdene's bathhouse, Zej saw Jūn hesitate and throw a measured glance in his direction. Zej thought that the Kulcan would stop him, but after a beat, Jūn left the room as well.

The silence that hung in the air was as heavy and opaque as the wall that had formed between the two of them.

'I . . .' started Zej.

'It was a mistake,' interrupted Keix. 'I shouldn't have kissed you and then left Atros without a word.'

Zej stood dumbfounded. Was Keix the one who initiated the kiss? Wasn't it mutual? He couldn't recall exactly who kissed whom at this moment. All he could do was to close his mouth and swallow the apology that he had prepared.

'I've been doing a lot of thinking since then . . . on the way to Tilsor, during the tournament, after Pod's . . .' Keix trailed off.

Zej didn't know what else he could do but nod. Pod's death was also weighing on his mind, and he didn't have the courage to face his jumble of emotions yet because he found himself lapsing into self-blame mode whenever he thought about his best friend.

'Your priority has been, and will always be, Atros and its people,' continued Keix.

'Keix, I . . .' Zej broke off. 'I'm sorry.'

'It's okay,' said Keix, her voice tired. 'I don't need your apology. Just go and do what you need to do. I promised to try to get the Kulcans to stand on our side, and I will do my best to ensure that this happens.'

Zej tried to process what Keix had said—to read between the lines and understand what it implied. Were they . . . over?

In a bid to buy himself some time, he blurted out the first thing that came to mind. 'I don't trust Iv't . . . I *won't* trust him,' he said. Was he trying to weaken Keix's resolution to draw a clear line between them or persuade himself to be more wary of Iv't? Even though the plan to take down ExA was already in motion, he could tell that everyone, including Maii, had their reservations about Iv't because they had been burned one too many times.

Even Seyfer, of whom they were the most distrustful, seemed like a much-preferred ally compared to the decades-old Ifarl, who hadn't aged since half a century ago. Zej was always catching Seyfer eye Iv't in a preoccupied manner, with a mixture of suspicion and awe. Seyfer also seemed to be still processing the possibility that the organization he served might have fallen to ExA. He couldn't conceal his worry as he raised questions about the feasibility of certain parts of the plan, especially when it concerned the civilians' safety. At times, Zej thought that he caught glimpses of himself in Seyfer, although he wished that he was as bold as the elite Atros trooper.

After a pause, Keix said softly, 'Yes, you shouldn't trust Iv't. When you head back to Atros, you should try to find out more about ExA. Granted, they killed . . .'

Pod and Lana, Zej completed Keix's sentence in his head, but no one uttered their names.

Keix took a deep breath and continued, 'It may appear like we're on opposite sides—us and ExA. But the real fight is between ExA, the current Atros and Iv't. We are just warm bodies caught in between their three-way power struggle. We don't even qualify as a number to them. People are not memorialized when they die; their loved ones are simply "notified" and life just goes on. Life is *expected* to go on.'

Keix's fervour made Zej's heart clench.

'You said it yourself,' continued Keix before Zej could respond. 'It's part of the reason why you joined Oka. Because Atros was covering up deaths and doing twisted experiments under the pretext of strengthening their defences for the safety of their citizens.'

Zej hung his head. He knew Keix was right. Even though it was the last thing he wanted to do, he forced himself to take stock of what he had lost in the past two years since he joined Oka and uncovered Atros's repulsive secrets.

Keix, Vin, and the families of the people he was helping when he was part of Oka—all of them had Atros turn its back on them. And now, he had lost Pod. His best friend had died because he felt the need to help Atros deal with a bigger enemy. An enemy painted with Maii's and Seyfer's words. An enemy that he hadn't even really met.

'Even if everything now points to ExA as the biggest villain here, we can't place our trust in Atros or Iv't. Seyfer doesn't need to know. But I've spoken to Maii privately and even she agrees,' said Keix.

Maii too? Zej thought. He hadn't expected the Ifarl to go against Iv't; just like him, who prioritized the lives of innocent people and the greater good, he thought that Maii's loyalties lay with Zenchi and the rest of her race. But an image of Maii, with her head bowed at Pod's memorial, overrode his thoughts. He suddenly felt ashamed that he didn't even have the courage to approach his friend's grave marker because he couldn't figure out how to face him . . .

'Trust Dace's instincts,' added Keix, her voice softening further, almost as if she could sense the hurt in Zej's silence.

At the mention of Dace, the awful memories which Zej had suppressed, resurfaced. Dace must blame him for Lana's death too.

'I . . .' started Zej, but he didn't know what he should say. *I will trust Dace? I am sorry?*

Keix sighed and turned to leave. When she was at the door, she halted and called over her shoulder solemnly, 'Take care, Zej. Vin will send regular updates whenever she can.'

Watching her retreating back, Zej felt a weight in his heart drop. Was it relief or disappointment? He couldn't tell. All he knew was that he had let Keix down. Again. He had let Pod down. And himself as well.

In some darkened recess in his mind, he knew that somehow, when he'd lowered his head to kiss Keix that night, that they were never meant to be. They'd missed their shot ages ago—when exactly, Zej didn't know. What he did know was that, once they crossed that invisible threshold, any second or subsequent chances they thought they had were just cruel jokes that destiny was playing on them.

22

Keix | Full Circle

Keix ran towards Jūn, who was standing atop a small hump on the vast grassland. The wind outpaced her and seemed determined to tease wayward strands of his hair out of his ponytail. It also caused the hemline of his heavy, black robe to sway gently.

The soft illumination of the morning sun highlighted his every feature—from his prominent cheekbones to angular jawline to the square set of his broad shoulders—and Keix grew suddenly conscious of how good he looked.

She gave a guilty cough when he turned to her, and stammered, 'Let's get going.'

From what she gathered, they would be on the road for at least a month or so. In preparation for the journey to Yurkordu, she had changed into a thicker robe—black and simple, like the one Jūn was wearing. Ma.erdene had also ordered another set in midnight blue, and that was packed in the bundle that she was bringing along.

She adjusted the parcel slung over her shoulder and her cheeks turned warm when the packaging of the food that she'd packed inside rustled loudly. Vin had bought a ton of Keix's favourite snacks and insisted that she haul everything along on the trip. Keix wasn't going to allow herself to go hungry again, so she had accepted her best friend's gesture gratefully.

When Jūn didn't tease her about the sounds her bundle emitted, Keix heaved a sigh of relief.

'Shall we go?' she asked breathlessly. Despite her having appeared in a flurry, Jūn didn't seem to be in a hurry to leave.

'Look what I found,' he said, extending his hand.

In his palm was a small, furry creature.

'A haagi?' laughed Keix. On closer look, she noticed that the tiny animal was grey and sported a white triangular spot on the tip of its right ear.

'It's the same one that we released?' she asked, pleasantly surprised. It seemed like aeons since she rescued the haagi which had been frozen with fright outside Atros.

'I think so,' replied Jūn with a smile. 'It's grown a bit plumper since we last saw it.'

Keix reached out to pat the animal on its head. 'Glad to see you're doing well,' she said affectionately.

'Shall we keep it?' asked Jūn.

At Keix's puzzled look, he added, 'As a pet.'

'Nah,' said Keix. She'd read somewhere about people keeping haagi as pets to serve as guides, but the wild animals would lose their navigating abilities after being cooped up in a cage for too long. 'It belongs in the wild.'

Jūn gave her a funny look before nodding in acquiescence.

Keix's heart skipped a beat when he flashed her a smile and then bent down to let the haagi hop down from his palm on to the ground.

'Take care,' he said, stroking the creature between its ears. In response, the ball of fur twitched its ears as it had previously done and scurried away.

When Jūn straightened up, he stretched out his hand in what Keix assumed was the direction of Yurkordu and inclined his head. 'Ready?' he asked.

Keix beamed. Seeing the haagi had somehow lifted her spirits. She was still trying to work past the loss of Pod, but the oppressive grief had eased a little over the past few days as they planned their strategy to take down ExA. She had every intention of double-crossing Iv't if the situation called for it. When Maii approached her in the middle of the night to confess that she didn't really trust the Ifarl, they had both vowed to never be used as pawns again.

While Keix hadn't planned to let Zej know about this deal, she found herself putting her cards on the table last night when he asked her to stay back for a word. She had never seen Zej at such a loss before. And she realized that she couldn't bear to let power-hungry people make use of him again. She didn't want him to sacrifice others or himself for the greater good—not when the terms were skewed to fit the agenda of a select group of people.

It was also then that Keix came to a decision regarding their relationship. There was a time when they could keep pace with each other. Then, Zej took a fork in the road. When they reunited, she was no longer the same person he had come to know. Neither was Zej. They tried to bridge that gap, mend that crack between them. Yet, what they could do was too little, too late. Zej seemed to want to stay where he was. His heart was in the right place, but his heart was blind. And Keix didn't want to be his eyes any longer. She wanted to, *needed to*, move forward.

In a sense, they still had the same goal, which was to bring peace, genuine peace, back to Atros—not peace that had been neatly packaged under layers of half-truths, or one that had been falsely obtained by oppression. Whether they would be able to do that remained to be seen, but Keix had a direction, and she had a plan.

She headed towards where Jūn had indicated, a bittersweet smile on her face. Her resolution was clear as she looked to the horizon, now coloured a vivid orange by the rising sun, and said, 'Come on. We've got a world to save, Kulcans to convince and a war to win.'

END

Acknowledgements

Sincerest thanks to everyone who made *The Light of Stars* possible:

- Nora and the teams at Penguin SEA and India (Chai, Garima, Ishani and more), for letting me bring the book to everyone
- Thatchaa, my structural editor, for being so thorough and patient throughout the structural editing process
- Jo and Jess, my colleagues and workshop partners; for sitting through hours listening to me ramble as I tried to figure out the plot for the story; for accommodating my intense schedule as a full-time employee, mother of two, and struggling novelist; for all the support and enthusiasm you guys have shown for TLOS before it even had a title. I'm eagerly awaiting the day you guys unleash your current WIPs on the world
- Bryan Choo, the boss of *TheSmartLocal*, for letting me go on a six-month sabbatical to complete TLOS and for being the most supporting and best boss anyone can ask for
- Joyce, Eva and Cat, for your unwavering support and for keeping me grounded as I constantly confided in you guys about the mini breakdowns I had as I navigated writing and marketing my books. I love how close we've gotten even as we're all in different parts of the world—Singapore, London and Manila :')
- Dave, my mentor for *The Night of Legends*. None of this would have been possible if you hadn't believed in my potential and accepted me as a mentee under National Arts Council's Mentor Access Project

- All the other author friends I've made on this journey—Audrey, Nabeel, Daryl, Ying Ping, Vivek, Nidhi, Sylvia, and more—for being so generous with your advice and in sharing resources as we try to get our books out to the world
- Eeling (@eeling.ink) and Valerie (@levairereads), two of my closest friends on Bookstagram, for letting me disturb them all the time with my nonsense; and my other bookstagram friends—@ywanderingreads, @wordwanderlust, @maireadingparty, @nofrigatelikeabookstagrammer, and more—who have been nothing but supportive of TNOL and TLOS
- Tammy Chew, my map illustrator and fellow Singaporean (@teechewpaper), for the amazing map included at the beginning of this book, and for making the art commissioning process a breeze; and Chinese illustrator 韶九， 谢谢你把我书里的人物画得那么有神
- My bestest friends in the world (even though you guys don't read my books!), Aries (my dar), TY (my dearest) and Ban, for being there for me all the time, for the past two decades (and more) of my life. I love y'all ♡♡♡
- My real-life, blood-related sister—you know I love you, and Hatch and Dou ♡♡♡
- My Low family—my husband, and Baby G and G-Shock—you guys are my life. I love you all. ♡♡♡
- Lastly, to you, my readers, for reading all the way till the end. I have so many more stories to share with you. If you liked TNOL and TLOS, follow me on Instagram (@lesliewwrites) and send me a DM anytime ☺